# Second

# To

# Sin

By Murray Bailey

# Second
# To
# Sin

Murray Bailey

Three Daggers
An imprint of
Heritage Books, Cornwall

# Chapter One

He'd suppressed the urges for a month. The gambling, the dangerous liaisons, and the free climbing kept the heart pumping. But he knew nothing could beat the ultimate thrill. And the more he forced them down, the more the urges pushed back up.

He'd taken the ferry to the mainland and walked out of Kowloon Harbour, past the Peninsula Hotel, through the commercial sector and into the heart of Chinatown.

The electric streetlights thinned to nothing, but the lanterns burned strongly. Despite the cloud enshrouded night sky, the red glow at street-level provided ample light.

Rowdy sailors lurched across the street in groups. Safety in numbers perhaps.

He bought a double shot of whisky from a bar and moved on. He was soon a solitary white man in a suit, out of place in a Chinese world.

He attracted attention, but they welcomed him in when he watched their game of craps. There was rowdy noise, laughter, hoots and howls. These were men who'd worked hard during the day and were now working hard at forgetting their troubles.

He played a while and made friends with men who were happy to take his money. Then he moved on. He found a bar and drank more rough whisky. A new friend, a wiry man, all twitchy with awkward arm movements, bought him another drink.

"Wacky," the man said, poking himself in the chest. "My name: Wacky."

"Charles. Charles Balcombe."

They knocked back another shot. Then Wacky was taking his hand and leading him to a game, betting and more drinking.

The night wore on. Wacky suggested he get a pretty girl, but Balcombe said no. He needed to get back to Hong Kong Island. To his own bed.

"Clean girl," Wacky said.

"Not tonight."

"Another game then, Master Balcombe. This time you will win big."

Balcombe didn't win big and was overly generous with his losses. Other men tried to befriend him but Wacky barked and pushed them away.

"They'd steal your money," the Chinese man said with a grin.

"I'm losing it anyway," Balcombe laughed. Wacky laughed and twitched.

After two more games, a win then a significant loss, Balcombe said, "I should go."

"One more game. You have more money?"

"Yes, but…" Balcombe blinked and thought, looking at the few notes he had in his hand. "I should stop now."

"I will lead you back to the hotel."

"The island," Balcombe said, his voice slurred.

"You need the ferry, Master Balcombe?" Wacky said, suddenly solemn. "Too late."

"A boat?"

Wacky nodded excitedly and waved his hands. "I will find a boat, Master Balcombe. Get you back to bed."

The twitchy Chinese man led the way, along passageways that smelled of rotten fish and human piss.

"Is this the way?" Balcombe asked, hesitating. The dock was in the other direction.

Wacky pulled his sleeve. "Yes, yes. Don't worry. Yes, yes."

As he walked, Balcombe swayed like a man at sea, the peculiar gait of someone whose legs and body weren't receiving perfect signals from the brain.

One more turn and the alley was dark. A cat wailed and scurried.

"Wacky, I don't think…" Balcombe began.

A big man pushed out of the darkness.

He was Balcombe's equal in height, over six feet tall, and he was wide. The big man looked twice the width of Wacky—who had since melted away.

Just the big Chinese man and the white man.

In a dark alley.

"You're my friend," the big man said.

Balcombe looked behind him.

No one around. No witnesses.

"I need a boat back to the island," Balcombe said, his voice slurred.

"It will cost you."

"How much."

"Everything you have." Despite the darkness, the movement of his right hand gave it away. The big man had a knife.

"Is this what you do?" Balcombe asked. His voice now clearer as though he'd suddenly sobered.

"What?"

3

"Lure people here and take their money."

The big man grunted, took a step closer. "Is your life worth a few pounds—for a friend?"

"No," Balcombe said.

He didn't move.

The big Chinese man didn't see a smile play on Balcombe's lips. Blood coursed through Balcombe's veins.

"Your money!" The knife came up, threatening.

Balcombe stuck a hand in his pocket and pulled something out; a bundle that looked like money in the darkness.

The big man's other hand came up.

"What?" he snapped as his fingers touched cloth. Not money, but a handkerchief.

The knife came up, thrusting.

Balcombe twisted. The handkerchief flapped open and towards the knife hand. Then he was holding the blade and yanking it.

The unexpected move left the big man gawping.

"Who are you?" the man finally said as he looked into Balcombe's cold eyes.

"BlackJack," he said. "I am BlackJack."

# Chapter Two

Fear is for pussies. It was a message Balcombe had heard in the army. Sergeant majors shouted it at raw recruits. But it wasn't true.

His friend had told Balcombe the truth.

He'd said, "Fear is God giving you the opportunity to be brave. What you feel is adrenaline getting you prepared. Don't worry, welcome it."

His name had been Charles. The real Charles Balcombe. Although Balcombe thought of him as Eric these days.

Eric had known excitement while free climbing. And he'd died doing the thing he loved more than anything else in the world.

"That feeling is what makes you live life to the full," Eric had said. "Fear is what proves you're alive."

Balcombe tossed the knife into the sea and washed blood off his hands. The tingle was still there. It would flow though his veins for days. Fear combined with death was the ultimate rush. One day it would be his own death, but not today.

Albert looked at him askance, reading his face as he approached on the dock. Everyone thought the rickshaw boy just had an effeminate face. He was lithe, young and strong. But *he* was really a young woman.

"You found what you needed," she said. It wasn't a question. It was a flat statement with no hint of judgement.

Balcombe said, "Get me home, Albert."

A sampan was at the dock, and they climbed aboard. With no instruction, the pilot of the boat untied it and headed across the strait. Moonlight danced over the gentle waves as Balcombe stood alone at the prow.

Dozens of boats moved across the water between the island and peninsula. Thousands more were moored along the coastline, behind and ahead. Sometimes as many as ten vessels deep. Referred to as the Boat People, they appeared to be an extension of the land. An amorphous mass that rarely stayed still.

On the island they were kept away from Victoria Harbour and the commercial docks. The marine police mostly left them alone providing they weren't blocking the waterways.

Balcombe could see their lights and hear the murmur of voices from almost half a mile away. The pilot steered for them, appearing to be another anonymous boat in the night.

Undoubtedly there was petty crime committed out there but providing the island inhabitants were safe the police didn't want to know. That was Balcombe's impression, anyway.

However tonight he was mistaken.

* * *

Detective Inspector Munro stood on the quay, his eyes sweeping over the sampans strung along Causeway Bay. Lanterns swayed in front of each one, creating ribbons of pale orange light. Beyond them he could see a handful of small boats crossing from Kowloon. None of those had lights. He saw their curved sails dance in the moonlight. There were probably ten times that number coming from the mainland, Canton and beyond. Boat People looking for a better life.

And some poor souls finding only death.

Munro removed his round spectacles and rubbed his eyes. It was midnight and he'd been working for a day and a half.

"We've recovered the body, sir," his sergeant said, stepping from the marine police boat and pointing behind him to a covered shape.

"Anyone see anything?" Munro asked.

The sergeant chortled and then stopped himself. They both knew these people wouldn't volunteer information. They wouldn't talk to the police for fear of deportation or worse. Munro didn't know of any recent cases, but these folks believed they were more likely to be found guilty of a crime they didn't commit than be punished by the true perpetrator.

"Not a word, sir." The sergeant took a breath. "If you ask me, the body could have travelled quite a way. These people will shove a body further along rather than report it."

"Someone else's problem," Munro said as he watched the body stretchered ashore. He could feel his chest tightening. Was this a BlackJack killing?

"He was floating in the shit," the sergeant said. "There's an eddy of it out there."

A Black Mariah waited with the back doors open. Munro stopped the men who stretchered the body then lifted the sacking that covered it.

He held his breath, not because of the odour but in case there were the tell-tale signs. He knew what a BlackJack corpse looked like.

The body was that of a malnourished Chinese man, his body white and bloated. Munro breathed. He could see a puncture wound in the man's side, deep and wide.

"All right, Sergeant," he said, dropping the sacking back over the body. "Let's get him to the morgue."

After the police van had left, Munro stood on the dock and rubbed his stiff leg that ached when there was a change in the weather on the way.

The distant sampans kept coming, although one caught his attention. It had veered off, now going West. Did they think they could pitch up in Victoria? He chuckled mirthlessly. If it didn't get mown down by a ship or ferry, an overenthusiastic citizen would put a hole in it. The police moved the boat people away, but sailors and others could take more permanent action.

The solitary sampan disappeared beyond the bay and Munro wondered if he'd be hearing about it in the morning.

\* \* \*

The wind had picked up and rain pelted him as Munro mounted the steps of the hospital. He shook out his Mackintosh before going down into the morgue.

"Good morning, Inspector Babyface," the assistant pathologist called cheerfully. Fai Yeung was in his early forties, the same as Munro, but looked ten years older with thinning hair and heavy eyes. However his demeanour was forever positive. A solidly built man, he had a thick neck and broad smile.

Everyone called Munro Babyface behind his back, except for Yeung. He said it to his face. In fact, Munro was sure his old friend had been the one to christen him with the name.

"Busy night, Fai?" Munro asked.

"I wouldn't know. I only started an hour ago. But a busy hour. Then again, when is it not busy? You police should stop picking up dead bodies."

"Or people should stop dying."

"Now that would be good," Yeung said. "Although then I'd be out of a job."

"And me too, probably."

"Then again, we could get better jobs. We could be wine tasters."

"I thought you wanted to be a chicken farmer."

"Or a fisherman or anything, providing I can sit back, watch other people do the work while I taste the wine."

"Tell me about our friend here," Munro said, pointing to the body on the slab—the man who'd been fished out of the sea seven hours earlier.

"He's called John Zeng, aged twenty-three, has five children but recently divorced his wife."

"Really? You know all that?"

"No." Yeung chuckled. "Except for the approximate age and the mark where he had a wedding band."

"Which was probably stolen."

"Most likely."

Munro walked around the body. He still only saw the one stab wound.

"Is that how he died?"

"Yes, although his head shows signs of a beating." Yeung parted the hair to expose lacerations. "Three blows pre-mortem, I think. The stabbing is deep, with a diameter that suggests a spear. He's been dead a couple of days and probably died slowly from the blood loss. He might have drowned, but I won't know that until I slice him open. Is it worth it?"

Munro nodded. Even though the examination would likely lead them nowhere, everything needed to be done properly. They'd have the record even though they'd have no perpetrator. Another statistic that the Chief of Police would be unhappy about.

"Did you hear about the murder last night?" Yeung said as he recovered the body.

Munro looked at his friend and wondered if this was going to be another joke.

"Over in Kowloon," the assistant pathologist said.

"No," Munro said cautiously.

"I'm being serious, Babyface." He paused, looking earnest. "I don't know any details, but it's another unusual killing."

Munro took a breath.

Yeung said, "Remember we thought a surgeon might have killed someone a month ago—the end of December?"

Munro said nothing. His mouth was becoming drier by the second.

"You know: the one with the chest incision and squeezed heart? Well, it sounds like they found another one like that last night."

# Chapter Three

At the end of his shift, Inspector Munro caught the ferry to the peninsula. As he left Star Ferry Pier, he wondered about the boat he'd seen last night. There was no sign of a rogue sampan here, and there had been no reported incident of one being maliciously damaged. Clearly it must have been travelling further around the coast, although he pondered at the unusual route it had taken. To head for Causeway Bay and then cut across towards Victoria, so close to shore, struck him as odd. Someone avoiding the marine police, but unlikely to be a smuggler. They wouldn't risk coming so close to the centre or passing the naval base.

A late-night passenger, he decided. Someone who'd missed the ferry. But that still didn't explain the subterfuge.

In Kowloon, Munro went into the police station asking about last night's murder. He expected to find the body in their morgue, but it wasn't there.

The police pathologist could only deal with two bodies at a time and the dead fat man found in Kwun Tong District had been number three. His body had been taken to the hospital on Waterloo Road.

"Busy night," Munro said to the police pathologist.

"Always a busy night," he grumbled. "You've got it easy on the island. I need a bigger morgue and two more of me." He shrugged resignedly. "Give my regards to Fai. Tell him he'll get fat if he doesn't work any harder."

Munro laughed and said he would pass on the advice. Once outside, he hailed a rickshaw to take him to the hospital on Waterloo Road. Regardless of its proximity to colonial developments, the civil hospital, more formally called Kwong Wah Hospital had been built by the Chinese for the Chinese. It didn't have the grandeur of the British-run hospitals, nor did it appear to have the discipline and organisation. However, Munro suspected it was a matter of volume versus capacity. The building was smaller than any of its counterparts and dealt with many times the number of people.

It further differed from the British hospitals, having its morgue above ground rather than below. The effect wasn't good despite the morgue being separate from the rest of the building. Munro could have followed the scent of death instead of the written signs to the morgue.

Before entering, he inserted the obligatory Vaseline into both nostrils.

When Munro asked to see the body, the assistant pathologist sighed hopefully.

"You're taking him now?"

"I'm afraid not," Munro said. "The police morgue is still occupied."

The other man shook his head. "Then why are you here?"

"Curiosity."

The assistant pathologist waited for more explanation. Eventually he shrugged and led Munro to a gurney and whipped back the sheet.

"Are you all right, Inspector?"

The tell-tale sign was there: a neat incision on the chest and no other obvious damage. Munro cleared his throat.

"I'm fine," Munro said. "The Vaseline blocks the smell, but I can taste the death in the back of my throat."

The assistant pathologist's face showed no sympathy.

Munro pointed to the body. "This just looks like a cut. What other injuries did he have?"

"A few cuts like he'd been in a knife fight. All superficial. He also took a blow to the head."

"Can I see the back of his neck?"

The pathologist frowned at the request but didn't question it. He rolled the man onto his side, exposing the neck. There was no expected puncture wound.

"Contented, Inspector?"

"How did he die?"

The body was rolled back. "The only deep cut is the incision on his chest, but he didn't die from exsanguination."

"The blow to the head then?"

"Look at his face," the assistant pathologist said. "That's shock. Without opening him up I won't know for certain, but I'd say he died from a massive heart attack."

"Shock? Heart attack?" Munro said.

"That's my cursory assessment."

Munro nodded. "That'll be it. No need to cut him open to determine that. Anything you can tell me about him."

"Thirty-one years old, six feet three and seventeen stone eight. His name is Feng Shubiao—apparently, he was identified."

"The name's familiar."

The assistant pathologist nodded. "Not surprising, since you're a policeman. He's a petty criminal."

"Gang related killing then," Munro said.

"That's your job."

"That's what it will have been. He's a big fat man. Heart problems, I suspect. Like I said, there's no need for further examination."

"Music to my ears," the assistant pathologist said. "It would be an even better tune if you'd take him away."

Munro rubbed his smooth chin as he considered it. Left here, the police might accept the heart attack verdict, but they might not. On the way back, he could complete the paperwork and have them transfer the body of Feng to Yeung's morgue. The pathologist here would be relieved, and the Kowloon police would be happy. One fewer case on their books. The only person Munro would have to deal with was Yeung. This mustn't be investigated. He'd do what he could to brush it under the carpet.

There was no doubt in Munro's mind. It confirmed his worst fears. The killer hadn't paralysed the victim with a stab to the neck. He hadn't needed to. Feng had been knocked out.

Munro knew the man who had committed by the man this murder.

And that man was BlackJack.

# Chapter Four

Munro had visited Charles Balcombe's apartment on Queen's Road. The man hadn't been there, but Albert, his coolie, had been. Munro told the effeminate boy to let Balcombe know they needed to speak urgently—at the usual place. He hadn't explained why.

The partially disused property sat at the end of the wharf off Connaught Road just after P&O Pier. The whole place was run-down, untouched from before the Japanese Invasion. Peeling paint and grimy windows seemed appropriate for his use.

He'd set up a table and chairs. A weak light bulb swayed from the cracked ceiling. The office's ownership was obscure. But it was Munro's place now. His secret place.

Munro had been here two days before that fateful day, forever known as Black Christmas. The Japanese had invaded on the same day they'd attacked Pearl Harbour, but it had taken ten days for them to land on Hong Kong Island and only a week more before the British surrendered.

An explosion on the mainland briefly flared in the darkness, aiding the return of the memories he sometimes welcomed in. Because most of the time he thought of his beautiful wife, Yan.

He could picture the Japanese warships in the bay, firing salvo after salvo into the city.

At first, he'd continued working—they all did. No one believed the Japanese would win. He'd investigated the use of this room by criminals benefiting from the distraction of the war.

He'd detailed the contraband he'd found there and returned to Victoria police station for support. But what he discovered was that the Japanese had taken the central station. They wouldn't win the war for another two days, but they were killing or capturing anyone in authority.

Most of the British were rounded up and held in Stanley Prison, but Chinese policemen were bayonetted on sight.

Despite his ethnic appearance—being half Korean—Munro's plain clothes had saved him. When he realized what had happened at the police station, he veered away, kept his head down, and hurried home.

He and Yan had holed up in their small apartment for two weeks, constantly afraid that a neighbour might give him away, but no one did. Finally, hunger forced them to leave the sanctity of their home and survive in the "New Hong Kong", as the Japanese were proclaiming it.

They'd taken over the banks and voided the old currency. However, people could still buy goods with Hong Kong dollars and money exchangers offered ridiculous terms, presumably hoping that normality would one day return, and they would become millionaires. And Munro suspected some of them did, eventually. For now, though, it was about survival and

Munro used the black market to barter valuables that he'd found in the run-down office.

Everything was bearable. He and Yan had each other—for a while at least. And perhaps they became complacent. The massacres had stopped.

The Japanese had ruled for three years before Yan made a mistake. They'd been out for a walk and passed a group of soldiers. She'd looked at one in *the wrong way* and he'd taken her life. Just like that. One moment Munro and Yan had each other and the hope for a brighter future and the next, she was lying on the ground in a pool of blood. He was beside her, crippled by their beating.

Now, nine years later, he stared at his reflection in the dirty window and said a silent prayer for his wife.

And then the light went out.

He hadn't heard the door open and now he could see nothing except the lights across the water.

"You came," he said, trying not to sound afraid.

There was no reply, but he knew the man was there.

And gradually his eyes adjusted so that he could see the other man's outline and a white face. Dressed all in black, he was standing by the door.

The man took a pace forward and Munro felt the menace. He strained to see whether the man had a knife in his hand.

"Are you BlackJack or Balcombe?" Munro asked.

The sound of the man's breathing crossed the room.

Finally, the other man said, "I could kill you."

*BlackJack then,* Munro thought.

"You could."

"No one else knows who I am. I could kill you and be done with it."

Munro said nothing.

BlackJack took another step.

Munro turned his back and looked across the water. Then his focus switched to the reflection in the window, and he imagined Yan was looking back at him. What would she think? What would she say?

He heard BlackJack take another step.

Munro said, "You could flee. Leave the country and change your identity. Do what you did before. Move on."

BlackJack said, "And keep on running?"

"You only have to run if you succumb to your urges. Stop killing and be a normal member of society."

BlackJack made a small sound, perhaps a grunt of derision.

"No?" Munro said. He thought of Yan again. He'd only ever been happy with her. Perhaps, if he had faith, he could be with her again. But no matter how hard he wanted to believe, he could not be religious.

He imagined BlackJack close now, right behind him.

"Then be done with it," Munro said. "Kill me."

He waited for a knife to pierce his back, maybe plunge as far as his heart. Perhaps that was for the best.

But nothing happened.

"You're out of control, Balcombe," Munro said, trying to see the other man's reflection in the glass. "You can't control the beast inside you."

Again, the grunt. Balcombe wasn't as close as Munro had assumed. He turned and paused, wondering if the knife would plunge into him now.

The man was two paces away.

Munro breathed in and out. "Are you in control?"

"Of course."

"You've been drinking. I can smell whisky on you."

Balcombe said nothing.

Munro said, "You have three choices, you know that. You're a smart man."

"Go on."

"Run away, kill me or kill for me."

"Isn't that what I'm supposed to be doing—killing for you?"

"Yes, you are. But you killed someone in Kowloon last night."

Balcombe was silent.

Munro took the opportunity to move sideways and put a table between him and the other man.

Balcombe moved to the opposite side and sat, his eyes always on Munro's. "He wasn't a nice man. And now he's dead. One less crook in Hong Kong."

"I didn't tell you to kill him." Munro said.

"And therein lies the problem. It's been three months—"

"More like nine weeks."

"We're in the third calendar month. Which is too long."

Munro shook his head. "So, you're admitting that you can't control BlackJack?"

"Stop talking like I'm some kind of Jekyll and Hyde character." Balcombe moved over to the table and sat at a chair. "I told you I'm in control. I don't kill just anyone."

"I don't want you to kill just anyone. I want you to kill the known serious criminals. The ones who are hard to catch. The ones who are hard to convict."

"That's what I did."

Munro sat at the table. "He was called Feng Shubiao. Yes, a criminal, but a minor one. Him being off the streets just means that someone else will step into his boots. And the more you act as an independent vigilante, the more likely you are to be caught."

"You'll cover for me." Balcombe leaned forward. "That's the deal, Munro."

Munro stared across the table to read Balcombe's facial expression, but it was too indistinct. "So you are Balcombe now. You *are* in control."

"Of course."

"Then stop drinking so much and await my instructions."

Balcombe said nothing for a moment, swayed back and then leaned forward again. "On one condition."

"What?"

"You don't leave it so long. Four weeks maximum."

"I—"

Balcombe slapped the table making Munro jump despite his resolve.

"Munro, you make sure it's no more than four weeks, otherwise I'll reconsider my three options." He stood and moved towards the door before speaking again. "Oh, and don't expect me to take option one. I won't run away."

# Chapter Five

"Dr. Swift!" Munro said, unable to hide the surprise in his voice. "I didn't know…"

Munro had arrived at the morgue expecting to find Fai Yeung, but his friend's boss was there. And so was the body of Feng Shubiao, the murder victim Munro had brought over from Kowloon.

The senior pathologist looked hassled, and his jowls seemed to sag even more than normal, giving him the look of a Basset Hound with unkempt grey hair.

"You were hoping for the assistant pathologist, Inspector? I'm afraid Yeung has reported in sick today."

Munro glanced at the bodies on the slabs, then turned for the stairs. "Another time then."

"Inspector?" Swift's challenging tone cut the rank air like a pathologist's scalpel. "You aren't here to discuss the body?"

*Not with you*, Munro thought.

"The full autopsy's done," Swift continued.

Munro turned back, his mind whirring. How could he get out of this? His plan involved Yeung doing him a favour. Involving the senior pathologist made things much more complicated.

Munro forced a smile. "I'll come back. I can see you're busy, Doctor."

Swift shook his head, and the jowls wobbled. "Rubbish man. Because I'm busy, I can get this case out and filed away. Delaying doesn't help anyone. You're here now and I was told this was a priority."

Munro thought to dispute the claim, but it wouldn't change things. Plus, it might highlight his attempted avoidance. He reluctantly took a step towards the largest covered body in the room.

Swift pulled back the sheet, revealing an open chest cavity. "You were correct," he said.

Munro peered at the gruesome sight.

Swift continued: "This is another Squeezed-heart case. No doubt about the similarity to the one in December. Seven-inch surgical incision in the chest; so precise it caused minor blood loss. A foreign body was inserted, and the heart squeezed." He pointed to a metal tray close by and Munro saw a heart.

"Not just a heart attack, then?" Munro said, giving up all hope of influencing the autopsy report.

Swift said, "Heart attacks don't result in contraction. No, when this organ stopped, it was less than half the normal size. Blood squeezed out. There are photographs in the report."

"Excellent."

"And you know what?" Swift said. "I would bet the foreign body was a hand. I think your killer opened the victim up just enough to get his hand inside and then squeezed the heart until it stopped." The doctor had his hand out, simulating a slow squeeze. "Can you imagine that, Inspector? Our killer would have felt the constriction, felt the atrial fibrillation and final cardiac arrest."

"I can't."

Swift dropped his hand and shook his head. "The sense of power…"

"It sounds like you admire the man."

The senior pathologist smiled in a lascivious way, as though jealous of BlackJack.

"It would take great skill. You dismissed the idea that it was a surgeon last time? The level of skill would make a surgeon my guess."

"It didn't fit the motive, but we can't rule it out." Munro paused. "How did he do it? The pathologist in the Chinese hospital said there was a blow to the head. It could be a copycat killing." It was his last throw of the dice to reduce the impact of the findings.

"Probably disabled through concussion," Swift said. "It's a minor injury, I'd say from a fall rather than a heavy, blunt weapon."

"That differs from December's case."

Swift nodded. "Puncture wound to the neck, paralysing the victim. Again, that takes some skill, Inspector. I don't want to do your job, but this has got to be the same killer."

# Chapter Six

Every Sunday, Charles Balcombe attended Mass at the Cathedral of the Immaculate Conception. His friend Roy Faulls accompanied him most of the time. Roy was the only one who knew about his romantic liaisons with the pretty, married women of Hong Kong. Apart from those ladies themselves, of course, and Albert, the rickshaw girl.

They'd been to the races yesterday. Faulls had placed safe bets as always and Balcombe had lost money. He didn't mind that so much. As far as he was concerned, gambling was for the thrill and to get that you needed to lose big sometimes so that winning big had the opposite impact. But yesterday, he just hadn't felt the rush.

For a change, there hadn't been a party that night. Faulls had gone off pursuing a photography hobby that Balcombe didn't share. Balcombe had spent the evening alone with his books and his whisky.

Today, he'd planned to free climb the crags at Victoria Peak, but the spirit hadn't taken him. Or at least, the spirit had. He strolled around the city, stopping at bars and sampling the single malts.

"What's up?" Faulls asked as they met outside the church.

"A drink too many."

"During the day?" There was disapproval in his tone. A couple of years his junior, Balcombe knew Faulls looked up to him. They we're both known to imbibe a considerable amount, but that was at clubs and parties. Rarely in the afternoon, and never alone.

When Balcombe didn't answer, Faulls went on: "Is there something wrong, Charles? Not money problems?"

Balcombe shook his head. They were striding towards the doors.

"Girl trouble, then?"

Balcombe gave a brief nod and then placed a finger to his lips because they were about to enter the cathedral. However, Faulls' expression suggested he thought there was a secret.

Faulls whispered, "If you ever want to share… a girl I mean."

Balcombe smiled weakly at his friend and took a pew near the back.

It would horrify his friend if he found out about BlackJack. Faulls wouldn't understand. He'd call Balcombe a hypocrite for sitting here and praying to God and acting as though he felt the Holy Spirit.

But there was no contradiction in Balcombe's mind. He'd been raised a Roman Catholic. He'd seen his parent's faith when their last baby had been stillborn. And when Balcombe's two brothers died on the beaches of Normandy, they prayed God had welcomed his servants into His arms.

Young Balcombe's faith had faltered when Eric died climbing, but soon afterwards, he'd heard his friend's voice, saving his life. Eric had urged him to face his fears, welcome the danger. Live his life to the extreme. And in doing so, Balcombe had felt His presence.

Now, years later, he sensed he was doing God's bidding. As he'd told Munro, he didn't kill anyone. He killed the bad people. The sinners.

The sermon—the coincidence snapped Balcombe out of his thoughts. Father Thomas was talking about saints and sinners.

"It takes a lifetime to be a saint," he said. "But it takes only a second to sin."

The priest paused for effect and Balcombe figured that the congregation was considering his words.

"Yes, we are all sinners. You have sinned. I have sinned." Again, the pause for reflection. "As a young man, I had impure thoughts. I confess it! That is the truth of human existence. And Christ died for our sins." He paused again before asking, "What does that mean?"

Father Thomas followed this by reading Galatians, chapter one, before he finished with: "Sin is a condition of the heart that is bent away from God in preference for other things, in our minds or attitudes or behaviours. Sin will be with us until that condition is wholly obliterated in the presence of Christ."

Father Thomas continued and started bringing Satan into the equation. Faulls leaned over and whispered under his breath, "A bit fire and brimstone today."

"That's what we like," Balcombe whispered back.

And then it became clear where Father Thomas was going with his sermon. By talking about Paul's Epistle to the Romans, he said that no one should emulate the saints but accept that they will transgress.

"Even though all of us have sinned and fallen short of God's glory, when we accept the gift of God's grace, we can still experience God's glory as if we had never sinned at all."

Then he talked about confession. He referred to John, chapter one. "If we confess our sins, He is faithful and just to forgive us our sins and to cleanse us from all unrighteousness."

Balcombe hadn't been to confessional in years. He didn't believe in it. He believed in God, and he believed in confessing to God, but not to a priest. Priests were just humans. They weren't special, in Balcombe's opinion. And they certainly wouldn't understand his need to kill.

After the service, the queue for confessional was longer than Balcombe had ever seen. Faulls lined up and beckoned for Balcombe to join him.

Balcombe shook his head and showed that he'd wait outside.

There was a young man, not yet twenty, who helped at the church, running youth classes and the like. He wore a simple white cassock and a genial smile. When he walked, Balcombe had noticed a limp.

"Everyone of us is a sinner," the boy said.

Balcombe nodded. "Jonah, isn't it?"

The young man held out his hand. It was cold and smooth.

Jonah pointed inside to the confessional queue. "He died for us, to defeat sin. All we need to do is face those sinful deeds and thoughts—"

Balcombe smiled kindly. "You'll make a good priest one day, I'm sure."

"I intend to." The young man flicked a glance at the queue. "Perhaps another time?"

"We have to be *ready* to confess, Jonah." Balcombe nodded. "There is no point in confessing and then returning to sinful ways."

The young man considered this and then turned his attention to the next person who passed through the entrance. As he left him, Jonah pulled a book from his bag and handed it to Balcombe.

"What've you got there?" Faulls asked as he joined Balcombe later.

"A book on the lives of saints," Balcombe said, having flicked through it. "It's homemade—by Jonah, I suspect."

"Interesting?"

"I've just learned that Saint Sebastian was murdered twice."

"That's a handy trick—although maybe murdered once and then surviving would be a better trick."

Balcombe signalled to Albert who was waiting with the rickshaw. "Coming for a drink, Roy?"

Faulls looked hard at his friend before speaking. "Don't you think you've had enough for today, Charles?"

"No." Albert pulled up and Balcombe addressed her. "Take me to the Wellington."

Faulls stepped back and shook his head. "Be careful, Charles."

"Never!" Balcombe said with a laugh and signalled for Albert to leave.

Minutes later, they were outside the inn. There was a mix of races inside, most middle class, all having a good time. Most would drink ale, but they had Glenfiddich single malt behind the bar and Balcombe could hear it calling.

Balcombe walked towards the door but then stopped. Inside, he could see Inspector Munro with a group of others—policemen, most likely.

For a fleeting moment, he felt like confronting the detective again, but he stopped himself. Munro had questioned his control. Balcombe had control over BlackJack. However Munro had control of him.

He spun on his heel, angry and frustrated.

"Albert," he barked.

"Sir," the girl bobbed her head obediently.

"Do you know the name Feng Shubiao?"

Albert shook her head, her dark eyes full of questions.

"Find out who he was. More importantly, find out who he worked for."

"Tomorrow?" Albert said uncertainly.

"Now, Albert."

Immediately accepting that he'd make his own way home, she set off, pulling the rickshaw down the hill. Balcombe watched her go, gritted his teeth and walked into the bar.

# Chapter Seven

In the morning, Balcombe free climbed the crags, pushing himself hard. Twice he slipped, the rock crumbling beneath his shoes, his fingers aching as they took his weight. Perspiration ran freely, and he was panting by the time he finished. He knew his heart rate was much higher than normal, much higher than it should be despite the exertion.

Last night, he'd had a double Glenfiddich at the bar, knowing that Munro's eyes were on him. Was he afraid of a public confrontation? Balcombe had closed his eyes and absorbed the atmosphere. He enjoyed the tension Munro must be feeling. There with his colleagues who knew nothing about BlackJack, wondering why Balcombe was there, wondering what he might do. Keeping the detective guessing was a good thing. The less predictable Balcombe was, the less control Munro would have.

He'd ordered another drink and then looked into the bar's mirror. Munro met his gaze and Balcombe cheekily toasted the detective.

The memory of Munro looking away made him smile. However he knew he'd drunk too much last night. He remembered getting home and having another, but he couldn't recall going to bed.

His heart rate was still too high and as he'd climbed, it had felt like the alcohol was leeching through his skin.

"Are you all right, Charles?" Faulls asked. The man was waiting outside the upper tram station at the Peak. He leaned against the bench with a camera around his neck.

"What are you doing here?"

"Out for a stroll… taking snaps… checking up on you. Albert said you'd gone climbing."

"You don't need to worry about me."

"What are friends for?" Faulls paused, then touched Balcombe's arm. "Sit down, old chap."

Balcombe sat and Faulls scooted up alongside him. The view of Victoria and the bays was both dramatic and spectacular in the sunshine: verdant hillside, city stone and glass, then an azure sea.

Neither man spoke for a while, both looking down the hill, both absorbed by their thoughts.

Finally, Faulls said, "You don't look well. Your skin's pallid and your eyes are bloodshot."

Balcombe nodded.

"And you stink of booze, Charles. It's not good for you."

"I thought I smelled good."

Faulls shook his head.

"All right, I had too much yesterday, and the exercise hasn't cured it."

"And drinking more won't cure it either."

"I learned that last night." Although it had really been the early hours of the morning, Balcombe admitted to himself.

The silence grew between them again and Balcombe was relieved Faulls didn't press him on what was wrong.

They were friends who bet on the ponies, went to parties and church together. That was it. Balcombe wasn't about to bare his soul to the man.

He was relieved when Faulls finally spoke again.

"You were an investigator," Faulls said. It was a statement of fact, with no probing.

Balcombe never provided details, never told anyone he was ex-military police, because then someone might put two and two together. They might discover his true identity. He said he worked for the government and left others to surmise that he was an undercover agent. It worked well on the ladies.

"You know when you were most enthusiastic?" Faulls said. "It was when you were looking for that missing young man. I know you enjoy climbing and the races and your little liaisons"—he flashed a knowing smile—"but I would say you were never more in your element than when you were being a detective."

Balcombe said nothing.

Faulls said, "I think you're a bit bored and we both know that drinking isn't the answer."

"It's not."

"Do you know Margaret Sotherland?"

Balcombe turned to his friend. "Should I?"

"Quite pretty. Curly brown hair and blue eyes. Catholic. Usually goes to Saint Jude's but also the cathedral now and again. You don't remember her?"

"No."

"I should say she *did go* to Saint Jude's."

"Because?"

"She's dead."

"Murdered?" Balcombe said, his interest piqued.

"No. Just died. She was only twenty-two."

"So, why the intrigue?"

Faulls shook his head. "I don't know, it just seems odd."

"People die all the time, Roy."

"Not young, fit people. Not unless there's an accident or suicide."

"Was it suicide?"

"You know the Catholic view on suicide? Purgatory. Burial without ceremony and not in consecrated ground. This didn't apply to Margaret."

Balcombe shook his head. "What are you suggesting?"

"If it *was* suicide, then it was covered up."

Balcombe rubbed his temple where an ache was building. "And that bothers you?"

"Someone covering up a suicide? Yes, it does."

"Because you want it to be reclassified?" Balcombe said dismissively.

"No, Charles. If it was suicide, then there's usually a reason for it. No one asked questions about her death. Not that I know of, anyway."

Balcombe sighed. He wanted to lie down, not debate the issues and motives associated with someone killing themselves. Faulls was looking at him expectantly.

Balcombe said, "How well did you know Margaret?"

"Not very. I spoke to her a few times a while back. Had tea with her, but it came to nothing." That meant Faulls had been interested in the girl, but the feelings hadn't been reciprocated. "Will you investigate?"

"Are you hiring me?" Balcombe chuckled.

"I know it's not about money."

Which was true. Balcombe had taken his previous assignment because of the sexy young wife. She'd offered much more than money for him to find her stepson.

"Are you offering to sleep with me, Roy?" Balcombe spluttered a laugh and regretted it. The headache worsened.

"No!" Faulls' face froze in a mask of horror. "How could you...? I'd just like to know what happened to Margaret—and it's a challenge for you. To keep you off the booze."

Balcombe stretched out his long legs and straightened his back on the bench. He breathed in the warm, fresh air. The squeak of a braking tram broke the tranquil moment.

"Let's go," Balcombe said. "I promise to cut down on the booze."

"And Margaret Sotherland?"

"I'll think about it," he said without conviction. "Maybe."

Faulls said nothing until they were on the tram and past the elevated section. He'd been staring out across the bay.

"You're not going to, are you?" he suddenly blurted.

"What?" Balcombe said, having put their last conversation out of his head.

"I keep your secrets," Faulls said, a whine in his voice. "I do a lot for you... as a friend. And as a friend, I'm asking you to look into Margaret's unusual death."

Balcombe suppressed his initial irritation. Faulls provided alibis that was for certain, but he didn't know everything. Faulls helped with introductions to pretty, bored wives occasionally, but he wasn't vital. In fact, he was more of a coat-tails follower than a best friend. Which made Balcombe wonder if he needed a genuine friend to confide in sometimes. Albert was a good foil at times and Munro was a challenge, but there was no one in his life who he could properly confide in. Maybe that was partly why he drank. Maybe it was a drunk's excuse that the bottom of a glass was his best companion.

"Charles? Are you listening?"

"You want me to investigate Margaret's death?"

"I do... as a friend. I don't ask much. I'd just like you to do this for me."

"All right," Balcombe said as the tram came to a halt at Barker Road. "I doubt there's anything, but I'll ask my police contact."

# Chapter Eight

Despite the early hour, the office already had a pall of blue smoke. Munro headed for his desk and the ever-growing pile of outstanding reports when he realized the Chief Carmichael was standing in his office, watching him.

The boss beckoned with a scowl etched on his face. Munro knew he was a great disappointment to Carmichael, and their meetings were rarely amicable.

"So here we are again," Carmichael said, now sitting behind his broad desk. He sounded weary.

"Sir?"

The Chief took time tidying the papers on his desk then looked up.

"Results, Munro. Results!"

Munro opened his mouth to speak but stopped.

"I don't want any more excuses," the Chief continued. "What were you bloody thinking, man? Bringing a body over from Kowloon and linking it to another murder"—he sighed—"and one which you haven't solved. Another one. Am I mistaken? Wasn't only a few weeks ago that I had you in here and you promised to improve your results?"

Munro bit his tongue. Carmichael was about to mention his predecessor. A man who was more interested in the numbers than bringing the true criminals to justice. Inspector Teags used to have a saying: "If you can't get them for what they did, get them for something else, lad." And that's why the justice system was creaking, the prisons overcrowded with men charged for petty crimes with scant regard for punishment for the actual crime. In Munro's opinion—which he wouldn't voice—the real problem lay with two things: the laws were too harsh for petty crimes and the burden of proof too high for serious ones. Of course, they created the former because of the latter. And they made matters worse and worse, like an unwanted feedback loop.

Carmichael continued: "It's a new year but the same governor. And that means the crackdown on crime must still happen. You need to start getting results, Munro. Or"—he paused—"or I'll have to do something about it. Before someone else does. Understood?"

"Yes, sir," Munro said only making half-sense of his boss's threat.

"The immigrant found in Causeway Bay at the end of last week. Definitely murdered?"

"Yes."

"Any leads?"

"No, sir."

Carmichael nodded and waggled a finger at Munro. "You've processed it the right way?" By that he meant it wasn't an Islander so, it wouldn't be part of the numbers.

"Yes, sir."

"What about the stabbing at the jeweller's on Saturday?"

"We're still processing it," Munro said. He read the Chief's expression, what he wanted. "No leads. No suspects," Munro added.

"How many cases have you got outstanding, Munro?"

"Nineteen."

"And the jewellers is the biggest?"

Munro knew the Squeezed-heart murder was the biggest, but that was in last year's statistics and officially he wasn't making progress.

"Yes, sir," he said.

"Then get people in for questioning. It's about time you solved some cases."

"Yes, sir."

"There's a fence who was charged with bodily harm last year. Get him in, Munro. He's your number one suspect."

Munro said nothing. He could sense where this would end up. The Governor wanted results, and the Chief was going to get them, whether they booked the guilty man or someone else.

"Munro?"

"Yes."

"Don't make me do your job for you. I promoted you for your reputation for getting the job done. What are you going to do?"

Munro took a breath to disguise his frustration. "I'm going to treat the fence we know as a suspect."

Chief Carmichael waved him out of the room and Munro was happy to be dismissed.

Balcombe was a problem. Last night he'd been provocative, going into Wellington Inn. Of course, the man could be seen in public, but why choose *his* pub? He'd taunted him with the raised glass. What was

Balcombe thinking? Was he out of control? Was he a problem that needed to be dealt with?

If Balcombe went down for the Squeezed-heart murders, what would he say? Would he pull Munro into it? Would he inform the court of their arrangement?

Munro had a pile of paperwork to complete, but his mind wouldn't focus on the job. The questions kept spinning through his head. Questions that he had no answers to.

However he eventually made doubly sure that nothing implicated him. No murder could ever be linked to him. And he would ensure that Balcombe didn't obtain any evidence to implicate him.

Carmichael kept looking at him throughout the day, probably checking he wasn't shirking. The idiot seemed to think that a low conviction rate equated to laziness.

By the end of the day, Munro had made good progress with his paperwork with few interruptions before he received a message. It made little sense, but Munro understood.

Balcombe wanted to meet.

# Chapter Nine

Balcombe visited Saint Michael's Cemetery in Happy Valley and located Margaret Sotherland's grave. He'd found her death registered four weeks ago in the obituary section of the *Daily Press*. It provided no detail except for the usual dates, that she'd been born in Kent and moved to Hong Kong with her parents in 1938. It said her parents had predeceased her and gave details of where and when she was to be buried.

Going through the newspaper archives, he also found a photograph of Margaret wearing a helmet. An ARP warden had an arm around her shoulder. A second man wore a Civil Defence Force helmet. The date of the piece was just days before the invasion. They were laughing and smiling as though they couldn't comprehend what was about to befall the colony. The caption read: *We're ready for anything!*

Margaret had been a young child with dark wavy hair and eyes that seemed to shine out of the picture. A pretty girl that no doubt became an attractive woman.

The sun was well past its zenith and dazzled off gold script. She had a stylish, grey marble headstone. The engraving didn't tell Balcombe anything new although he noted an interesting phrase. It referred to Margaret as a *Stanley Survivor*.

There was a double grave beside Margaret's. Its simple tombstone was for Jack and Olive Sotherland who'd died in January 1941 and May 1942, respectively. He'd been thirty-eight and his wife thirty-two. The inscription included: *loving parents of Margaret*.

Balcombe's next visit was to Government House and the records section, where he located Margaret's death certificate. As a detective, he instinctively crosschecked the details, and they tallied. There was nothing unusual except perhaps the registered cause of death.

It said, *heart failure by misadventure*.

He noted the name of the doctor who had signed the certificate.

Three hours later, he was in Inspector Munro's abandoned property by the wharf. He'd sent an anonymous coded message that Munro would understand.

The detective arrived thirty minutes later than requested and he was scowling.

"What's your game, Balcombe? If this has anything to do with that stunt you pulled at Wellington Inn—"

"It's not."

Munro's features relaxed slightly. "And if you're going to threaten me." He lifted his jacket to expose his gun. "I won't hesitate to use this."

Balcombe smiled. If he came for Munro, the inspector wouldn't be expecting him. He wouldn't call him to a meeting first.

"I'm just doing a favour for a friend." Balcombe opened his hands and gave a shrug. "Probably pointless, but I'm just looking for a distraction. I'm sure you would appreciate that."

"The death of Margaret Sotherland?"

Balcombe's note had mentioned the girl's name as well as who the examining doctor had been.

"Misadventure," Balcombe said. "That's what the death certificate states."

Munro nodded. "I pulled the file. The police report as well as the medical record. Sotherland died of an overdose. Opium. You know how it is. Most of the population is taking opium. People die from overdoses every day."

"But not most white people."

"True, it's less common, but it doesn't mean it didn't happen. She had an empty bottle of Paregoric beside her. Took one too many swigs, it seems."

"Can Paregoric kill you? I thought it was medicinal."

"Anything in the right quantity can kill you. But you're right, normally it's not enough, but it was the final straw or someone using."

"Was there a note?" Balcombe asked.

"What, like a suicide note? You're investigating this as a suicide?"

"That's the question."

"There was no note."

Balcombe waited a beat. "Did you investigate or are you just telling me what's in the report?"

Munro sighed. "It wasn't my case. There are multiple incidents like this each week, and I don't get involved unless there's something suspicious."

"And the death of a young, fit girl doesn't raise suspicions?"

"No. Not if she was a user."

Munro pulled a slip of paper from his pocket. "You may already have this, but since you're looking into her death, I thought you'd need this."

Balcombe took the slip. On it was the address of a boarding house on Wan Chai Road.

"Where she lived?"

Munro nodded.

"Thank you."

"Anything else?" Munro asked with a hint of sarcasm.

"I'd like to know if there's been anything similar in the recent past. Suicides or overdose misadventures"— Balcombe made quotation marks in the air—"of young, white females."

Munro shook his head slowly. "I don't mind you wasting your time, Balcombe, but not mine. I'm far too busy to worry about creating additional work for myself."

★ ★ ★

Albert was waiting for him when Balcombe returned home. He'd not seen her for two days since dismissing her at the Wellington.

She walked into the alley beside his apartment block, and he followed.

"You have something for me?" he asked.

"You wanted the name of Feng's boss."

"You found it."

She hesitated. "Nie Pingping."

"Is that a real name?"

"What's a *real* name?" she said with more impudence than he liked. "It's the name he goes by. Have you heard of him?"

"No. Should I have?"

She paused again and lowered her already hushed voice even further.

"Pardon?" Balcombe said, leaning closer.

"Triad," she whispered. "He's from the Walled City with Triad links."

"All right," Balcombe said.

Albert said nothing.

"Where do I find Mr. Pingpong?"

"Pingping," she said. "And, as I'm sure you know, it would be Mr. *Nie.*"

"Where, Albert?"

"The Walled City. And you aren't going there."

No, he wasn't. It was an enclave of China, surrounded by Kowloon, a weird lawless block of housing squeezed into the area of three football pitches.

"But you're going to tell me where he goes. People like him don't stay in the Walled City. Not people who run businesses in Kowloon—at least I know he's running people in Kowloon."

Albert shook her head. "This is a mistake."

"Tell me!"

And so she listed Pingping's gambling, alcohol and prostitution operations. Six of them. And she said he had links to smuggling but hadn't dared pursue it any further. Balcombe paid her well, but not that well.

"My life is worth at least three times the amount you pay me."

Balcombe laughed but then realized she was being serious.

"All right," he said. "Just tell me where he's most vulnerable."

"I don't know."

He pulled a sheaf of dollars from his wallet. "Here's three times what I normally pay you. Now go and find me an opportunity."

"An opportunity?"

"You know what I mean, Albert."

"What about tomorrow? Do you need me?"

"No," he said. "I'll just be poking around an old house on Wan Chai Road."

# Chapter Ten

Munro sat at his desk. Balcombe was right. Keeping him busy would have its benefits. BlackJack was less likely to act if Balcombe was occupied.

Munro wrote out a request for a search of the files. Specifically, he wanted any single white females who had died under suspicious circumstances in the last year.

Once submitted, he turned his attention to the outstanding investigations on his desk. After flicking through the top three, hoping for inspiration, he picked up the file on the body he'd brought over from Kowloon: Feng Shubiao. He glanced at Doctor Swift's report and again wished he'd got his friend to perform the autopsy. Yeung was never unwell, but he'd chosen that damn day to be sick.

Munro shook his head at his bad luck. At least Yeung was soon over the virus that had kept him from work.

"Penny for them," a gruff voice said, cutting into his thoughts.

Munro's eyes jerked from the report.

The man towering over him was Inspector Gordon Garrett. Under their breaths, the men called him

Garrotte although it seemed a little unfair. The man was on secondment from the Suez, having been in Mandatory Palestine until the handover to Israel. He had tanned skin and bright blue eyes, although the good looks ended there. Garrett's grey hair tended to be unkempt, and his beard irregularly trimmed. His clothes took a higher priority than his personal grooming. As though he was hiding behind a suit. Or perhaps his self-esteem didn't warrant attention to the state of his facial hair.

When asked why there wasn't a Mrs. Garrett, the inspector responded that wives got in the way of travel and career. Which was true. Although Munro suspected there was more to the story. There probably had been a Mrs. Garrett years ago, and he'd let himself go since it ended. That was Munro's private theory, anyway.

It would also explain why Garrett wasn't overly friendly, although racism seemed to run strongly through the man's veins. Then again, it was something to be expected in the British colonies.

"Munro?" Garrett said in a challenging tone. They were the same rank and yet, the way the other man spoke to Munro, anyone listening would think he was the superior.

"Yes?"

Garrett said nothing for a moment. Then he said just one word: "Tooki."

It was a Korean word, and one that Munro hadn't heard for two decades. It meant *alien devil* and was used as a derogative name for anyone of mixed race. He'd been called it many times in his youth. Munro met Garrett's gaze and tried to hide his feelings.

"I beg your pardon?"

"Nothing."

Munro forced a smile. "How can I help you, Garrett?"

"Tell me about your interesting case," Garrett said, sounding like he expected Munro to report to him.

"Which one?"

"The one you've just been reading. You looked intrigued."

"Just another one for the pile," Munro said dismissively, closing the Feng Shubiao report and sliding it to the other end of the desk, away from Garrett.

The other inspector patted, then leaned on the bundle sitting on Munro's desk.

"Too much for you?"

"Too much paperwork," Munro said.

Garrett nodded although his eyes remained unfriendly.

"You live here in the single officer's quarters?"

"I do."

"We should have a drink sometime," Garrett said.

"I'd like that," Munro lied.

"Good." Garrett nodded again, pushed off the pile of folders, towered over Munro for a minute and then finally strolled out of the office.

Two of the junior men were staring.

"Back to work!" Munro snapped, and the men put their heads down.

He pulled the next report from the top of his pile.

*What the heck?*

It was an old case, dating back six months ago. In fact, it had Munro's predecessor's name on it: DI Bill Teags.

Someone was playing games. Someone was messing with him. Munro looked around to see who was watching. But his men had their heads down. And then he got it. Garrett. That's why the man had his hand on the pile. He'd used sleight of hand to slip the old file onto the top.

Munro opened it. He couldn't help himself. Then the memories came flooding back.

# Chapter Eleven

The boarding house on Wan Chai Road was called Homeville, although it looked anything but homely. It appeared old, built of mismatched bricks, probably from other demolished or war-damaged buildings. Or perhaps they were leftovers, and it was built by someone who didn't care about aesthetics. There were four floors, the lower two of which had bars at the windows.

Balcombe went into the entrance hall and knocked on a door marked "Caretaker".

"One minute," a lady mumbled before he heard someone scuffling to the door. A floral scent wafted out as she opened the door. An astringent edge made Balcombe suspect that the scent wasn't natural or perhaps was covering the smell of something less pleasant.

She was in her fifties with grey hair pinned up in circles around her head. Along with excessive makeup, she wore a brightly coloured house coat. A row of expensive-looking pearls hung around her sagging neck. A monkey on a silver chain hopped and chattered behind her.

"Yes?" Her accent was fake, trying to sound posh. She looked him up and down and frowned. "You're not here for the apartment, then?"

The monkey scrambled up her coat and perched on her shoulder and studied Balcombe with its head cocked to one side.

"Margaret Sotherland used to live here," he said. "Flat ten."

"Yes, that's right. And who might you be?"

"A relative," he lied. The idea came to him, thinking that the woman might be more likely to let him into the flat. As a random investigator, he doubted he'd gain access.

Her eyes widened. "Her brother?"

"Cousin from Kent. The family lived there before Rosyth in Scotland." He added details to make his subterfuge more convincing.

She didn't look like she needed to be convinced.

"Good," she said. "I'm supposed to let the room, but it's got her junk in it. That and the fact she died in there puts people off, see?" He noticed that the posh accent slipped at the end.

"Would you show me her rooms?"

"Toby, down!" she said, and the monkey jumped down. She detached the chain from a wrist and reached behind the door. Her hand came back with a bunch of keys.

"This way," she said as she stepped into the hallway and shut her door.

They turned left and went up a flight of stairs. At the top they went right past two doors before stopping at number 10. He noticed a communal kitchen and shared toilet. There was no bathroom or tub that he could see.

The door to number 8 opened and an elderly woman peered out. Balcombe caught a waft of stale cigarette smoke, and when she spoke, the woman had a smoker's deep, crackly voice.

"Hello? Are you showing the room?"

The caretaker swivelled and glared. "Nothing to do with you, Mrs. Gallshaw. Go inside."

The old woman grunted and shut her door.

"Nosey old busybody," the caretaker said and unlocked the door to Margaret's room. The door swung inwards.

Balcombe stepped toward it and the woman barred his way.

"Since her stuff is here and... well, there's two months' rent that's due."

"She's only been dead one month."

The caretaker tapped her bright red lips before speaking. "We're into the fifth week and it's a month in advance."

Balcombe stepped around her and into the room.

The woman grabbed his arm. "Money first, young man! You might be a cousin, but the rent is overdue."

He wondered what she thought she could do if he brushed her off. Maybe she had a weapon. It was unlikely to be a gun since she'd need a licence or be ex-services. And as a woman, she wouldn't qualify, anyway. However, he didn't want trouble.

"How much?" he said.

"Eighteen dollars."

That was cheap for a typical island apartment, but from the look of it this wasn't typical. It was a bedsit, a single room on the second floor, facing inland. He saw barred windows that made it feel like a prison cell. It was hot and stuffy too, but it was clean and tidy.

Balcombe peeled off ten dollars and held them out. The amount didn't bother him. It was small change but make it hard to get and it would be all the more appreciated. That was his experience. So, he always let them haggle.

"Fifteen," she said, eyeing the money but not taking it.

He waited. The money wasn't for rent. It wouldn't go in the books and reach the landlord. This was her pocket money.

"Fine," she said eventually and snatched the cash from his hand. "But you clear it all out by tomorrow."

She handed him a key ring. It had the door key and another. "For the window bars," she said.

"Thank you." He shut the door with the caretaker on the far side.

Before doing anything else, he put gloves on, just in case. Then he surveyed the room.

It had a bed, a sink, a chest of drawers, and a chair. Beside the bed was a table with a lamp, a brown bottle with a screw cap, a glass and a book.

There were hooks on the wall behind the door. From them hung eight dresses. He wasn't an expert on ladies' clothes, but the dresses were well-made, quality items. There were also four pairs of nice shoes.

He paused, wondering why someone would live in this dump but have expensive clothes.

The chest of drawers was full of nice things, too. They smelled fresh. One drawer had a vanity bag with make-up.

There was a double photo frame on top of the drawers, a man on the left and a woman on the right. The man was older and, despite the smile, didn't look well. It was the same man who'd been in the photograph in the newspaper; the one with his arm around Margaret.

The woman was pretty, with the same bright eyes as her daughter. Jack and Olive Sotherland, Balcombe figured.

He turned his attention to the bed. Despite being slightly crumpled, the bottom sheet was clean. Another white sheet lay heaped on the floor. The chair was turned beside the bed, facing it. The bottle was four inches tall. The yellow label had a red cross on it, symbolizing its exemption from laws concerning opium despite being a camphorated tincture of opium. This was Paregoric, containing the drug that she'd overdosed on. He glanced at the label and noted a long list of purposes, including stress and insomnia.

A miracle drug, it seemed.

He unscrewed the top and sniffed the bottle, detecting a sweet honey scent. The glass was empty except for a tiny drop of clear liquid. He tilted the glass and noted a viscosity to the liquid. The glass also smelled slightly of honey, but he may have imagined it.

Balcombe checked under the bed. The pillow and a cushion were under it, and he wondered why. It was possible the people who'd removed the body had just thrown everything onto the floor and kicked them out of the way.

His search found no more bottles of the medication or any other evidence of opium abuse. And he found nothing in writing, no suicide note. No notes of any kind.

He looked at the window. Although on the second floor, the ground rose steeply behind the property and the drop was less than four feet. That explained the bars on the outside of the window—in case of attempted break-in. Burglar-bars, some people called them.

The window was shut with the latch down. However the bars were against the window but appeared unlocked.

He lifted the window latch and it opened easily, swinging inwards. He pushed the bars. Corroded hinges creaked but it took little effort to move them out and back. He could see a round hole where the key fit. Closing the bars, he inserted the key and locked them.

He stepped back to the door and surveyed the room again. What had happened here? Was it a simple matter of an overdose?

It troubled him. The setup of the room, and the bottle. Maybe it was nothing, but his detective's mind asked why Margaret had screwed the top back on the bottle. If it was suicide, she wouldn't care. If she was a heavy opium user, drugged to the eyeballs, would she even think of it?

And there was the window. Why would the bars be unlocked?

# Chapter Twelve

Bill, better known as Old Bill, Teags hadn't always been conscientious. He had served as a detective in Hong Kong for thirty years and people said that the war affected him. It affected everyone, but Teags' spirit had been crushed by the invasion and his subsequent incarceration. While some people, like the Governor, came out of Stanley Prison, full of energy and enthusiasm for rebuilding Hong Kong, Old Bill turned to drink.

People who knew him best said that he suffered night terrors although he denied it. All Munro had noticed were the hand tremors and occasional tics.

An incident during the Karen Vaughn case had forced his retirement. It had also seen the death of the case. Teags had spent too long on it.

Which may have explained his breakdown.

He beat up a suspect and deliberately drove a car into a wall, almost killing himself. The assault victim didn't press charges and Munro suspected senior people had been involved to protect him. *Diminished responsibility due to psychiatric reasons* was the formal pronouncement and Teags slipped away into obscurity.

When Munro was promoted as his replacement, the Chief made it clear that results were required and set a rule that any case more than three months old, had to be dropped unless progress was being made. Of course, he was still insisting on results.

So why had Garrett sneaked the file onto Munro's desk?

Munro picked up the file. He knew the story.

Geoffrey Prisgrove had taken his daughter, Nicola and her friend, Karen to the cinema. The Saturday Morning Matinee was their regular treat and had been for almost a year. And then came September 12th. Three of them went into the cinema but only two came out. Geoff and Nicola Prisgrove. Dad and daughter. Karen Vaughn never returned home. She had been ten years old.

The version in the newspapers reported that she'd *never been seen again* although there were over a hundred people who reported seeing Karen on that day. Ninety-three people gave witness statements. Some of them reported seeing her during the matinee, most of them later in the day. And ten witnesses claimed to have seen Karen days later.

The later ones were all ruled out as mistaken identity. The photograph in the newspaper showed Karen in her school uniform of a blue, pleated skirt and white blouse. And each of the later witnesses claimed to have seen her in that same uniform. Which was impossible since the uniform was still at her home.

On the day she disappeared, Karen had been wearing a blue and white top with a brown skirt. Her black hair had been in a single bunch rather than her usual two. Nicola had worn a red dress and many sightings mentioned that.

Teags had marked all the sightings on a map. They spread from the North Point to Sheung Wan in the west. But the majority were in Central Victoria along Queens Road and Garden Road, with a cluster around the lower Peak tram station.

Munro read the daughter's statement. Nicola Prisgrove said they'd watched the newsreel, followed by Heckle and Jeckle and Mighty Mouse—which she loved. The cliff-hangers of the main feature were always ridiculous, but they didn't mind. After the serial came the final programme: a slapstick comedy. And of course, it all wrapped up with everyone standing and singing *God Save The Queen*.

But they hadn't stayed till the end. Geoffrey and Nicola didn't enjoy Norman Wisdom and left ahead of the crush. Karen wanted to stay and so they waited outside for her.

"She's lovely, isn't she—the new queen, I mean?" Nicola had said to Teags. "That's one reason why Karen wanted to stay—to sing the national anthem. *God Save The Queen*—it's so amazing to have a queen!"

Over a thousand people poured out onto the street, but Karen wasn't among them. When the ushers shut the doors, Geoffrey decided they must have missed Karen and they set off home.

Nicola said that they looked out for her friend all the way back.

Inspector Teags had questioned why they didn't immediately go to Karen's home to check if she was there. Nicola hadn't had an answer.

Geoffrey Prisgrove, on the other hand, explained that he felt guilty for leaving Karen in the cinema. He didn't want to turn up at Karen's home and get berated by her mother.

"She's Chinese and has a fiery temper!" Prisgrove had told Teags.

"You didn't report Karen missing until seven hours later," Teags said.

"Yes. That's when Simon Vaughn, Karen's father, came to our house to collect her."

"And you weren't worried until then?"

"Not really. Because—as I have already stated—I believed Karen had gone home without us."

"Had she ever done that before?"

"Yes. Well, I don't know."

"What does that mean?"

"She's an independent child, known to do her own thing. You know, go off. A bit naughty, I suppose. So I wasn't too surprised that she'd go ahead without us."

Teags had questioned Nicola again and didn't like that she used the same expression about Karen being *a bit naughty* and wasn't too surprised that she'd go ahead without them.

He'd written in his notes: *I think the dad told Nicola what to say.*

He'd interviewed Geoffrey Prisgrove no less than five times and Teags developed a theory. Mrs. Prisgrove worked on Saturdays. She wasn't there when Geoffrey and his daughter got home, and so there were no witnesses. Had Karen been with them? Was Prisgrove covering something up? Teags suspected so.

"What happened, Geoff?" Teags had asked in his fourth interview. "What really happened to Karen?"

"I don't know what you mean or are implying."

Teags noted Prisgrove's defensiveness, but a search of the home found no trace of blood and Nicola's response afterwards was the first Bill Teags believed.

"That's daft," she'd said almost relieved, when he asked her.

Teags also questioned Prisgrove about his movements after returning home. The man claimed that he and Nicola had spent time wandering around the markets in the central district.

Once again, Teags noted the similarity in the father and daughter's statements. He wrote: Prisgrove is coaching his daughter. Does that make him guilty?

The Prisgroves lived on Bowen Road. The route from Queens Theatre to Bowen Road could have taken them past the Peak tram lower station.

Teags must have walked the route a hundred times after Karen's disappearance. He focused on Saturdays and various timings, hoping to find someone who would speak rather than be a formal witness. The Chinese community, in particular, was wary of the police. Too many times—in their view—innocent people were charged with a crime, just because they came forward with information. Raise your hand and look guilty.

Teags had made some interesting discoveries. A handful of people said they remembered two girls on their own in the vicinity of Garden Road and Kennedy. Three people said they'd seen Prisgrove with a girl during the afternoon. However no one described Karen. The missing girl was Eurasian with darker skin than her friend, Nicola Prisgrove. Karen had worn a brown skirt and Nicola a more distinctive red one. People remembered the red one.

Teags concluded the couple seen were Prisgrove and Nicola although based on the description, this was not two people off shopping. They looked as though they'd lost something—or someone, Teags concluded.

He questioned Prisgrove a final time and was told that they had an eye out in case they bumped into Karen.

Teags didn't like the explanation. On the one hand, they weren't worried but on the other, they were looking for her. Why would they do that? However Teags questioning had led nowhere.

What did lead to his next suspect was an alleged sighting of a girl, answering to the description of Karen, outside the Masonic Hall on Zetland Street.

One unofficial witness reported seeing a girl go inside. A second witness said he'd seen a man talking to a dark-skinned, young girl on the steps. Neither came forward to be interviewed. However a third provided a statement that she'd seen a girl in a brown skirt go up the steps, speak to someone she called the doorman, and go inside.

Eric Cattles was in his sixties. He wore a smart black suit every day to work, and he was the curator of Zetland Hall.

And Eric Cattles was known to the police. It was said that he had an unhealthy interest in children, although he'd never been arrested or charged.

The police had been called when he'd been spotted outside school premises. He would hang around at the end of the school day handing out sweets.

He claimed it was innocent, and when asked to move on, he'd turn up outside another school a few days later.

There had also been complaints about him at work. On three occasions that the police knew about, Cattles had invited a child off the street and given them a tour of the Masonic meeting hall. Nothing had happened, as far as Munro was aware, but parents had complained.

Was he just an innocent, sad old man who wanted to give children sweets? Maybe he longed to be a grandfather and vicariously enjoy the enthusiasm and carefree happiness of youth.

Or maybe there was something more sinister about the old man. Teags thought so. Particularly when Cattles panicked when he was picked up by police and accompanied them to the station.

In the first interview, he denied seeing Karen.

Teags had revisited the witness statements and re-interviewed the lady who had thought she'd seen Karen near the lower station. He concluded that Karen might have been heading for the Masonic Hall.

When presented with this in the second interview, Cattles said that he'd seen two girls and maybe one of them was Karen. She'd entered the foyer of Zetland Hall, then changed her mind and left.

In the third interview, he changed his story and claimed to have been off work with a stomach bug that day. He produced evidence that transpired to show he was at work until lunchtime.

Cattles' excuse for the discrepancy was his poor memory. Teags had taken the opportunity to search Cattles' house and found what he'd thought was the evidence. On a top shelf, Cattles kept a small wooden casket, inside which were suspicious objects including a plastic ring and pair of knickers.

Karen Vaughn's parents didn't recognize the ring although Karen's friend. Nicola did. But it was not reliable evidence since such rings were ten-a-penny and the one found couldn't be directly linked to Karen. The underwear too. Mr. Vaughn could only say that the knickers were possibly Karen's. There was no name inside, and they were widely available.

Teags was convinced the items were trophies and grilled him in the fourth session after holding him in a cell for two days. The man continued to deny wrongdoing.

"It's all family ephemera," Cattles said. "Nothing more, nothing less."

They released him. The items found weren't evidence. Plus, the Chief had noticed the timing issues. Karen couldn't have been near the Masonic Hall before Cattles went home with sickness. At the time she was allegedly going inside and meeting him, she was still at the cinema with Nicola and Geoffrey Prisgrove.

However, at this point, Teags was already showing signs of stress. The case was months old, and Karen was undoubtedly dead. Munro remembered they'd all discussed it and concluded the same thing.

After too many beers, Teags had turned up at Cattles' home and beaten him. He wrecked the house as well, using a sledgehammer, claiming the old man must have a secret hiding place behind the walls.

Teags had hoped to get a confession. He'd hoped to find a body. But he got nothing except a reprimand. And the following night, Teags drove his car at full speed into a wall. Munro had seen the crash site as East Point. Teags had been aiming for the water and missed. He'd intended to drown but instead faced the ignominy of a medical assessment that pointed to psychiatric problems.

It was a duff, cold case. There could be no happy outcome because Karen Vaughn was undoubtedly dead.

And Inspector Garrett had put it on Munro's desk. There could be only one explanation. Garrett was trying to intimidate him.

# Chapter Thirteen

Balcombe went downstairs and knocked on the caretaker's door again. The woman bustled out with a scowl. "What now?"

"Who found Margaret Sotherland's body?"

"I did," the woman said as Toby the monkey scampered onto her shoulder. She fed him a peanut. "Although she'd been dead for three days. The room smelled really bad, I can tell you."

"She was lying on the bed?"

"Naked as the day she was born." She chuckled, then her face dropped. "Oh sorry, you being a cousin and all, you don't want—"

"It's all right," Balcombe said, putting on a sorrowful voice. "I can cope. I'd just like to understand what happened to poor Margaret."

The caretaker's eyes narrowed slightly, a thought crossing her face.

Balcombe said, "Was she covered by the white sheet on the floor?"

"Yes."

"Is anything else different—from then to now?"

The caretaker's eyes flickered enough to let Balcombe know she was about to lie. "No, not that I've noticed."

"What's different?" he said firmly.

Her face set hard. "Who are you again?"

Balcombe smiled sweetly. "Her cousin. I just want to get to know her. It's been such a long time..." He handed the woman another five dollars. "Please."

"All right."

"So, what changed apart from the sheet?"

"Nothing," she blurted.

Balcombe waited and decided not to pursue it for the time being. The monkey chattered, and she fed it another peanut.

Balcombe said, "What was Margaret like as a tenant?"

"Hardly knew the girl," the caretaker said. "Wasn't here long. Most people aren't."

A man came in through the front door. He was dressed like a labourer, although his demeanour and depressed slouch suggested he was looking for work rather than doing any. He nodded politely as he passed and then climbed the stairs.

Balcombe said, "Is this a halfway house?"

"What ex-cons?" she said gruffly, as though he'd insulted her.

"No, sorry. People with a drink or drugs problem?"

"Doesn't everyone... have a drink or drugs problem around here?"

Balcombe peeled off another five dollars. "Tell me something worthwhile about Margaret."

"Thought she were a bit of a lady," the caretaker said raising an eyebrow. "Could be a bit hoity-toity, a bit lardy-da. Looked down her nose at the likes of me—at most people here."

"Did she have any visitors?"

"Not that I paid any mind to."

"Friends?"

"Gladys might know. I saw them talking from time to time."

"Gladys?"

The caretaker held out a hand for the money. Balcombe let her take it.

"She's in number fifteen, third floor. But she won't be back until after six tonight."

★ ★ ★

At six, Balcombe was on Wan Chai Road outside the boarding house. He watched people come and go and concluded the building was somewhere Europeans, down on their luck, stayed. Maybe not forever, if they could help it. Cheap rent for a while, still on the island. A place to use until things got better again—hopefully.

"Gladys?" he said as a young woman approached the front door with a brown parcel under her arm. He recognized her from the caretaker's description. Gladys was a few years older than Margaret would have been. She was smartly dressed and had a respectful air about her.

She stopped and looked at Balcombe with suspicion.

"Do I know you?"

"No," he said. "But I'm hoping you can tell me about Margaret Sotherland."

She continued to look dubious, and Balcombe spoke honestly this time.

"I'm an investigator. I'm just—"

Gladys blinked. "Oh, thank goodness. I was so shocked at her death. It didn't seem right."

"She wasn't a user?"

66

"Drugs? I doubt it." She glanced around, then back. "Look, I'll just take this meat up to my husband and be straight back down. Then we can talk."

Less than ten minutes later, Balcombe and Gladys were in a teashop. She said she didn't have long because her husband wanted his dinner, but she gratefully accepted Balcombe's offer of tea and a slice of fruit cake.

"She was a lovely girl," Gladys said once they'd sat down. "Really lovely. Such a sweet nature, and pretty too."

"What happened to her?"

Gladys shook her head. "You mean how did she die? Well, as I said, it wasn't drugs, I'm sure of it. She wasn't the sort—and you get to see them all in Homeville. You get used to spotting it. No, she wasn't using drugs."

"The death certificate said heart failure."

"Then I suppose that was what it was." She shook her head again and took a sip of tea. "I'm not medically trained, so I wouldn't know. We didn't talk much, just the occasional hello although we'd both lost our fathers about the same time. Her father died of heart trouble. They say stress and the Hong Kong climate got to him. Perhaps it was inherited?"

"Was she under stress?"

Gladys sighed. "Aren't we all?"

"Why was she was living in the boarding house?"

"She didn't say. I got the sense she was ashamed about whatever the reason was."

"Ashamed?"

"Of course. My husband lost his job at the dockyard last year. He doesn't talk about it. It's like someone whipped away his manhood."

Those last words came out more falteringly and Balcombe wondered if she was about to cry, but she didn't. She breathed in and straightened her back.

"We soldier on," she said, and he figured it was her personal mantra.

Balcombe waited a moment before saying, "Who do you work for, Gladys?"

"I'm a housemaid." She tried to make it sound better than it was, but he could see she was embarrassed.

"What about Margaret?"

"She didn't work."

Balcombe waited in case the friend would reveal more, but she didn't.

"Margaret had nice shoes and clothes," he said as a prompt.

"Yes, she did. I think she came from money. Must have been to afford the clothes and jewellery she had."

Balcombe said nothing and Gladys seemed to think as she drank her tea. Then she said, "Maybe she used to work. Perhaps she also lost her job, although she didn't tell me."

"She moved to the boarding house about eleven weeks ago," he said.

"Yes, she wasn't with us long."

"Do you know where she came from?"

Gladys thought, took another sip and then gave Balcombe an address on Seymour Road. "I think that's what she told me and at the time I wasn't sure it was the truth. You know how it can be? People make up stories rather than be honest about their past. However, yes, I think she probably did live there."

She glanced up at the clock on the wall and panicked. "Oh goodness, I must get back and cook his nibs his dinner!"

She hadn't previously touched her cake and she quickly wrapped it in a napkin and placed it in her handbag. Balcombe suspected that it would be shared with her husband—at least, he hoped she'd get half of it.

Darkness was rushing in, which wasn't the best time to start knocking on people's doors. He was close to Queens Road East and its regular trams, so he caught the next one going west and travelled with workers heading home for the evening.

When he got back to his apartment, Albert was waiting outside.

"I hope you're not ditching me for the tram," Albert said.

Balcombe shook his head. "Don't worry, you've still got a job."

"Good." Albert handed him a piece of paper with an address. "And this didn't cost me my life after all—although there are no refunds!"

"Very funny." Balcombe chuckled, then dropped his voice. "Is this where I'll find our Pingpong friend?"

"You know it's Pingping and yes. But it's a secure building," Albert said. "There are no connected buildings. There are no windows on the ground floor. The windows on the first floor have shutters and probably don't even open. That's what I was told."

"That does sound secure."

She ignored him and continued: "There is one entrance on the ground floor. Two men guard this. Inside there will be at least two more men guarding the stairs. Pingping uses the first floor for his fun so no one goes up and—"

"What's his *fun*?" Balcombe interrupted.

"That part wasn't clear. Although, I suspect it's only him who has the fun. And not the teenagers he has sent up. Boys and girls. He spends an hour with them and

69

then goes to the top floor for a massage. The masseur is hand-picked, always the same, goes in advance and leaves later. If you are thinking you will go in before and lie in wait, forget it. You can't. They always search it from top to bottom before Pingping arrives."

"Secure and cautious."

"There was once an attempt on his life, apparently."

"Wait here." Balcombe said before disappearing inside his building. A few minutes later, he reappeared carrying a Kodak Brownie.

"A camera?" she said.

"Take it. Walk around and take photos of all sides of the building. And don't get caught."

She shook her head with derision. "I won't get caught. I'm invisible."

"Then don't be overconfident." He saw her shrug. "I mean it, Albert!"

"All right, I'll be especially careful."

"And when you're done, take the camera to Mr. Faulls."

"Your friend."

"He'll process the film. And tell you when you'll be able to collect the photos."

# Chapter Fourteen

Munro found Garrett in a bar, alone and reading a newspaper.

Munro slapped the folder on the table.

"So, Garrett, it's time we had a chat."

The other man looked up slowly, his face impassive. Munro noted long grey hairs sprouting from his nostrils and wondered whether Garrett didn't care or hadn't noticed them.

Garrett said nothing, waiting. He took a sip of beer.

"The Karen Vaughn case," Munro said, jabbing a finger at the file. "You left it on my desk."

Garrett's fish-cold eyes studied him.

Munro said, "What's your game?"

Garrett looked over his shoulder and waved. "A beer for my colleague," he called to the barman. Then, turning back to Munro, said, "It's a heads-up."

"A heads-up?"

"Have you read the file?"

"I lived the file. It was one of my boss's cases."

Garrett took another sip. "Ah, DI Teags. I hear he had problems."

Munro's beer arrived, but he didn't touch it.

"He's a good man."

"Aren't we all?" Garrett asked. Munro didn't comment.

Garrett took a longer drink and pointed to the stool opposite. "Sit down, Munro. It's time we got properly acquainted. I read your file. You came here in thirty-three... Half Korean..."

Munro expected to be called Tooki again, but Garrett pointed to the stool again and said, "Your surname's Scottish, is it?"

Munro sat. "My real name is Jo Munro. Since I'm Korean, Munro is my given name. Jo without an 'e' is my family name. When I registered for work in Hong Kong, the clerk was confused. He thought my first name was Joe."

Garrett nodded, as though the information was more interesting than it really was. "And your wife was killed during the occupation."

Munro gritted his teeth. "Why are you messing with me, Garrett?"

The other man smiled. "You misunderstand me, old chap."

"Do I?"

"I want us to have a better working relationship."

"We don't have *any* working relationship," Munro said. Garrett was civil police rather than CID. They didn't need to work together.

"Have your drink," Garrett said, and Munro's thirst overcame his stubbornness. He downed a third of the glass and felt the warm ale ease the tension in his gullet.

Garrett watched him and smiled.

"It's tough out here," he said. "Even tougher than usual for the police. Do you like Westerns?"

"Westerns?" Munro said taken by surprise. Thoughts of the Karen Vaughn case rushed in. Red

Ryder was the cliff-hanger cowboy series that the girls had watched with Geoffrey Prisgrove.

"The loneliness of the lawman," Garrett said more quietly.

"Is that a film?"

"Perhaps. If it is, I haven't seen it, but it would be a good title because it describes us—as well as most of the Westerns with lawmen. Have you noticed that the plots are often the same? Young man sees wrong and takes up the fight—sometimes he becomes the sheriff but often it's unnecessary. We know the goodie is on the side of the law. He tracks down the baddies and there's a fight. There's always a point at which you think he's going to lose, but in the end, he wins through. The baddies are defeated, and the good guy gets the girl."

"That doesn't sound lonely."

"Well, he usually loses the girl, or you realize it's not a long-term relationship. There's always another fight and a different girl. They don't have friends."

"The good guys have partners, don't they? Sidekicks, I think they're called."

Garrett shook his head. "Yes, but they aren't really friends. You take the Lone Ranger. He has Tonto for support, but he isn't called Lone for nothing."

"I don't watch Westerns," Munro said, taking another gulp of beer.

"Maybe you should," Garrett said, "but that's not the point. The lawman can't let people get too close to him—not unless he changes career. Unlike the Silver Screen, there's never a happy ending. Like in the Karen Vaughn case—like for William Teags."

"Bill," Munro corrected. "He never liked to be called William."

Garrett shrugged, unconcerned.

Munro said, "So you gave me the file because what…? You're telling me it's time for me to change my career?"

Garrett finished his beer and ordered more. Munro declined the offer.

Garrett opened the file and glanced at it although Munro knew he wasn't reading. He was delaying.

The fresh glass of beer arrived.

"I've been here for almost four weeks," Garrett said. "And I already know the problem."

"What's that?"

"Too many criminals and not enough law enforcement."

Munro said nothing. The population of Hong Kong had exploded. More than a million people had flooded into the colony since the end of the war and the country couldn't cope. There wasn't the infrastructure and there weren't the jobs. Poverty led to crime, although Munro had learned that it wasn't so straightforward. People needed food and shelter and could commit crime to survive. However the real problem was vulnerability. Those same desperate people were susceptible to use by hardened criminals. It was the criminal organisations that were the root cause and not the petty criminals.

"The prisons are overcrowded. Victoria Gaol has three times the number of inmates than it was designed for. Stanley Prison is as bad."

Munro finished his drink. He wasn't getting drawn into a conversation about the failings of the criminal justice system.

Garrett said, "The solution is a new prison. The Commissioner is going to announce the building of a massive open prison on Lantau Island."

Munro had heard this before. It had come from someone with alleged connections with the Governor and he suspected Garrett was doing the same—implying connections.

"Interesting," Munro said.

Garrett looked at him hard. "Here's my message, Munro. You can be part of a brighter policing future, or you can end up like William Teags." He shrugged a shoulder. "It's as simple as that."

Munro stood. He picked up the file. "Thank you for the drink and the *heads-up*, Garrett."

"Oh that wasn't the heads-up, old chap." Garrett smiled. "I wanted to warn you that I'm taking your job."

# Chapter Fifteen

Seymour Road wasn't as prestigious an address as the nearby Robinson or Cairn roads, but it was a world apart from the boarding house. The houses had walled gardens and a stunning view across the harbour.

Had Margaret really sunk from such a property to the near slum on Wan Chai Road?

There were four apartments in the property and Balcombe didn't know which one had been Margaret's. He knocked on the first door and got no answer. Nothing from the second either. He went upstairs and door three was answered.

"Did Margaret Sotherland used to live here?" he asked the elderly lady who stood looking at him uncertainly. "I'm a friend trying to trace her," he added.

"Pardon?" she said with a hand to her ear. "You want to live here?"

Balcombe spoke slowly and clearly. "I am looking for Margaret. Margaret Sotherland."

The elderly lady shook her head, confused. Then she pointed to door four. "Try there." And without a farewell, the door was shut in his face.

Balcombe knocked on the door opposite. A slim middle-aged man swept it open. He wore a silk kimono with little underneath, Balcombe surmised. The man smiled slightly after an appraising glance.

"Well now, how may I help you?"

Balcombe repeated his story about being a friend of Margaret's.

"Oh, you should come in," the man said, swept the door open, and with a flourish, spun and walked into a sumptuous lounge. Then he turned sharply with a flick of his head and held out a soft hand. "I'm Marcus."

"Balcombe. Charles Balcombe."

Windows faced east and west so that the apartment had views of both the sea and mountain. Windowsills were covered in trinkets and photographs with elaborate silver frames. Covering a quarter of a feature wall was an oil painting—something very colourful and arty that Balcombe had no appreciation of. There were rugs and throws and cushions that may have been Persian themed. There were chaise lounges and pouffe stools. A giant footstool acted like a central table.

Marcus flopped onto a chaise and Balcombe perched on a nearby pouffe.

"Do tell me about yourself," Marcus said. He waived a hand in the air as though trying to waft away a lazy fly. "For background, you understand?"

"I'm a friend looking for Margaret," Balcombe said.

"Come, come, Charles, there's more to it than that."

"What do you mean?"

"You're a good-looking chap. She's a good-looking girl, if you know what I mean?"

Balcombe took a breath. "Margaret is dead."

"What? No!" Marcus sat up; the back of his hand pressed to his mouth. "What happened? How? An accident?"

"Heart failure, I believe."

Marcus stood and walked unsteadily to another room. A second later, he was back with two crystal glasses and a bottle of brandy. It wasn't Balcombe's drink of choice, but he accepted the large measure and took a sip.

"I'm shocked," Marcus said eventually. "Of course, it happens to us all, but you just don't expect it... Not someone so young."

"What can you tell me about her?"

"Lovely girl. Always polite. Always a friendly smile. Although I did catch her crying once."

"Once?"

"I was passing her door and heard the sobbing, that was only a few days before she left. You don't think...?"

"What don't I think, Marcus?"

"That was why she was crying. Some reason to do with moving out."

"Did she tell you why she was moving?"

"No. I got the sense that it was sudden. Of course, she didn't own the apartment—as you know, she couldn't get a mortgage without a man's signature."

"There wasn't a man in her life?"

"Not that I know of."

"How could she afford to live here?"

Marcus frowned, as though he hadn't considered the question. "I don't know if she had a job. I think... I thought she had a job, I suppose. And then again, I always assumed she came from money. You know, sometimes you can just tell. People of class, if you know what I mean?"

Balcombe thought about that. The parents' grave didn't suggest the money came from them. He doubted their estate amounted to much—especially since they'd died years ago, during the war.

"Have you asked Katie?" Marcus asked.

"Katie?"

"Katie Halpern. She's the new tenant. Moved in after Margaret left—although come to think of it there may have been an overlap."

That sounded strange.

"Margaret gave up the apartment to a lodger? Is that what you're suggesting?"

Marcus looked confused. "No, I don't know. I never thought about it. But it does seem strange. Anyway, I know they knew each other before because... You know, I can't quite remember."

"Where did Margaret work?"

Marcus pouted and frowned. "You know I can't remember if she told me that either. Katie would know, I'm sure." Marcus shook his head. "Poor Margaret. I can't believe it."

Balcombe waited a moment as Marcus knocked back his brandy. The host offered another drink, but Balcombe declined.

"Will you be honest with me, Marcus?"

The other man smiled coyly. "Of course, Charles. Whatever do you want to know?"

"Whether Margaret ever took drugs."

Marcus frowned, looked skywards, then frowned again. "No, I wouldn't have said so. She was fun, but I doubt she'd do anything like that. Why do you ask?"

"You said there wasn't a man in her life. Surely someone so pretty would have a boyfriend."

"Well yes, I'm sure she did. More than one probably, but she never mentioned anyone to me or Timothy." He hesitated and looked guilty.

"It's fine, Marcus. I guessed you shared the apartment with... a friend."

Marcus smiled with relief. "Well, Margaret was fun, but she was also a Catholic. We did wonder if she was

79

embarrassed about… you know… urges. We decided she couldn't admit she was seeing anyone."

Balcombe nodded.

"We often used to comment on how lucky she was. Her apartment has a backdoor. Anyone could secretly come and go through there." Marcus chuckled lightly.

"Who might know about a boyfriend?"

"Only Katie. They're quite similar, really. She also keeps herself to herself—although, come to think of it she's never mentioned her religion. And"—he screwed up his face—"if I'm honest, Katie doesn't have that same *je ne sais quoi*."

Balcombe asked what time Katie returned home and Marcus said it was between six and six-thirty on weekdays. About the same time as Timothy.

"Which means I have a lot of time on my hands during the day," Marcus added.

Balcombe decided it was time to leave. Too early to speak to Katie Halpern, but he wanted to revisit Margaret's grave. Someone had spent a lot of money on it.

# Chapter Sixteen

"I've seen you before," Father Thomas said. He'd seen Balcombe walk through to the cemetery.

"I attend Mass most Sundays," Balcombe said. He shook the priest's hand and gave his name.

"Ah yes, that's why you look familiar, Charles. Although we've never spoken, have we?"

"No."

The priest smiled and nodded, waiting for Balcombe to say more. The man had warm eyes beneath bushy grey eyebrows. His steel-coloured hair was trim and thick with no sign of balding. He looked fit for a man Balcombe guessed to be in his fifties. The priest's eyes stayed on his, as though he could see into his soul.

"I enjoyed your sermon on Sunday," Balcombe said eventually, breaking the spell.

"About sin."

"It only takes a second," Balcombe said.

Father Thomas nodded. "We are all sinners, Charles, and the hardest part is not the confession. Do you know what it is?"

"Admitting it to ourselves."

Father Thomas smiled then tapped first his heart then his head. "In here and in here. Attitude and behaviour. By admitting it, by confessing it, God will cleanse us."

Balcombe said, "And I'm enjoying the book of saints stories."

"Ah, Jonah gave you a copy," the priest said. "One day I'm sure he will make a fine minister. Do you know why he gave it to you?"

"Because he thinks I should confess."

The priest smiled as though waiting for more.

Balcombe didn't continue with the topic. Instead, he said, "Could you tell me about Margaret Sotherland?"

For the first time, Father Thomas's demeanour changed; his face darkened, his head angled, and his posture shifted.

"Father?" Balcombe said, studying the priest.

Then the man's expression reverted to that of the kindly priest. "You took me by surprise," he said. "Why would you want to know about Margaret Sotherland?"

"I'd just like to know what happened to her. A lovely girl, taken too young."

Father Thomas said, "Yes. I understand it was heart failure. An inherited problem."

Balcombe nodded. "I saw her tombstone. In fact, that's why I'm here again. I wondered if she had any family remaining. Who paid for the burial and stone?"

The priest thought for a moment. "Yes, the Lammys, as I recall. Nice couple, although not Catholics themselves."

"You don't happen to know where they live?"

Father Thomas said he didn't, but their details would be in the register. He directed Balcombe to the administration building and suggested he speak to the warden who administered the churchyard and burials.

Father Thomas was about to leave him when Balcombe asked another question. One he already knew the answer to.

"Father, what's the Church's attitude to suicide?"

The priest showed his other character again with the angled head and awkward stance before looking back at Balcombe.

"Why?"

"Because there's a suggestion—"

"That Margaret killed herself? No, I don't believe it."

"You knew her that well?"

Father Thomas backed away. "I have things to attend to. A pleasure finally speaking to you, Charles."

Balcombe watched the man walk away and sensed his pace was faster than normal. He couldn't help thinking that the priest knew something he wasn't saying.

# Chapter Seventeen

Chief Carmichael stretched in his chair as Munro waited for his boss to say why he'd been called into the office.

"How many times have I warned you, Munro?"

"Warned me about what, sir?"

The Chief took a breath. "Results, Munro, damned results. I spoke to you only two days ago and now I find you are picking up cases rather than solving them!"

Munro waited, hoping that Carmichael was referring to the old case. But he wasn't.

"You took a case from Kowloon CID. The murder of a Chinese man and now it's been linked to that case you didn't solve at the end of last year. The one they're calling the Squeezed-heart murder. Now you've made it look like we've got a multiple murderer on our hands. Brilliant!"

So the Chief had learned about Feng Shubiao—the petty criminal who'd been killed by BlackJack. He kicked himself for not speaking to Fai Yeung about it, trying to get Doctor Swift's autopsy findings buried before anyone realized what he was doing.

He quickly decided how to handle it.

"Sir, you want results. As you say, it's another Squeezed-heart murder. If I can solve it... the Commissioner—"

"Shut up, Munro!" Carmichael's face was flushed crimson. He took a took a deep breath and blew it out equally slowly.

"Sir I—"

"You are no longer the lead on the case," he said, controlling his temper. "You will provide DI Garrett with any support he needs. Apart from that, you're confined to desk duty until further notice. Get out of my room. Get out of my sight and do not piss me off anymore." He paused before barking loud enough for the people outside could hear. "Get out. Now!"

All the staff in the CID office were looking at the Chief's door as Munro passed through it. Garrett wasn't smiling, but Munro imagined the man was grinning behind that messy beard.

Garrett pointed at Munro and then the door. He led the way to the small office that he'd made his own. Six months ago, it was a storage room. It was hot with no windows and smelled of the old paper that used to be stored there. It had one desk, two chairs and an oversized wastepaper basket.

"I tried to warn you last night," Garrett said in a conciliatory tone. "I wasn't allowed—"

"Don't worry yourself about it," Munro said. He took the spare chair when Garrett waved in its direction. "I think the Chief's been looking for an excuse ever since he promoted me."

"It was out of his hands," Garrett said. "The Commissioner found out about the multiple murder case."

Garrett had documents spread on his desk and started picking them up. "You've not made it easy for the Chief. He needs results just like you do. His head is on the block, just like everyone else's. Now tell me about the Squeezed-heart case."

Munro talked through the original murder. A man called Chen Chee-hwa was stabbed in the neck to paralyse him before his chest was cut open and his heart apparently squeezed.

"You thought the killer might be a surgeon."

"That's right."

Garrett put down the paper and picked up another. "This latest case. I've got the autopsy report, and it looks like the same killer."

"Except this one wasn't stabbed in the neck."

"Correct. However that doesn't mean much. In fact, in my experience, killers may have a preferred technique, but they can improvise, and they can adapt."

Munro nodded and tensed as Garrett picked up another report. Had he found another BlackJack murder?

"This one is interesting," Garrett said then pursed his lips as though thinking. "The butcher who killed the immigrant girl. That was one of your cases, right, Munro?"

"It was, although we couldn't convict him for the murder. You'll know that we resort to lesser charges in order to get a conviction."

Garrett nodded. "Meat hygiene issues. So, he was locked up for three days and was found dead on the day of his release."

"Yes. We think it was retribution. Probably someone who knew the victim."

"Or someone who had his rotten meat?" Garrett laughed at his own joke, then stopped abruptly. "It was a gruesome murder, don't you agree?"

Munro did. The butcher had been hung on a meat hook and Yeung judged that it had been pre-mortem. The man's belly had been sliced open so that his guts ran down his legs. The piss mingled with the blood implied he'd been alive when this human butchery had taken place.

The memory of it turned Munro's stomach and he tried to force the image from his mind. The butcher hadn't been adequately punished by the courts, but BlackJack's version of justice kept him awake at night.

"Munro?"

"Yes?"

"Do you agree that we've got a vicious bastard murderer on our hands?"

Munro nodded, then took a breath before speaking. "This last one's in Kowloon. My theory—"

"A Chinese surgeon. Yes, I know. Although I haven't heard anyone work out that the man must be very strong. Lifting that butcher onto a meat hook wasn't something you could easily do, Munro. No disrespect. So, were looking for a big Chinese man and that he is based on the mainland. Despite increasing the department's workload, I for one, think you did the right thing bringing the latest body here."

Munro said nothing and Garrett's beard twitched with a smile.

"It'll look good for us if we find the murderer."

*Look good for you, you mean*, Munro thought.

Garrett continued: "And we could do with the Commissioner's approval for a change, don't you think?"

Munro said nothing and Garrett turned his attention to the reports on his desk.

"Are we finished?" Munro stood.

Garrett looked up with the hard eyes once more. "I'm focusing on the surgeons. I've requested Kowloon send us all murder reports for the past two years. I want you to go through them, Munro and pull out anything that looks gruesome or matching the skills of a surgeon. Understood?"

"Yes," Munro said and tensed in case Garrett expected to be called *sir*.

"Clear the rest of your backlog," Garrett said. "And if you have any time, see if you can't solve the Karen Vaughn case." He winked and jabbed the air. "You do that, and the Chief will love you again"

Munro returned to find a hand-delivered package on his desk. He recognized the writing to be that of Charles Balcombe's. Inside was a brown bottle with Paregoric on the label.

An accompanying note asked him to test the opium concentration.

# Chapter Eighteen

The clerk responsible for the cemetery gave Balcombe the address of the Lammys. They lived in a grand house on Robinson Road.

A butler introduced him to Simon Lammy who received him in a drawing room. The man looked to be around forty, with thinning brown hair and grey eyes. His cheeks were as rosy as his nose and Balcombe judged him to be a drinker. His portly five-eight figure suggested he liked his food as well. He was dressed smartly in a black suit with a shocking-pink tie. The clothes appeared custom-made.

"Lucky to catch me home," Lammy said after introductions. "So, you're a journalist, you say, Mr. Balcombe?"

"A struggling one," Balcombe said disarmingly. "I'm writing a story about Margaret Sotherland."

"Really? Why would you choose Margaret?"

"Well, not specifically her. It's about Brits falling on hard times and Margaret died recently."

"Yes." His face dropped and Balcombe watched the man's Adam's apple bob up and down before he spoke again. "Very sad. If we'd known…"

"You paid for her burial."

"The least we could do."

Balcombe took out a pad and pencil. "She came to Hong Kong in thirty-eight?"

"That's right. With her parents. Her father worked in the Naval dockyards. You know the chimney? The generating station at the dockyards? That was where his office was. He worked at Rosyth dockyard before being transferred here."

Balcombe knew the latter from his research. "Tell me about Margaret," he prompted.

"Well, I mention Jack Sotherland because he was the reason they came—and why they were still here when the Japs invaded."

Balcombe waited for more, pencil poised.

"Well, they evacuated, Margaret and her mother. All non-essential British women and children were shipped out in 1940. They didn't want to go and made it as far as the Philippines. Margaret's mother, Olive, was an auxiliary nurse and was trying desperately to get an exemption."

"They didn't want to leave Hong Kong with the threat of Japan's invasion?"

"Most of us didn't think it would happen. And bear in mind the Blitz was happening in London. Leaving the luxury and apparent safety of Hong Kong for that didn't seem an attractive option. Anyway, while they were docked in the Philippines, Olive got the message that as an ANS, her exception was approved. My goodness, they were off that ship and back here before you could say Jack Robinson. We couldn't imagine that little island could defeat the Royal Navy. We thought Hong Kong was the safest place on Earth."

Balcombe pretended to write. "Let's skip forward, shall we?"

"Er… right. Well, Jack Sotherland died of a heart attack. The heat and—"

"I heard he had a heart problem."

"Right… That was just before the invasion. We were all rounded up and taken to Stanley Internment Camp, although Olive arrived two weeks later. People tell stories about the Japs killing people mercilessly, but they didn't. Not here anyway. They kept the doctors and nurses on during a handover of sorts."

"So, she had two weeks without family. How old was Margaret then?"

"Eleven. Wait, no ten. She celebrated her fourteenth birthday just days before we were released."

"Then what?"

"Then we took her in. Olive died within the first six months and my wife, and I cared for Margaret like she was our own. And after Stanley, she came to live with us."

"She was like a daughter?"

"That's right."

"And she moved out… when?"

"Shortly after her seventeenth birthday. Could be a bit headstrong." He smiled at what Balcombe guessed was the memory. "Very independent girl. The war did that—then again, it's not all a bad thing."

"Did she move to Seymour Road from here?" Balcombe asked, thinking it would be an expensive place for a girl in a new job.

"Hmm… no, I don't think so." He rubbed his temple. "To be honest, I can't recall where she lived before there. Was it 44 Seymour?"

"Number 24," Balcombe said.

"Ah, right."

"And where did she work?"

"She got a job as a clerk, working for the civil service at first I think."

"You're not sure?"

"Well, she moved about a bit. Mrs. Lammy and I advised her against it but, as I said, she was a little headstrong. Wouldn't take advice. Anyway, it seems she did all right."

"Until she didn't," Balcombe said.

Lammy said nothing, as though waiting for a question.

"Do you know what happened?"

"No."

"You know she moved to Wan Chai?"

He screwed up his nose. "No, I didn't. Not a nice neighbourhood. If I'd known…"

"Are you aware whether she ever took drugs?"

Lammy's eyes narrowed, and Balcombe wondered if the man looked worried. "Why ask that? For your story? Look, Mr. Balcombe, I think you'd be better off writing about Jack Sotherland and—"

Balcombe interrupted. "It's just a standard question, sir. Lots of people take opium… for various reasons."

"Opium? Margaret?" Lammy shook his head. "I doubt it. I doubt it very much."

"Boyfriends?" Balcombe asked.

"Boyfriends? Do you mean, do I know whether she had any? No, I'm afraid she wouldn't have shared anything personal like that with me. Anyway, what's that got to do with it?"

"What about Mrs. Lammy? Would Margaret have confided in her?"

"No, I wouldn't want to trouble my wife with something like this. She's sensitive, you know. Talking about poor Margaret would upset her."

Lammy stood and called his butler.

"I trust I've been of help, Mr. Balcombe."

Balcombe didn't move for a moment, his eyes locked on Lammy's.

"One more thing."

Lammy looked nervous.

Balcombe said, "You spent a lot of money on Margaret's grave. You must have felt very guilty."

"What?"

"She was like a daughter, and you let her live in Wan Chai."

Lammy's jaw tensed, and spittle appeared on his lower lip. "Goodbye, Mr. Balcombe. I'd appreciate it if you do not come back."

# Chapter Nineteen

Bill Teags sat alone in the pretty garden of Oceanview nursing home outside Aberdeen to the south of the island. The chair had wheels and with a blanket over his knees, Teags looked considerably older than his sixty-odd years.

A nurse had directed Munro to where Teags like to sit.

"Don't worry him," she said. "Please don't make Bill upset or excited."

There were other people spread about in chairs and a couple of orderlies watching over them all. Munro wondered why the patients weren't allowed to sit together. Maybe it's what they wanted.

"How are you doing?" Munro asked as he approached. The flower garden was all shades of pink and the grass stretched for forty yards, then dipped, creating the illusion that the sea was just beyond.

Teags didn't turn and his eyes were staring fixedly ahead when Munro rounded the chair.

"Old Bill, how are you?"

Teags' pale grey eyes drifted from the vista to meet Munro's. He blinked and rubbed his temple before speaking. "Babyface Munro!"

"You're looking well," Munro lied.

"It's the pills," Teags said after a pause. "Slow the heart but dull the brain, sorry."

Munro smiled kindly and waited.

"My mind… it's not what it was. And all I have to do is sleep, eat and shit." Teags chuckled quietly. "And stay calm, they tell me. I'm not even allowed to read the newspaper these days because I can get *too agitated*. That's what they say. I'm allowed to listen to the radio, but again, never the news. The orderlies here are worse than the Japs, you know."

Munro looked out to sea, wondering if this had been a wasted visit.

"Would you push me?" Teags asked.

"Of course." Munro took hold of the handles and pushed. The chair moved sluggishly on the turf.

"They won't push me around here," Teags said, conspiratorially. "Too difficult, they say. But a strong man like you, Babyface…"

After ten paces, Teags said, "Right, now we can talk quietly. You're not here for a social visit. Unless you remembered it's my birthday?"

"Sorry? It's your birthday?"

"No, I'm just teasing." Teags snorted his amusement. "Go on then, tell me."

"Karen Vaughn."

Teags put a hand on the right wheel so that the chair turned. His eyes were brighter now. "Go on."

Munro glanced around and started pushing again.

"I've picked up the case."

Teags shook his head.

Munro said, "What was your theory?"

"You know, I've thought of little else since I've been retired," Teags said, rubbing his temple. "I had a theory."

Munro waited, hoping that the ex-detective wouldn't say it was the Masonic Hall man, Eric Cattles.

Teags said, "I'm trying to remember it. These pills mess with my mind. I think I remember it all but keep forgetting and getting the timings and people all mixed up.

"What was your theory?" Munro prompted after a pause.

"I think... Well, it doesn't make sense. Why would Karen be at Zetland Hall? Her home was the other way. That was the way the friend would go."

"You think it was Nicola not Karen?"

"Shush!" Teags whispered and Munro saw an orderly looking in their direction.

Munro pointed at the island across the strait and said something banal. Teags went along with the pretend conversation until he'd been pushed a little further and away from prying eyes.

"I think it's all messed up," Teags said. "The people and the times. Someone is lying."

"The witnesses?" Munro said, dubious.

"The dad and friend," Teags whispered. "Maybe it's my befuddled head, Munro, but none of it makes sense. I should have questioned them more."

More than five times? Munro thought, remembering how many interviews Geoffrey Prisgrove had given. Teags' first suspect had been questioned over and over but his story never varied, not the key facts anyway.

"Nicola?" Munro said. Teags had been suspicious of her statements. She'd seemed coached.

"Yes, Nicola was hiding something!" Teags said too loudly, causing an orderly to sprint across the lawn towards them.

"What are you doing?" the man challenged. He looked at Teags and took his wrist, checking his pulse. "Bill, your heart-rate…"

"I'm fine!"

"Nurse!" the orderly bellowed then stepped between Munro and the back of the chair. "You can go now, sir. And you'll be barred from returning."

Munro took a step back as a nurse hurried across the lawn, her wimple flying like a white flag from her head.

She started talking, the orderly was talking, and Munro stepped back again.

"Babyface!" Teags said, straining in his chair to see Munro. "Question the timings. Question Eric Cattles again!"

# Chapter Twenty

"Katie?" Balcombe called as a young woman climbed from a rickshaw outside number 24 Seymour Road. "Katie Halpern?" She had black, patent leather high heels and a speckled black skirt that showed off a firm backside and shapely legs. When she turned and flicked back her curly blonde hair, he saw she had an attractive face, too. Twenty-years old, if that.

"Yes?"

He stepped towards her and felt her appreciative gaze.

"Hello." He said in a voice suggesting intrigue.

She smiled demurely. "Can I help you?"

"I hope so. I've been waiting for you."

"Oh?" She looked less keen suddenly. "Why?"

"Just for a chat. If that's all right?"

"About what, Mr.—?"

"Balcombe. Charles Balcombe."

"What's this about, Mr. Balcombe?"

"Please call me Charles," he said. "I met Marcus earlier and… could I come in rather than talk on the street?"

She chuckled. "Good try, mister, but out here will have to suffice. Unless you'd like to chat over tea."

"Better still," he said. "Have you eaten? I'll buy you dinner."

She paused with pouted lips and thoughtful eyes. Then she chuckled lightly again. "All right, mysterious Charles let's go and eat. I hope you like Chinese."

They descended steps to Bridge Street, and she took him into her *regular*, as she called it. They ordered food and he made small talk, flirting a little.

"You must have an amazing job," he said eventually.

"I do. I work for the accountancy firm of Lowe, Bingham and Matthews, offices on the fifth floor of number one Queens Road Central. Founded in Shanghai in oh-three."

She was proud and sounded like an advertisement, reeling off a company's credentials. It surprised him when she didn't continue.

"Impressive," he said.

"It's an excellent company."

"You've clearly done well."

"What do you mean?"

The food arrived, and he was grateful for the interlude before answering.

"Your rooms—24 Seymour is a good address."

She thanked him.

He waited another beat before telling her he was a journalist.

"That's why I wanted to talk to you," he said.

Her face dropped. "Oh."

"But not why I asked you to dinner," he said charmingly. "I hope it's not impertinent to say that you're rather attractive."

"Only rather?"

He flashed a smile. "All right, that was an understatement."

They ate for a minute, and he resumed the small talk before telling her he was interested in various riches-to-rags stories.

"I've got a few interesting cases," he said. "But I've come across Margaret Sotherland's name and spoke to your neighbour, Marcus, about her."

"Yes, he knew her better than I did."

"She lived in your house before you. Is that right?"

"It is."

"Marcus mentioned an overlap."

Katie finished what she was eating. "That's right. She had me as a... as a lodger, I suppose, for a few weeks."

"To help her pay rent?"

"I suppose."

"Did she lose her job? What happened?"

Katie pondered for a moment. "I'm not sure she worked."

"Oh? Marcus said you would know."

She laughed lightly. "No, I don't think she ever told me about work."

"So, what happened to her, do you think?"

"I don't know that either." Katie stopped eating and looked uncomfortable.

"I'm sorry," Balcombe said. "I hope you don't mind the line of questioning."

She forced a smile. "I just don't think I can help you, Charles."

"Did she have a boyfriend?"

"I suppose... but I never saw him."

"Did she take drugs?"

"I never saw her taking drugs. Why?"

"Because she died from an opium overdose."

Katie put her hand to her mouth, her eyes wide. When she spoke again, she said, "Do you mind if we talk about other things?"

Balcombe didn't. He doubted he could learn anything more from Katie Halpern and enjoyed her company for the rest of the meal.

Afterwards, he walked her home, and she asked if she would see him again.

"Undoubtedly," he said. "A pretty girl like you? I'll definitely be in touch." He knew where she lived and worked. He never gave out his address to the ladies. It was far too dangerous to have one of them coming round. And regarding Miss Halpern, he probably wouldn't see her again, anyway.

She was too young and too single. Although there was also the mystery of her wealth. She wasn't senior at the accountancy firm and yet she could afford the prestigious address. Which made him think of Margaret Sotherland. She'd lived in the same expensive house.

He leaned in and kissed her cheek. It wasn't a peck. He pulled away, realizing his lips had made contact for longer than he'd intended. Her fingers made light contact with his.

As he walked away, he wondered whether he was involuntarily feeling something for her. Then he decided it didn't hurt to keep her keen, just in case he needed to question her again.

# Chapter Twenty-One

Munro wasn't a theatre goer. He'd been once before the war and didn't enjoy the experience, being packed in with a thousand other people all smoking and talking. He remembered the smell of rubber beneath the blue haze of tobacco fumes. It was even more distinctive now that Queens theatre was empty.

Dim lighting and stillness made the hall feel even bigger than it was. Munro had the sensation of a man alone in an unmoving, endless ocean at night.

The next show would be in an hour. The early afternoon performance of some nonsense called *How to Marry a Millionaire*. It would be shown again in the evening and no doubt the cinema would be stacked. Most people loved the cinema, no matter how trashy the story, providing there were film stars living fake glamorous lives.

This was where Karen Vaughn had watched the Saturday Morning Matinee which ran from 10 am for an hour and a half. A random thought came to Munro. *Matinee* referred to an afternoon performance and yet the kids' Saturday cinema was in the morning.

Old Bill Teags had told him to question Cattles again. Munro wouldn't do that without excellent cause.

Cattles had connections and upsetting him again would undoubtedly end Munro's career.

But Teags had also said to question timings. That made sense and so Munro was in the cinema, at the start of it all.

He sat in a chair and looked at the red velvet curtains, imagining they'd been pulled back to reveal the screen. Wouldn't it be amazing if they could reveal the answer. What had happened?

*What had you been thinking on that day, Karen?*
*Why didn't you leave with your friend and her dad?*

Munro got up and walked down to the front, stopping at chest-high black panelling. Beyond was the orchestra pit. There were chairs and an organ to the left.

His eye caught something in the side wall; a door, snug-fitting, almost invisible.

*There's more than one exit!* Of course, there was. Munro walked to the side door and noticed a light-fitting above it. It was off now but would come on at the end of the show. The door had no handle but opened when he pushed. On the other side was a black, square tunnel. It sloped down and at an angle. He felt his way along because it was even darker than the hall. Light edged a door at the far end. He reached it and found a handle. The metal door was locked.

He stood with his hand on the door as though secrets could be felt through the metal.

*Did you come out this way, onto Theatre Lane, Karen?*

If she did, then Nicola and her father wouldn't have seen her. They waited on Queens Road and Karen could have slipped out and round. Although that did raise the question: Why? Why come out a different way? Did Karen want to avoid the others?

Munro walked back up the slope and returned to the theatre hall. Despite seeming slightly brighter after the dark tunnel, Munro still felt an oppressive atmosphere. He really had no desire to stay here any longer.

In the lobby was a manager's office. He'd spoken to the man to gain access, and now he found him again. He was busy with a clerk checking schedules or takings or whatever fascinating things staff did outside of show times.

"Everything satisfactory, detective?" the manager asked with an obsequious smile. He stood with a ramrod-straight back and tried to look smart despite wearing a cheap blue suit accompanied by a red and black striped tie. His shirt looked off white although it could have been the lighting.

"The exit onto Theatre Lane..." Munro said. "The door is locked."

"Of course."

"When is it unlocked?"

"It's an emergency exit, so it's unlocked for every show. We put the exit light on at the end so people know they can go that way. It eases the congestion, of course."

Munro nodded. "But isn't that a problem? Couldn't people sneak in that way once the show has started?"

The manager smiled again. "There's no handle on the outside. Although we've caught kids sneaking in. One kid pays, goes down the tunnel and lets the others in. Every now and then I'll have a member of staff there."

"When?"

"Certainly, for the Saturday Morning Matinees and—"

"What about Saturday, the twelfth of September?"

"For the kid's matinee, definitely."

"The whole time?"

"No, just the first half an hour, give or take. That's when they try to get in."

"What about someone getting out."

He frowned. "Why would... We wouldn't stop anyone going out, although in the first half an hour, we'd be suspicious of their motives. After that, they can leave whenever they want although..." The manager paused.

"Yes?"

"Why would anyone, eh?"

Munro pushed for more: "Why would anyone leave that way?"

"Right? Why go down that way when you can come out through the foyer. There would be no crowd until the show's end."

"But—" Munro started to say, then saw something in the manager's eyes. The man was willing him to believe the story. He stopped and waited.

"Yes?" the manager asked nervously.

"You won't get into trouble. I just want the truth."

The manager blinked and wet his lips.

Munro said: "Because of kids getting in without paying, you don't unlock the doors until later on Saturday mornings."

The manager still said nothing.

Munro said, "You opened the doors right at the end." Again, he paused. "I really just need the truth. You can change your practices after this meeting, and we'll leave it as a warning."

The manager nodded. "Just before."

"How long before?"

"Fifteen minutes? No more than twenty before the end."

"Thank you," Munro said. "That helps." He was about to leave the office when a thought struck him. "Do you have the show timings for the Saturday Morning Matinee on that day?"

"It will have started at ten and the running time is an hour and a half, give or take."

"I mean specifically."

"Specifically?"

"When each—what do you call them? Episodes?"

"Programmes."

"When each programme started and finished."

"On the twelfth of September?" the manager said sceptically.

Munro nodded and waited while the manager seemed to have a mouse scrabbling about in his brain. Eventually, the man shrugged.

"Tony might know."

"Tony?"

"The projectionist. He checks timings, but whether he took a note of them—or kept them... it's been months!"

Tony wasn't available and Munro asked the manager to call Victoria police station and let him know whether the projectionist could help.

# Chapter Twenty-Two

Balcombe returned to Homeville in Wan Chai and knocked on the door number 8.

The old lady came out, holding a cigarette. "Yes?"

He hadn't smelled it before, but now he caught the whiff of cats and stale smoke. He could see two cats lounging on the chair behind her. "I was here yesterday," Balcombe said. "I'm Margaret's cousin."

"Oh yes. I heard you talking before."

She could have just said that she saw him with the caretaker. But she'd heard him say he was Margaret's cousin. A nosy neighbour.

"You see and hear what's going on?" Balcombe said, cocking an eyebrow and flashing a smile.

"I do!" she said before taking a puff on her cigarette. Then she looked Balcombe up and down with approval.

Balcombe said, "Did Margaret have many visitors?"

"She had a few."

"Men?"

"Men and women. Gladys from upstairs visited most."

"I guess, I'd like to know if"—Balcombe hesitated, wondering how the old lady would take the question—"Margaret got paid by any of her men friends?"

She chuckled and then gave a phlegm-filled cough. She stopped it by sucking on her cigarette. Then she cleared her throat.

Balcombe waited.

"That wouldn't surprise me," the woman said. "A lot of the girls... the pretty ones... well, you can't blame them."

"Do you have any names for me?"

"No. I didn't ask."

"You didn't hear."

"No, that neither."

He paused for thought.

Unprompted, she filled the silence. "It was odd at the end. You know I was the one who reported the bad smell coming from the room?"

"Did you go in?"

"Oh no, the door was locked. The key was on the inside. I know that because the caretaker—nobody likes her and her stupid Toby monkey—had to jiggle the key in the lock to knock it through." She sucked on her cigarette again and seemed to have lost her train of thought.

"You were saying it was odd at the end."

"Ah yes. Before she died—it must have been that very same evening—I could hear a lot of chanting or something, maybe reading the Bible out loud. I think she was troubled."

"She was Roman Catholic," Balcombe said.

"Ah that explains it." She raised her hands to the sky. "Hail Mary."

"Explains what?"

"There was a priest here." She laughed and coughed. "I don't think he was the paying sort, if you know what I mean."

# Chapter Twenty-Three

The official witness who had excited Bill Teags was a flower seller. She worked Garden Road between the lower Peak tram station and Kennedy Road. She'd seen someone matching Karen Vaughn's description. Her statement said she'd seen a girl go up the steps of Zetland Hall and been met by the doorman. She'd spoken to him, gone inside and then a few minutes later come scurrying out.

She'd said the time had been somewhere between 11 and 11:30.

The Saturday Morning Matinee finished around 11:30 and the distance from the theatre was less than half a mile. So, if Karen had left just a few minutes early, she could easily have reached the masonic hall and been seen on the steps.

Munro had read through all ninety-three witness statements and fully understood why Teags had become obsessed by the curator. To anyone who didn't know his job, they'd think he was a doorman.

One of the people who had called in, but left no name, had mentioned seeing a girl in a brown skirt go into Zetland Hall. The timing hadn't been clear, although the caller hadn't mentioned a man, nor had they said that the girl had come out again.

"Mrs. Song?" he said, approaching a little Chinese lady with a tray of flowers hanging around her neck.

"Yes?" she said suspiciously.

Munro explained who he was and his interest in the case of the missing girl.

"You're sure it was Karen Vaughn?"

"Yes. She didn't have the same clothes as in the newspaper photographs and her hair was different, but it was her." She puffed up her diminutive figure, proud and confident.

"Do you remember Saturday, the twelfth of September?"

"Not especially, but I remember her."

"Was it busy that day?"

"It's busy every day, but especially on Saturdays. All day."

"How is it you noticed that one girl in a crowd?"

"I watch."

Munro blinked. "You watch?"

"Him." She pointed to Zetland Hall, a cream block of a building on the corner of Kennedy. "The doorman."

Munro couldn't see anyone but knew who she meant. "Eric Cattles?"

"If that's his name, yes. I don't trust him. I don't trust any man who dyes his hair!"

She went on to say that she thought he paid too much attention to the children. He would stand on the steps and watch them. Sometimes he would beckon them over.

"Did it happen on that Saturday?"

"I didn't see him until after."

"After?"

"Two girls went up the steps, but he wasn't there then. He came out a few minutes later. Perhaps he'd seen them."

"Two girls?"

"Yes."

"Karen and another?"

Mrs. Song screwed up her face in thought. "No, maybe that was earlier."

"But you saw Karen go up the steps?"

"Yes, that man was at the door, looking through the glass. She walked up the steps, he opened the door and I think she said something to him, then they went inside."

"For how long?"

"A few minutes," Mrs. Song said, confirming what she'd said in her witness statement. "If it had been much longer, I would have sent one of the boys to check."

"And what time was this?"

"I'm not sure. The papers said she'd gone missing around half past eleven."

"You told my colleague it was between eleven and eleven-thirty."

"I wasn't sure."

"What happened after she came out of the hall?"

"Well, she scampered, like she was excited."

"Excited?"

Mrs. Song shrugged. "That's what I thought."

"All right. And did you see where she went afterwards?"

She pointed beyond the hall. "Up the hill. They went up the hill."

"Sorry, you said *they*?"

Mrs. Song frowned in thought. "Yes," she said slowly, "I did just say *they*. I may be imagining it now. It's been a long time."

"What are you imagining?"

"The girl with another girl. The white girl in the red dress."

★ ★ ★

Munro returned to his desk and wrote up his notes before instructing a sergeant to bring in Prisgrove and his daughter for questioning again.

It was only when he'd set aside the Karen Vaughn file that he noticed a new one on his desk. The name on the front was Theresa Pell. The file had come from archives in response to his query.

He opened it.

Single, white female died five months ago. Cause of death deemed to be an opium overdose. The main difference between this and the one Balcombe had mentioned was that this had been classed as a suicide.

Munro didn't have the time or inclination to give it any more consideration. He stuck the file in an envelope and wrote Balcombe's address on the front. He'd have someone he trusted deliver it discretely.

# Chapter Twenty-Four

Munro had Geoffrey Prisgrove and his daughter Nicola at the Victoria police station. They were in separate interview rooms.

Geoffrey Prisgrove was very unhappy about being called in. Munro sat opposite the self-important mid ranking manager for a major shipping broker. The file said he was thirty-seven, but his pasty-white skin and thinning hair made him look older. He had a goatee beard that was thicker than the usual style, giving him an Elizabethan appearance. His clothes stressed the period look; he wore a brown suit and a sombre, dark crimson necktie.

Munro was accompanied by DC James Tattersall, a white junior officer. It was standard practice to have a white officer present when interviewing a white gentleman.

"I don't appreciate this," Prisgrove said, making eye contact with the other officer.

Munro said, "Just a formality, sir. I've taken over the investigation and just need to make sure all the t's are crossed and i's dotted. I apologize for the inconvenience."

Prisgrove breathed in heavily. "I've told the police everything I know."

"Would you mind telling me again, sir? What happened on Saturday the twelfth, when Karen Vaughn disappeared?"

Prisgrove repeated his original statement about waiting outside for Karen, but she didn't show.

"We thought we'd just missed her," he added. "There were a hell of a lot of kids."

"You didn't think to go inside and look for her?"

Prisgrove pouted and spoke with indignance. "No, I didn't."

"Why not?"

"Because… because I assumed she'd gone home by herself. I wasn't going to go scrabbling around inside a theatre hall looking for a kid."

"And you didn't report her missing until her father came to your house seven hours later?"

"That's correct." He paused. "Because I wasn't concerned. I didn't think she *was* missing."

"You thought she'd just gone home."

"Yes."

"Was that usual?"

"Usual?" Prisgrove stretched his neck, which appeared to be longer than most people's. Perhaps it was the combination: a beard and crimson tie separated by a white throat.

"When you normally went to the cinema. You went every Saturday, isn't that right?"

"It is—although we haven't been since. It doesn't seem appropriate."

"So," Munro said patiently, "did Karen often go home without you?"

Prisgrove frowned but said nothing. He looked at the white officer.

"It's a simple question, sir," Munro said.

Prisgrove gaze crawled back to Munro. "Is it? I suppose. I don't recall." He paused, looked at the other officer and slowly back to Munro again. Then he shook his head. "Look... Munro, you said, right?"

"Inspector Munro."

"It's all very distressing. I can't remember. I can't think straight."

"That's all right," DC Tattersall said. "I understand. If anything occurs to you later, please let us know."

"Where's my daughter?"

"In the next room," Munro said, standing. "I'll only keep her a few minutes."

Prisgrove bristled. "Make sure you do. I'll be waiting right outside

★ ★ ★

Nicola had large green eyes and brown hair pulled into bunches. She'd come straight from school and was wearing the uniform of a blue pleated skirt and white blouse.

Munro started by introducing himself and Tattersall and then apologized for the delay. Nicola looked at him with unfocussed eyes.

"How old are you, Nicola?" Munro asked.

"Eleven."

"Karen would have been eleven by now, too. When was her birthday?"

"December. Sixteenth."

"Could you tell me in your own words what happened on the day she disappeared?"

Nicola spoke, and Munro checked her witness statement. It was almost the same, word for word.

When she finished, Munro said, "You haven't thought of anything new?"

For a second, the girl's eyes gained focus. "No, why would I?"

"Because people remember things they forgot at the time," Munro said kindly.

Nicola shook her head.

"You recognized Karen's ring," Munro said, referring to the one found in the box in Eric Cattles's house.

Nicola blinked her eyes and nodded.

"You're sure it was hers?"

"It could have been. She had one just like it."

"Did she give it to the man at Zetland Hall?"

"She might have."

Munro waited in case Nicola would say anything more, but she didn't. Munro had hoped that the faraway stare meant she was thinking back, but her mind didn't seem to be full of thoughts.

"Tell me about the man there, Nicola."

"He's creepy."

"Anything else?"

She shook her head.

Munro said, "Why would Karen have been at Zetland Hall after the cinema? That wasn't the way home for her."

The focus briefly returned to the girl's eyes as she looked at Munro. "Because she just went that way."

Munro waited. She'd accepted it as fact, rather than question Karen's movements.

When the girl said nothing else, he pushed: "Where did she go after going into Zetland Hall?"

Nicola breathed loudly but said nothing.

"Nicola?"

"I don't know."

Munro tried other angles but got nothing. Then he thought about what Mrs. Song, the flower seller, had said. He repeated it: "Karen was seen with another girl."

Nicola met his eyes, and he read the surprise in hers.

"Could she have left the cinema with another friend?"

"It's possible."

Munro said, "Was that a smile, Nicola?"

She frowned and shook her head.

"Why would that make you smile?"

"It didn't. Maybe I thought *Good, she went off with another friend.*"

Munro waited, but Nicola didn't say more. However her eyes showed more interest than any time previously.

"Who were her other friends, Nicola?"

"It could have been anyone," she replied. "Karen had lots of friends. Anyone in our class. Anyone in the school."

Munro could feel Tattersall looking at him. This was new. Bill Teags hadn't pursued the idea of Karen being with another girl. There had been two alleged sightings of Karen further up the hill. Two girls were seen at the MacDonnell Road tram stop, although on the wrong side to get on and too early. A second witness had said they'd seen a girl at the front of the tram at around 11:20. Could they be connected?

"Nicola, did Karen ever go on the Peak tram?"

"No," she said quickly. "Neither of us are allowed on without an adult."

"That's not what I asked," Munro said gently.

"I don't understand."

"I'm asking if she *ever* went on the Peak tram?"

The girl looked at him with narrowed eyes, like he'd asked a trick question.

"Nicola?"

Her eyes brimmed with tears before one spilled over. "I want to go home," she said. "I want to go home now."

Her father greeted her with a comforting arm and a scowl for Munro.

After they'd gone, Tattersall said, "That was odd."

"Yes, James, it was."

"What did it mean, sir?"

Munro didn't know, but he was sure of his next moves. He was going to talk to the witness who'd seen a girl at the front of the tram. And he was going to interview the tram driver.

# Chapter Twenty-Five

Balcombe met Roy Faulls at the Jazzles Club for lunch. It was two buildings along from the Hong Kong Club. Exclusive, but not as restrictive as the latter. Roy and Balcombe were still waiting for membership of the most prestigious club in Hong Kong. That one was for formal occasions, dinners and meetings with the upper class of the island. Jazzles had a pool, allowed non-whites as members and regularly put on a jazz band for dances.

Roy had been swimming and Balcombe waited with a glass of single malt while his friend dried off and reappeared fully dressed. His hair was a tousled mess, and the grin on his face was wider than a Cheshire cat's.

"Life is good," he said, sitting beside his friend and waving for a waiter. They ordered food and settled to watch the men frolic in the pool and the sailboats in the harbour.

"I've got the film from Albert," Faulls said as the food arrived. "I hope it wasn't urgent."

"No."

"They're... if you don't mind me saying Charles... not very good. If you ever want lessons..."

"I don't, thanks."

"Good. Should be ready for you by tonight. Any particular size?"

"Just big enough to see."

He nodded as though relieved, then asked how Balcombe was getting on with his investigation into Margaret Sotherland's death.

"It is bemusing," Balcombe said, "and terribly sad. She seemed to have everything, living on Seymour in a lovely house. The neighbours liked her and then it all went wrong. She shared for a few weeks and then just moved out and into a dive in Wan Chai."

"Something happened," Faulls said.

"You're not wrong, but I can't find out what it was. She had friends. She had nice neighbours, she didn't have parents anymore, but her adoptive parents were well-off and caring. They were devastated by her death."

Faulls asked, and Balcombe gave him some of the details. He laughed when told about Marcus and shook his head at the description of the caretaker and her monkey.

"Don't judge a woman by the monkey on her shoulder," he said. "She sounds a charmer."

"The old dear in number 8 Homeville was also pretty rough," Balcombe said, thinking of the old lady who the caretaker had described as a busybody.

"And the cause of death?"

Balcombe shrugged, distracted for a moment by a young woman's shapely backside as she walked past the club. Undoubtedly parading with a purpose.

"Overdose?" Faulls pressed.

"Yes, but I'm not convinced she was a user."

Faulls looked at him side on, one eyebrow raised. "You think it was suicide."

"Maybe. It would explain a lot. But then…"

"What?"

"Her last dose of tincture of opium was weak—Paregoric. An entire bottle of the stuff wouldn't kill you. So she had to have had more."

"But there was no evidence."

"Nothing."

"No evidence of suicide?"

The way he said it made Balcombe think his friend was holding something back. "Why are you so convinced it was suicide, Roy?"

"Have you heard of Theresa Pell?"

"No, should I have?"

"She used to go to our church, died a few months ago."

"OK?"

"Suicide. What are the chances, Charles? Two single young women from our church die of unnatural causes."

Charles shook his head. "I don't know. I guess there's a probability. Two incidents don't imply a link, Roy."

"No, but it does make me think. Anyway… I'm just asking that you use your contacts. Find out what happened to Theresa. Maybe it'll help with your investigation into Margaret."

A band struck up and Balcombe let the music wash over them for a while as he thought. He was convinced his friend was still playing games—with the best intensions. He wanted Balcombe distracted from destructive activities. In that he was like Munro, only Faulls thought it was just excessive booze.

Balcombe admitted that his investigative instincts were piqued. He wanted answers. He needed to understand what had happened to Margaret, whether or not it was suicide.

"This Katie Halpern, sounds nice." Faulls said, breaking into his thoughts and the way he said it implied more than her being a nice girl. "Double entry, you said?"

"I think I described it as accountancy." Balcombe chuckled at his friend's keenness.

"Maybe…" Faulls said, raising an eyebrow and giving Balcombe a cockeyed smile.

"Maybe what, Roy?"

"Maybe you should try an ordinary girl for a change."

He meant a change from the married wives. But Balcombe enjoyed the thrill of their dangerous liaisons. He was a risk taker after all. However, the excitement had been wearing thin lately. Routines had crept in and what had once been dangerous was dangerously close to slipping into safe and dull. Perhaps Faulls was right. Perhaps it was time to find out if a feisty young thing like Katie Halpern could be a thrill.

That could wait because he was visiting a woman friend called Pamela Amey this afternoon. Maybe he'd spice it up a little with her, see how far he could take it.

Later, he'd get in touch with Munro and ask about Theresa Pell. How much of a similarity was there between the two girl's deaths?

# Chapter Twenty-Six

The concierge grinned at Balcombe when he got back from seeing Pamela Amey. The man couldn't know what he'd been up to, but maybe he was reflecting the look on Balcombe's face. Amy had renewed his faith in his sexual liaisons and, no doubt, he was beaming.

"Hand-delivered letter, Mr. Balcombe," the concierge said.

Balcombe took the thick, over-sized envelope and tipped the man generously.

It had come from the police station, and he hurried upstairs to open it.

Inside was an autopsy report for Theresa Pell.

*How the hell?* Balcombe thought. Munro had sent the file before he'd asked for it. Then he remembered asking the detective to look for cases like Margaret Sotherland's.

And Faulls had been right. The similarity was clear. Theresa was white-British, aged twenty-three and single. Her religion was confirmed as Roman Catholic.

She'd died before Balcombe had arrived in Hong Kong, over four months ago.

The cause of death was recorded as pulmonary failure and cardiac arrest because of a drug overdose. The drug: opium.

Balcombe's pulse quickened.

The difference between this and Margaret Sotherland's death was that the coroner had classed it as suicide, there being no evidence of prior drug abuse.

*But there was no evidence of Margaret's prior use either!*

Munro had included police notes taken at the scene by an officer called Tam. Theresa Pell had been found in her bed, covered by a sheet. It said that no pills or powder or bottle was found in her property, suggesting that she had ingested the drugs elsewhere. Tam had interviewed the housemate who'd found the body, and they provided a written statement to the effect that they hadn't taken anything or disturbed the scene. The witness said that Theresa had looked peaceful, as though she was sleeping.

There was a photograph of a suicide note.

It said:

*Forgive me, Father.*

*No one can see the kingdom of God unless they are born again.*

*He said, for I will forgive their wickedness and will remember their sins no more.*

*He is faithful and just to forgive us our sins and to cleanse us from all unrighteousness.*

*I lay myself down to sleep and will awake, my soul renewed.*

It was the strangest suicide note Balcombe had ever seen. Most were letters aimed at someone, explaining why they'd done it. Or blaming them. Or the world.

This note was more like extracts from the Bible. Was that surprising? Theresa Pell was a Catholic, after all.

One of the photographs of the room showed a chair beside the bed. It reminded him of the chair next to Margaret Sotherland's bed.

# Chapter Twenty-Seven

The address Balcombe found for Theresa Pell was on MacDonnell Road. It was a nice red brick building that had once been a single home but now comprised eight apartments.

A woman answered the door, opening it just enough for him to see her face. It was round and friendly, with warm brown eyes and a generous mouth. "Hello?"

"Good evening," Balcombe said. "Is this where Theresa Pell used to live?"

"It is." She squinted with suspicion.

"I'm a reporter. Charles Balcombe."

"OK?"

"And I'm investigating a series of suspicious deaths."

The woman said nothing.

He said, "Theresa was a Catholic and—"

"And suicide"—the woman took a shuddering breath—"is a sin."

"It is. What's concerning is that another girl has also died recently of a drug overdose. She was also Catholic."

"Another suicide?"

"May I come in and talk?"

She hesitated, then nodded and opened the door enough for him to enter. She was wearing a pink and white floral dress with house shoes. He gauged her to be in her early thirties with a good upbringing. She had an air of style that was reflected in the well-decorated living room she led him to. Watercolour paintings on the walls were of the Peak and coast. Not great works of art, but pleasant amateur efforts.

There was a partial view of the Royal Docks and the water beyond. A reasonable vista that he enjoyed once seated.

"So, Mr.—"

"Call me Charles."

She smiled. "All right, Charles. So, you're an investigative reporter. What's your angle? I won't talk to you if you're looking to write a nasty piece about Theresa."

"That's not my intention."

"She was such a lovely person, maybe too good for this world."

"My angle," he said, "is to understand what happened. Why would she do it? What happened to her?"

"All right," she said, although her eyes narrowed as though dubious.

"First, I didn't catch your name." He knew she hadn't provided it.

"Mary Pilkington," she said after a hesitation. "Although I don't want—"

"Don't worry, Mary. I won't use your name unless you're happy for me to do so. In fact, I won't use anything you're not happy with." He felt a frisson of guilt lying about his purpose to someone who didn't seem capable of imagining he could do anything untoward, not least pretend to be a reporter to get her talking. He already knew her name. He'd found out before visiting the house. He also knew that she worked as a typist for the Whiteway & Laidlaw solicitors.

"All right," she said.

"Tell me how you met."

"I'm not supposed to sublet, but there are two rooms, and everyone does it."

"You advertised?"

"Yes, in the paper. The *Daily Press*, of course. Is that your newspaper, Charles?"

"No," he said just in case she knew someone who worked there. "*Manchester Guardian.*"

"Ooo!" she said, impressed.

"And how long did she room with you?"

"Four months."

"Did you know she was taking opium?"

"No! At first, Theresa didn't even drink. I used to call her Saint Theresa, although she didn't like that."

"Why not?"

Mary shifted uncomfortably in her chair. "I don't think I can talk about that."

"You said *at first* when you said she didn't drink."

"Yes. She didn't touch a drop. Perhaps it was my bad influence, but she started drinking a lot. She particularly liked gin."

"Were you surprised she took her own life?"

Mary took a breath and her eyes suddenly brimmed with tears.

"It's all right. Take your time," he said.

She breathed and blinked and eventually made eye contact with him. "I found her. I couldn't believe it. I knew she was unhappy but couldn't imagine… She just didn't seem the sort."

Balcombe wondered if anyone could easily spot the sort—unless it was a cry for help, perhaps.

"If you can, Mary… How long had she been dead before you found her? Did they tell you?"

"I came home at ten past seven. I always work late on Thursdays." She paused and collected herself. "Anyway, I think they said she'd been dead for five hours."

"So, she took the overdose around two in the afternoon?"

"I suppose."

"She wasn't at work?"

"She didn't work."

"Oh?"

"You're wondering how she could afford to live here."

"I am."

"She had money. She'd come here from England. Arrived early July last year." She paused, perhaps wondering what to say. "She came because of her boyfriend."

"Her boyfriend?"

"That's right. He got transferred here with the Navy. Mary said she came here to be with him. Only…"

"Only?"

Again, she looked uncertain about what to say. "I think… I know he didn't want to have anything to do with her. She came all this way, and he didn't want to know."

"What did she do with her time?"

"She was looking for work towards the end."

"Did she have any visitors here?"

The question took Mary by surprise. "I… I don't know. You mean men?"

Balcombe nodded.

"Are you suggesting…?"

"I'm just asking."

"No, she wasn't like that. She made one mistake with one man and she…" Mary's face froze as she realized she's said something she hadn't intended.

"It won't go into print, I promise."

Balcombe connected the dots. Theresa didn't drink. She'd gone halfway around the world to follow a boyfriend who didn't want to know her anymore. She'd made a mistake. She started drinking gin. Mother's ruin.

"She was pregnant," Balcombe said. But even as the words left his lips, he realized the autopsy hadn't mentioned a foetus. So she hadn't been pregnant. He could read Mary's face and nodded. *Of course.*

"She got rid of it."

"Broke her heart, it did." Mary breathed and shook her head. "I really shouldn't talk to you about it."

"It's important, Mary. It may help with other cases."

She nodded. "She was distressed. It was against her religion of course and I heard her crying about it— much worse than worrying about how her Davey didn't love her anymore. This was serious. I wondered if she got rid of the baby to spite him. Maybe she threatened him. She didn't tell me straight off about getting rid of it. I heard her crying and the next day thought she'd cut herself because of the blood. Then she said, "Silly girl had gone back-street because of the embarrassment.""

"How long was this before she killed herself?"

Mary blew through her lips. "I would say… yes, it was about a month."

"Did she ever mention the name Margaret Sotherland?"

"No. I think I'd remember that name. Wait, was that the other girl—the other one from church who took an overdose?"

"Yes."

Mary shook her head sorrowfully. "It's so sad."

"Could you show me where Theresa stayed?"

"Her room? Yes, of course." Mary led the way to a small bedroom. It was just long enough for a single bed. There was a narrow wardrobe and a wooden chair with a straw seat.

"Is this how it was?"

"Exactly," Mary said. "I haven't had the heart to rent it since. And I doubt anyone would be happy staying in a room where a young woman died. Would you?"

Balcombe ignored the question. He let his senses go to work, imagining the woman, dead on the bed. It didn't smell of death anymore. Not after so long. Instead, there was a hint of lavender. The bed had a white sheet and pillow. A wooden cross hung over it. There was also a photo frame with a copy of the painting with Jesus holding a lantern: *The Light of the World*.

"Were these Theresa's?" he asked pointing at the religious symbols.

"Yes. I couldn't bring myself to throw them away." Those last words came out slowly and she then added: "I had to give the rest to charity. I couldn't keep her clothes in the wardrobe." She sounded remorseful.

"It's all right, Mary," Balcombe said. "Everyone would understand."

"Thank you."

"Could you think back to when you found her?" She frowned, then closed her eyes, and he guessed she was picturing it. He saw her swallow hard and give her head a slightly regretful shake.

"What do you see?" Balcombe asked.

"Theresa on the bed. Well actually, I didn't see *her*, if you know what I mean?"

"No."

"She was covered by her sheet—from head to toe. She looked so peaceful, like she was sleeping."

Balcombe thought about what Mary had said and about Margaret Sotherland. It's not easy to cover your own head with a sheet. "Her head was covered?"

"That's right. And on her chest was her Bible."

There was a small window, about twenty inches wide and a little over double that in height. He stepped over to it. It faced northeast and at an angle, he could see the docks and a sliver of water.

Instinctively, he tested the window.

"Was this shut when you found her?"

"Yes. As far as I know, Theresa never opened it. It's a bit stiff you see."

Balcombe lifted the latch and pushed. The wooden frame had warped over time and was jammed shut. He gave it a few sharp knocks, but it didn't budge.

"All right, could you tell me where the bottle of medicine was?"

"What bottle?"

"A packet? Something that had contained the opium she took?"

Mary shook her head, frowning. "There wasn't anything."

"And, if you don't mind me asking again, did she ever take drugs before?"

"Not that I know of except for headache pills, that is."

Balcombe looked around the room again and wished he'd seen it immediately after Theresa was found.

"You mentioned her boyfriend was Davey. Do you know his surname?"

Mary shook her head. "But there was a photograph... there is a photograph of him." She opened a drawer, took out a passport-size photo and handed it to him.

"May I keep this?"

She hitched a shoulder. "I've no need of it. Be my guest."

"Thank you," he said. They exited the room. "You've been very helpful, Mary."

"You promise not to use anything without me checking first."

"I do," Balcombe said, "but a word to the wise, Mary, don't believe any reporters in the future. I wouldn't want them to abuse your trust."

"You're different?"

"I am definitely that."

She looked demure before leading him to the front door. He wondered if she'd ask for his contact details, but she appeared too shy for that.

Before leaving, he asked, "One more thing."

"Yes?" There was a glint of hope in her eyes.

"The suicide note was definitely in Theresa's handwriting."

"Yes." Her eyes dimmed. "Is that all you need?"

He smiled and shook her hand. "You really have been a great help, Mary. If I need to come back, would that be all right?"

"Oh yes please," she said and then looked guilty at her obvious delight.

# Chapter Twenty-Eight

Munro interviewed the witness who'd provided a statement about seeing Karen Vaughn at MacDonnell Road tram stop. He was a young Frenchman called Gerrard who had been on his way to a meeting at the Peak Hotel.

"You're sure about the time?" Munro asked him in the hotel lobby. DC Tattersall was in attendance but hung back.

"Yes, it was just before half past ten," Gerrard said.

That was over an hour too early. Karen had still been with Nicola in the cinema at that point. However in his witness statement at the time, he said he'd seen a mixed-race girl with a brown dress. He'd even confirmed the hair: black in a single ponytail.

"You're certain?" Munro pressed.

"Of course."

"Two girls?"

"Yes."

"You were on which tram?"

"The B-tram," Gerrard said without hesitation.

"Did they get onboard the B-tram?"

He shook his head. "No, as I said before, they were on the wrong side for getting on."

"You saw them as you passed? They were still there?"

He pouted, pensively. "Well… I… You know, thinking about it, I don't remember seeing them both."

"Both?"

"Well, I saw them both as we were stationary at MacDonnell Road, but then afterwards… I wonder if I saw them again on the offside at May Road. Or perhaps it was just one girl then. He pulled an apologetic expression.

"I thought I remembered so well, but now I'm mixed up."

★ ★ ★

"What do you think, sir?" Tattersall asked as they walked down from the hotel to the tram station. "Did Karen Vaughn catch the tram?"

"I don't know," was all Munro said. "But since we're here, let's talk to the tram driver."

Philip Slater worked for the Peak Tram Company. He'd been the driver that day and given a statement that he hadn't seen any unaccompanied girls join the tram and he certainly hadn't let any ride up front. It was against regulations.

Munro asked for him at the Peak tram station and was told to wait until the next one came up.

Munro watched the driver as the tram rounded the curve and approached its destination. The man was young, with a gaunt face and wide eyes. His blue uniform looked a size too large.

Munro flashed his credentials as Slater stepped out and stretched.

"What's this about?" he said nervously.

"Just a chat about the day that girl went missing last September."

He rolled his eyes, "I gave a statement back then. I don't know anything."

"It'll just take a few minutes, sir," Munro said.

Slater's eyes shot between Munro and Tattersall then he checked his watch.

"Less than five minutes," he said.

Munro shook his head. "It'll take as long as—"

"Everything all right, Phil?" An older man in uniform had approached along the platform.

Slater shrugged. "Just more stupid questions," he said. "Trevor, would you mind…?"

"Taking Betty back down? Of course not."

"Who was that?" Tattersall asked as the other man went back into the tram.

"Trevor Weston. The conductor. He shouldn't drive but if you're insisting—"

"I am." Munro nodded to the waiting-room so they could talk out of the sun's glare. "I presume Betty is what you call the tram."

"Yes. Betty and Alice," Slater said as they walked into the room.

It smelled of hot metal and varnished wood. Once they were settled in a quiet corner, Slater sitting on a bench at right angles to the police, Munro started asking questions.

"You were driving Betty, the B-tram, on Saturday the twelfth of September?"

"Yes."

"Did you see any children—boys or girls—trying to get on at MacDonnell Road?"

"No."

"What about on the wrong side?"

"Trying to get on?" He shook his head. "No."

"Did you let anyone go upfront?"

"No."

"There are seats up there—" Munro started before Slater spoke over him.

"Yes. Used to be reserved for the Governor—still is, but anyone can sit up there now as long as it's the last second. We don't stop them."

"Children?"

"Sometimes." His eyes narrowed. "But not on that day and not without an adult."

"But a witness saw a girl up front."

Slater took a breath. "What time?"

"Between eleven and twelve," Munro said, being generous with the window of time.

"No."

"How can you be so sure?"

"I'd remember. And—"

Munro waited expectantly. When nothing was forthcoming, he prompted: "And what, Mr. Slater?"

"Nothing. I'd remember, that's all."

"Why, specifically that day? Or have you got an extraordinary memory?"

"Because it was the day after my birthday." He shrugged. "So, I remember."

"In that case, what do you remember about that day?"

Slater shook his head.

Tattersall said, "Anything out of the ordinary?"

"No."

Munro watched and waited. When nothing was forthcoming, he prompted, "Did Karen Vaughn ride in your tram, Slater?"

"No."

Munro waited another beat and saw the man's eyes flick from side to side. A bead of sweat formed on Slater's upper lip.

"I think you're lying, Slater," Munro said directly.

"Sir!" Tattersall hissed. A line had been crossed.

Slater set his jaw, then stood. Looking at the junior detective, he said, "This interview is over."

★ ★ ★

Bill Teags had become obsessed with Zetland Hall and Eric Cattles. Now Munro felt like he was becoming obsessed by the tram. He didn't like the way Nicola Prisgrove had reacted when asked about the tram and a possible other friend. Now he didn't like Slater. Would Munro start punching witnesses and get into trouble like Teags?

He rested with his head in his hands. Slater was outside on the platform, looking down the track. Did he know something?

Witnesses were notoriously unreliable. Gerrard undoubtedly had the time wrong. Or he'd seen someone else. Or it was the A-tram.

He sucked in the sour waiting-room air. "We'll question the other tram driver," Munro announced.

"No, sir," Tattersall said firmly.

Munro shot him a glance.

Tattersall shook his head. "You need to take a break from the case, sir. No disrespect, but I think it's getting to you."

Munro pushed down the sense of anger he felt rise in his chest.

"I've heard you say it to others, sir," Tattersall said. "Take a break from this case. Let your thoughts settle and maybe, just maybe, things will come a little clearer."

It was the smart move, what with the Chief on his case and Garrett threatening to take his job, Munro couldn't afford to go round upsetting people—even lowly tram drivers.

As the junior officer drove him back to the police station, Munro kept thinking about the tram. There were so many discrepancies, not least with the timing, both at Zetland Hall and MacDonnell Road.

Perhaps all of it was a red herring. Perhaps Karen Vaughn really did go into Zetland Hall and never came out again. Or perhaps the sighting at the North Point fair a day later was genuine.

When Munro got back, there was a note of the cinema programme timings on his desk. It was hand written in a barely legible scrawl. He could see that Norman Wisdom started at 10:58. Prisgrove and his daughter left at this time to avoid the programme, which meant that Karen could have slipped out through the Theatre Lane exit at the same time or just after. If she ran up to Zetland Hall…

Munro shook his head. He didn't know what he was looking for. He put the note in his desk drawer.

It would be another two days before he'd question something else that would change everything.

# Chapter Twenty-Nine

On Sunday morning, Albert handed Balcombe the pile of photographs she'd collected from Roy Faulls. She'd used all twenty-four exposures on the roll of film. Balcombe considered each photo and stopped at one of the rear of the building.

"What's that?" he asked, pointing.

She held the picture close and studied the mark on the wall that he'd spotted. "I don't know."

He riffled through the paper and pulled out another of the rear. It was a slightly different angle, and he could see it clearly now. One brick was sightly proud.

"How high up is this?" He pointed to the bottom of the first-floor window.

"Twelve feet up, perhaps?"

The prominent brick was less than two feet below it. In his mind, he ran up, right foot on the wall, jump and grab the brick. Then immediately pull up and grab for the window ledge. Neither were wide. Could he hold on? If he could, he could use the brick for a toe. He imagined himself working around the frame, using it to pull up and stand on the ledge. Once there, he'd need to get onto the top of the frame and jump for the next floor's window. Which was open. No one could scale that without a ladder. That's what they would think. And that's where they would be wrong.

Then he realized the flaw in his thinking. He could climb the edge of the window frame, but he couldn't reach beyond it. With his feet so close to his hands, as soon as he took them off, his centre of balance would be moving away from the wall. His body would follow. He'd simply topple backwards.

There was no hope.

"When will Pingping be there?"

"Tonight," Albert said, "Expect him at the building after midnight." She paused. "Tell me you're not doing this."

"Arrange a sampan taxi for ten-thirty from Blake Pier."

Albert nodded. "And I'm coming with you."

"It's too dangerous." Balcombe went to open the apartment block's front door. Albert stepped in the way.

"Yes, it is, but I'm coming. Someone needs to keep a lookout for you."

Balcombe nodded his acceptance. Albert was an amazing asset. He was lucky to have her, but he also found himself concerned. Risking his own life was one thing, but the more Albert got involved, the more dangerous it would be for her.

"I've another job for you," he said.

She narrowed one eye. "Three times my pay again?" she said.

"No, this one's more straightforward." He handed her the passport-sized photograph of Theresa Pell's boyfriend, told her his name was Davey and that he was shore-based in the Royal Navy. Balcombe didn't know whether he'd need to speak to the young man, but it kept Albert busy and out of trouble.

He left Albert in the alley and took the other photographs to his rooms. After flinging them aside, he poured a glass of whisky and sat in his favourite armchair. The photograph of the three boy-climbers looked down upon him. The friend he called Eric, had disappointment in his eyes.

Balcombe knocked back his drink and felt the angry fire burn his throat and then all the way down inside.

He looked back at Eric as he stood to pour another drink.

*How would I do it?* Eric said in Balcombe's mind. *What would I do?*

"You'd find the impossible handhold, the impossible crevice."

*Then look for it, my friend.*

Balcombe breathed deeply, letting his chest swell, his muscles tense. Could there be a way?

He pulled a magnifying glass from a drawer and spread the photographs before him on a table. The ones showing the window were the important ones.

Yes, there! To the right of the frame was a line, barely discernible. He focused through the magnifying glass. It was a thin, shallow gap in the mortar. Balcombe visualized himself on the frame. If he could get purchase on the gap... A knife-hand, perhaps? Could he wedge his little finger and the edge of his right hand in there? It would be hard. That fine purchase would need to take his weight as he raised his legs, but then he'd need something more.

Yes! Another gap higher to the left of the first. Again, it would be a tough move and partial grip, but if he could... Balcombe breathed again and felt Eric's spirit. It was possible, and it was extreme. It was the reason he climbed. Too easy and there was no satisfaction.

# Chapter Thirty

"It's Saints Cyril and Methodius's day today," Jonah said, standing by the church doors and catching Balcombe as he waited. "February isn't a great month for saints. I didn't include them in the book. Last week was Saint Colette. I didn't include her either."

"Why not, Jonah?" Balcombe said out of politeness rather than any genuine interest.

Jonah gave a small, guilty shrug. "If I remember, Colette was a nun who founded many nunneries and predicted her own death. All a bit boring. And as for Cyrill and Methodious, all they did was to translate the Bible into Slavonic."

A man cleared his throat and Balcombe turned to see Father Thomas. "That might sound easy, Jonah, but you must remember that the Liturgy used to be in Latin and Greek. Other languages weren't allowed. Cyril and Methodius suffered considerable prejudice for trying to spread the word of God. We'd probably be conducting the whole service in Latin if it weren't for them."

Jonah bobbed his head in acceptance. "Yes, Father."

The priest turned his attention to Balcombe as Jonah went to accost another parishioner. Munro's bad leg had been caused by a beating. As Jonah walked away,

Balcombe suspected the boy had been born with his problem. His left leg seemed shorter than the right.

Father Thomas said, "Enjoy the sermon today, Mr. Balcombe?"

"Always," Balcombe said unconvincingly. "But I'd like a chat with you, if you have the time?"

"Now?"

"Please."

Father Thomas smiled beatifically. "How can I help you today?"

"Margaret Sotherland."

"Again?" The priest exhaled loudly. "All right, you can have ten minutes in my room."

Balcombe followed Father Thomas through a series of oak doors and into a small office that smelled of wood polish and dust. Vestments hung from a cloak stand. There was a table piled with Bibles and documents. A statue of a lamb looked up at him from beneath the table. It carried a cross and pennant with the words *Agnus Dei*.

The priest closed the door but kept one hand on it as though he'd swing it open again at any moment.

Balcombe said, "It looks like Margaret Sotherland committed suicide."

"We've had this conversation, Charles." The priest waved his free hand. "Margaret did not kill herself."

"How can you be so sure?"

Father Thomas shook his head sadly. "Death certificates don't lie."

Balcombe had a different opinion but didn't bother questioning the statement. Instead, he said, "Margaret wasn't a drug user, Father. She took a large dose one night and it killed her."

Father Thomas said nothing.

"Did she confess to you, Father?"

"Most of the congregation confess at one time or other."

"Specifically, Margaret."

The priest said nothing.

"Had she sinned?" Balcombe asked. "Did she need redemption?"

"It wouldn't be appropriate for me to betray a confidence."

"Even though she's dead?"

The priest smiled kindly. "If people thought their private conversations came out after their deaths, do you think they would confess in confidence? Of course, they wouldn't. That trust and confidence goes beyond the grave, Charles."

"Did you visit Margaret in her home?"

"I do home visits," he said noncommittally.

"Specifically, did you visit Margaret in her home?"

Father Thomas looked like he was going to speak but then didn't.

Balcombe said, "You were seen."

"Where?"

"Homeville, where Margaret lived."

"I really don't appreciate your tone, Charles."

Balcombe shook his head. "Because it looks like a suicide has been covered up?"

Father Thomas opened the door and looked like he was going to dismiss Balcombe but paused and took a breath. "If a suicide did occur, then it's still a tragedy. But I can assure you there was no coverup by the Church."

"What about Theresa Pell?"

"Theresa Pell?" Father Thomas closed the door again.

"She was also from this congregation. She killed herself four months ago."

Father Thomas frowned. "That wasn't *covered up,* as you called it. I don't see—"

"Did she confess to you?"

Father Thomas said nothing. The frown remained.

"Did you visit her in her home before she died, Father?"

"All right, Mr. Balcombe, that's enough. You may take your leave now."

Jonah was still on the steps when Balcombe emerged from the church. No doubt he was peddling his books again.

"Ah, Mr. Balcombe," Jonah called as Balcombe tried to slip past.

"Another time, Jonah."

The young man limped over. "I just wanted to suggest another saint for you." He dropped his voice. "Instead of today's official saints. Read the chapter on Perpetua and Felicity."

Balcombe nodded kindly. "I'll do that, Jonah."

★ ★ ★

Balcombe met Munro in the run-down secret office at the end of the wharf.

Munro looked more hassled than usual when he came into the dusty, old office. He was carrying the brown package Balcombe had sent him. The one that contained the bottle of Paregoric from Margaret Sotherland's room.

Balcombe could read that he was right. No evidence of previous use. No evidence of other medication. "The tincture in the bottle… it's too strong, isn't it?"

"About ten times stronger than it should be," Munro said. "This isn't what it says on the bottle. Where's it from?"

Balcombe told him.

146

Munro nodded. "A small bottle of this will kill you for certain."

"It looks like suicide," Balcombe said. "Classed as death by misadventure—an overdose. But the Sotherland girl wasn't a known user. This may have been the first time. She replaced the weak tincture with a stronger concentrate so that no one would guess what she was doing. Like a drunk will hide his bottle."

Munro raised an eyebrow.

Balcombe shook his head at the implication. "I like my whisky, Munro. That doesn't make me a drunk."

"If you say so."

Balcombe ignored him. "I think there's a coverup."

"So that's why you're involving me in your little investigation. You're not just finding things that weren't there to be found."

"It was suicide!" Balcombe said.

"So?"

"Misclassified." He could see that the policeman still didn't get it. "Margaret Sotherland was a Roman Catholic. Suicide is a sin."

"Ah."

"It looks like she may have been a prostitute. She was getting counselling. She was probably getting home visits from Father Thomas.

"Father Thomas?"

"He's a Catholic priest... from the cathedral." Balcombe paused, letting that sink in. "This is big, Munro. They buried Margaret in consecrated ground— a lovely grave and tombstone. Now, I don't have a problem with it, but the Church does."

"I can't prosecute a priest for covering up a suicide."

"I don't expect you to, Munro. I'm just wondering how big an issue this is. I'd like you to look through old cases and check for similar deaths—not just suicides like

Theresa Pell's, but any misadventure that could have been suicide."

\* \* \*

Back in his rooms, Balcombe checked his watch. With an hour to spare, he poured a shot of whisky and sat in his favourite chair and read the medical analysis report on the contents of the Paregoric bottle from Margaret Sotherland's room.

The bottle's label said it was a tincture of opium containing 0.14 ounces per fluid ounce. The volume of the bottle was 2 fluid ounces.

The report said the contents were ethanol, honey, some trace elements and anhydrous morphine. The concentration according to the report was twenty-five times what it stated on the bottle.

Someone had written a note beside the analysis. It said: *The bottle contained enough opium to be a fatal dose. In fact, half a bottle could be fatal for someone unused to the drug.*

No need to be an addict then. Just a bottle of this would have done it. Which raised a massive question: How had Margaret obtained a bottle of Paregoric with such a high concentration of opium?

With plenty of time and wanting a distraction, Balcombe set aside the analysis report and picked up the book of saints that Jonah had given him.

What was the story he'd recommended? Saints Perpetua and Felicity. Balcombe found the page and read the brief passage.

Perpetua had been a noble woman and Felicity her slave. When they refused to renounce their faith, the Romans put them in the arena to be savaged by wild animals. They survived and, after being cleaned up, they were reintroduced to the crowd to face the gladiators. Both women were stabbed, and the slave died quickly. Perpetua took a sword and slit her own throat.

However, it wasn't their devotion to Christ that intrigued Balcombe; it was a vision Perpetua allegedly received. A golden ladder reached up to heaven. Along its length were swords, daggers, and hooks. At the foot was a dragon ready to strike. She said the words: "In the name of Jesus Christ, he will not hurt me," and the dragon lowered his head.

The story appealed to Balcombe because Chinese gangs often used the dragon as a symbol. He wasn't going to pray, but he did toast the photograph of the boy he called Eric. It wasn't the climber who would be afraid tonight. It would be the dragon.

Tonight, Balcombe told himself, he would release BlackJack.

# Chapter Thirty-One

Nie Pingping lay face down on the bed. It had been a good day, probably one of the best. The masseur applied oil and started working up and down his back. Pingping sighed and smiled into the pillow. Yes, it had been good. The two boys had been well-matched. Naked except for the body straps, they had fought for their lives. A three-foot pole connected them, attached to their chest straps so they couldn't run away. They had to twist and deceive. They could kick, but with smart moves, they could pull the other close enough to punch. The skinnier one had worked it out first and caught the other by surprise. However the second one, a pretty boy, was a quick learner, and he pulled the same stunt to get revenge.

The smartest move was to sweep the other's legs, and they went down in a tangle of limbs for the first time. The sweeper had lost the advantage. It took three goes before one of them solved the technique.

So equally matched were they that they'd kept going for almost an hour. By the end, both boys were exhausted but the skinny one had forced Pretty-boy to the ground and managed to stay on his feet. He used the pole to pin his opponent before stamping on his neck and leaving it there. The stamp hadn't done much damage but, too exhausted to escape, Pretty-boy had been throttled by a foot.

Pingping grinned at the memory. So, Skinny had won, which was a shame, because the other boy was not only pretty, but had a better body. Never mind. In victory, Skinny did not know what his prize would be. Perhaps he thought he'd be set free. Pingping had unlatched the pole and gripped the strap-ring on Skinny's shoulders. Then he slit Pretty-boy's throat. Blood didn't spurt and pump, so he must have been dead already, but the demonstration served a purpose. It showed Skinny what would happen to him if he disobeyed.

Pingping pulled the Skinny over to the chair where he'd been enjoying the spectacle. He pushed the boy down, and Skinny's exhaustion showed as his legs buckled.

Pingping opened his gown and laughed at the look on the boy's face. But Skinny understood what he needed to do. He understood he had no choice when Pingping gripped the face straps and pulled him into position and made the boy use his mouth on him.

Pingping closed his eyes and relaxed into the massage. The memory of the boy's performance sent a shiver of pleasure down his spine. What a shame Pingping had to take his life afterwards. It would have been good to experience that exquisite pleasure again. But he knew it was never the same the second time. He'd let a girl live once, because she'd been so good at fellatio. But the second time had been a disappointment. She'd known what was going to happen. Of course, she wanted to live, but she'd known what was coming after her fight. There had been no surprise, and he loved the shock when they realized what was expected of the winner. So he'd killed her after the second time. A chuckle grunted into the pillow. Now that had surprised her!

The masseur paused and Pingping was about to complain when he started again. This time the man worked his neck.

Hey! The fool peasant had gripped too hard.

Pingping tried to turn his head and complain. But the hand was like a vice, pinning him. How dare the masseur be so rough? He'd die for this.

"Stop!" Pingping growled, but his voice seemed lost in the pillow.

The grip tightened. He thrashed his legs, but the grip was too strong and there was weight on his back. The man was on his back! Pingping felt knees on his shoulder blades.

"Guards! Help!" he yelled.

Stars flashed in the darkness of his vision. He knew what was happening. He'd done the same himself. The person gripping his neck was stopping the blood flow.

"Who are you?" Pingping mumbled. The darkness was coming in waves now. "Who are you?"

"Your worst nightmare," a voice said. Then just before he lost consciousness, Pingping thought he heard the name BlackJack.

# Chapter Thirty-Two

Twenty minutes earlier, BlackJack's first attempt failed. He was at the rear of Pingping's building in Kowloon. He'd sprung at the wall, kicked up, grabbed the protruding brick and then jerked upwards. He'd planned for the momentum to take him up to the lowest window ledge. His fingers touched it but couldn't hold on. In his mind, he'd done this over and over to the point of considering it done. The hard part was moving between the window frames and floors, not this.

He looked up, hoping the photographs had been wrong, hoping a lower window might be open, hoping he could somehow use the climbing rope he had around his waist. There was nothing. He could just about see the dips between the bricks. Perhaps he wouldn't be able to use them either? Eric would have said, "use the fear," but this wasn't fear, it was doubt.

Eric laughed derisively in his mind. *What use is doubt?*

BlackJack ran at the wall again and jumped. The second time, he was closer but still fell back. The third time, he placed his springboard foot a touch higher, and it worked. He was dangling by his fingertips from the first-floor window frame. Using the edge, he pulled up with one hand and then the other. He found purchase at the top and was able to stand. He paused for breath. Through the slats he couldn't see the room beyond because of darkness. Before he'd gone to the rear, he'd seen the two bodyguards at the door—just like Albert had said. If it weren't for them, he'd now question whether Pingping was inside. However, there was also faint light coming through the second and third-floor shutters. Pingping was up there all right, enjoying whatever "fun" he sought here.

BlackJack saw the dip between the bricks and managed to wedge his knife-hand into it. It wouldn't take his weight, but it was enough. He moved up until he balanced on top of the frame. He could reach the next frame now and within seconds, he was standing on it, his hands on either side of the frame, creating compression. He breathed again and let the muscles relax. But it was only for two breaths, because he could see a sliver of light. There was movement in the room and BlackJack pressed his eye to the slit.

Then all the efforts at relaxation failed. He could see two young people naked except for black straps around their heads and chests and waists. Vertical straps held them together, including two between the legs. They looked like weird, kinky packages. Toys, BlackJack thought, or a tethered dogfight.

The boys were attached at the chest by a pole that swivelled. He saw them twist and turn, throw wild punches and kicks. A flash of crimson. There was another figure in the room. The man moved into view, and BlackJack saw he fitted the description of Pingping. Tall and lithe but with a head impossibly large for his shoulders and one sticking out ear. He was wearing a gaping crimson robe, beneath which he also seemed naked.

Blood spewed from one of the boys' mouths and Pingping got aroused. BlackJack's breathing became ragged, and he forced himself away from the spectacle. The next part of the climb was the trickiest since he'd seen no gaps in the mortar to help him onto the frame and grab the third-floor window. He edged right, his left fingers straining on the fine edge of the frame, his right arm reaching sideways, his right leg also out, feeling the brick and air until they found the edge of the next window. Now he was spreadeagled against the wall, one hand and foot on one window, the other on the next. His fingers inched up to the top and gripped. Then he pulled, using his feet to push inwards, creating enough friction to hold. Halfway up, he found a slit between the windows and jammed his left hand into it. With an urgent push, he went right, grabbing a new hold with his right hand and snatching the same upper frame with his left.

He let his legs drop to the bottom of the window frame and rested. All he'd done was transverse the wall, moving from one window to another. But this one had gaps between bricks to the right and above. After a flex of the fingers, he was pulling up and clambering to the top of the frame, then pulling himself on to the third-floor one.

Inside the top room, he saw a low bed and a little plump man dressed in white. Candles burned and he could smell incense or medicinal oil. There were stairs to the left and two doors on the right. When the man in white disappeared through one door, BlackJack was in the room and darting for the second door. He entered, left the door ajar, and looked around. It was a storeroom with everything needed for massage treatment, including towels and a white gown. BlackJack slipped one over his dark clothes.

After a flushing sound, the plump man left the other room and stood by the bed. BlackJack waited behind the door.

Fifteen minutes later, Pingping appeared. He dropped his crimson robe and wiped bloody hands on a towel that he also tossed aside. The plump masseur said nothing, keeping his eyes down.

Once on the bed and settled, the masseur rubbed oils into Pingping's skin before massaging Pingping's back. He worked the man's legs for a few minutes and then paused to refresh the oils.

BlackJack moved. He whipped a towel around the masseur's face to smother noise, then used the pommel of his knife to knock the man out. In his head, it took a second, but laying the man down without a noise also took time and Pingping got restless.

Acting fast, BlackJack gripped Pingping's neck and placed the other hand on the man's back. Then as soon as Pingping became suspicious, BlackJack climbed onto his back and pinned his neck harder, squeezing. But this wasn't about throttling the repugnant man, it was to hold the carotid artery. He wanted Pingping asleep while he operated.

He hadn't planned how he would kill him. But the sight of the man's evil debauchery downstairs drove BlackJack's hand.

# Chapter Thirty-Three

Two years of murder files from the whole of Hong Kong were beside Garrett's original desk. He'd given up his sweatbox of an office to Munro.

Munro wanted to spend more time on the Karen Vaughn case. It was in his blood now, like it had been in Old Bill Teags'. Instead, he had to work for someone of the same rank and do the grunt work.

Garrett arrived in the main office. He glanced at Munro, probably checking that he was reviewing the files before sitting down at Munro's desk in the main office. The other men noticed. They must have recognized it was a statement. Garrett had taken Munro's job.

*Not yet,* Munro thought. *Not ever.*

After sitting for ten minutes, the other inspector strolled around, talking to the other men before heading toward Munro.

"How's it going? Solved the case yet?"

"Good morning," Munro said.

Garrett stood over the desk and spread out the files there, ruining Munro's organised piles.

"Found anything interesting?" Garrett asked, flicking his eyes over the file names.

"Not yet. I'm going through, slowly and carefully."

"And spending time on that cold case."

Munro nodded. "Karen Vaughn. I think—"

"All right, Munro, just don't spend all your time on it. We have a multiple murderer on our hands, not just a missing girl." Garrett smiled with his mouth only.

Munro nodded.

"Let me help," Garrett said. "Have you found the Sham Shui Murders file?"

"Why that one?"

Garrett already had his hand on the file. The title in bold black type on the front was: *Sham Shui Murders.*

Munro held his breath as Garrett opened it. The man had clearly seen the file before and probably reviewed it. He'd been waiting for Munro to mention it or maybe he was just pretending to be clever.

Garrett flicked through it and seemed to study the photographs.

"Six gruesome murders in one house. You *have* seen this file, Munro?"

"Not yet. I'm only midway through last year's." He thought he sounded nervous, but Garrett didn't seem to notice.

"Ugly," Garrett said and handed Munro a photograph from the file. It showed a man minus his genitalia. "Looks surgically removed, don't you think, Munro?"

Munro breathed. "I can't tell. Perhaps."

"That's interesting," Garrett said pulling the photograph back. "Although the PM says that he had a broken neck."

Munro's brain finally started working. "Six murders," he said as though pondering. "Gang war. You're aware of the trouble in the Sham Shui district? I

158

would guess that a third of the cases here relate to that district."

Garrett nodded, also thinking. "A surgeon working within a gang." Then he smiled. "All right, I think we're making progress. As you review, think about that. Go back and look at gang-related murders and possible connections with a surgical cut."

But Garrett was only there for a few minutes before a clerk bustled into the room and handed him a note. Within seconds, the detective was on his feet and darting for the door.

"What's happened?" Munro asked when he cornered the clerk a few minutes later.

"The inspector has gone to Kowloon, sir."

"Because?" Munro said impatiently.

"The note just said there was an horrific murder last night."

Munro's guts constricted. *Please don't let it have been BlackJack.*

# Chapter Thirty-Four

Balcombe was in Mary Pilkington's apartment on MacDonnell Road, where Theresa Pell had lived. She had recently returned from work and drawn the curtains against the darkness outside.

Mary didn't hide her excitement at his visit. She fussed that she'd have put on makeup if she'd known he was coming. She was in her work clothes, and he said she looked smart.

She gave him a cup of tea and chatted about the influx of Chinese refugees and the pressures on housing.

"I'm so lucky to live here with protected rent."

He nodded politely.

"But you hear of people claiming properties just by squatting in them," she said. "I really don't understand the Hong Kong laws. You couldn't get away with that in England!"

"No, you couldn't."

She continued, and he listened until she seemed to be out of small talk. Then he said, "Mary?"

"Yes, Charles."

"The other death—"

"Margaret Sotherland. Yes, I looked her up in the papers."

"There are a lot more similarities between the cases than we... and the police"—he quickly added—"first thought. That's why I'm back. I want to clarify some things."

"Oh," she said, deflated.

"Do you think someone else was to blame for her suicide?"

"What do you mean?"

"The boyfriend? What was he called?"

"Davey... Let me think... No, I can't recall a surname if Theresa ever told me."

"Could it be his fault?"

"I don't know. I never met him and despite... no, maybe because what had happened, she talked about going home to England rather than find work. I remember her saying 'what's the point, now?' Do you think that was the indicator that she was going to take her life? But then why go to confessional?"

"Confessional?"

"Yes, Theresa said the vicar or... no, I mean, the priest was really helpful. She attended Saint Jude's but also the cathedral, I think."

"Have you heard the name Father Thomas?"

She shook her head. "I didn't pay attention to the names."

"Did the priest come here?"

She shook her head, frowning. "Do priests do that?"

"The other case I'm looking into... Father Thomas visited Margaret Sotherland before her death."

She shook her head again.

"Have you heard the name Lammy?"

"Is that a nickname?"

"A surname."

"It's not familiar."

"What about the company Lowe, Bingham and Matthews?"

"The big accountancy firm based in the Hong Kong and Shanghai Bank building?"

"That's right," he said, appreciating that she knew the company. "Did Theresa go for an interview there?"

"She didn't say, although she did visit a lot of firms looking for work. So, it is possible."

Balcombe described Simon Lammy as being of moderate height, tubby with thinning hair, grey eyes and a ruddy complexion. "He would have been well-dressed," Balcombe concluded."

"Apart from being well-dressed, he doesn't sound too appealing. I don't think Theresa would have had anything to do with a man like that. I gave you the picture of her Davey. He was a real looker."

Balcombe waited a beat. "I don't mean to speak ill of the dead but is it possible that Theresa needed money? After all, she was looking for a job and needed to pay rent."

"A prostitute, you mean?"

He nodded, relieved at her frankness.

"No." She shook her head firmly. "She was lovely and anyway she would have been out walking the streets and she only ever went to church in the evenings."

"Some girls limit it to a few wealthy clients," Balcombe suggested.

Mary thought for a moment, then shrugged. "I suppose... You never really know anyone, do you? I wouldn't have guessed she'd get herself into trouble. But a lovely girl. I hope she wasn't. I prefer to retain my memory of her."

"And yet she took opium and killed herself."

Mary shook her head. "It really doesn't fit, does it, Charles? She wasn't the sort, and her death came as such a shock."

\* \* \*

Balcombe stepped out onto MacDonnell Road. His head was full of thoughts about religion and religious people. He turned and Mary Pilkington smiled and waved goodbye. She clearly hoped he'd be back. However he was sure he'd learned all there was to learn from her. Maybe he'd come back another time when she wasn't home. He could ask the neighbours whether they'd seen anyone enter the house. Unlike Margaret Sotherland's rooms, Mary's apartment was the first one. Anyone coming inside wouldn't pass the other front doors. In particular, they wouldn't pass a nosey neighbour like the cat woman in 8 Homeville.

There was a pool of streetlight to his left. Two men were chatting and smoking as they leaned against it. Balcombe turned right towards Kennedy Road. He'd taken five, maybe six steps before he realized there was someone behind him.

He turned in time to see a flying fist. A twist made it glance off his head, and he was reaching for his handy knife when another blow struck. Two men, one on each side.

He took a punch to the temple and two to the gut.

His knife was in his hand now as he twisted to avoid the blows raining down. He took a step back for respite and defence, but something hit his leg as he transferred the weight.

Balcombe went down.

A boot drove into his ribs, and another caught the back of his head.

Roll and get up, he told himself, but as he started, the kicks landed again and all he could do was curl up and protect his head.

Suddenly, the attack stopped.

A gruff voice said, "Keep investigating and next time will be final."

They both laughed and their boots clattered off into the darkness.

# Chapter Thirty-Five

*Has BlackJack struck again?*

Munro returned to his desk and took half an hour before deciding that he should make use of the time rather than sit around fretting, fearing the worst.

He picked up the Karen Vaughn case and reviewed his notes. He worked on the timings and then called the Peak Tram Company. He arranged a meeting with the driver, Philip Slater. This time, he'd have the man in an interview room at the station.

Two hours after dashing off, Garrett came back into the office carrying a file.

Munro watched the other detective get a drink of water then go into the records room. When he emerged, he was carrying another file and walked directly to the sweatbox of an office. He put one file on the desk in front of Munro.

The top file was that of Fung Haoran's, the murdered butcher.

Garrett indicted he should open it.

Inside were the reports about the immigrant girl who'd been found dead in the cold-storage room. The butcher had been a suspect—as far as detectives were concerned, he'd been the murderer. It also had the conviction details of the hygiene offence that had put him in prison for three days.

But Garrett wasn't interested in those. He reached out and slid a photograph from the pile: the body of the butcher hanging from a meat hook.

"I'd never seen anything like this in my life," Garrett said. "And now I've seen it twice."

He slid the second file across the table. The name on the front was Nie Pingping.

Munro's heart pounded hard. He felt sweat prickle on clammy skin. Would Garrett notice? But the other man seemed to be in a state of shock, his eyes too glazed to register anyone else's condition.

Munro opened the file and saw his worse fears realized. The crime-scene was grotesque: an overweight man on the floor with a trail of guts longer than his body. Other photographs showed the abdomen, clinically sliced from sternum to pubis. There was a path of blood to a table. Without reading the report, Munro knew what had happened. He forced himself to speak.

"It's almost the same—without the meat hook."

"Yes."

"Nie Pingping," Munro said, pretending to read the front sheet. "It's a familiar name."

"Kowloon CID say he's a high-ranking gang member from the Walled City. He was still alive when he was cut open."

Munro nodded. "It's got to be the same killer. The cuts are surgical." He paused a beat. "You're thinking it's the same—another gang killing?"

"I saw the body, Munro. My God, who is capable of such a thing?"

Munro shook his head but said nothing.

"A gang killing. Retribution. A power-grab? But here's what I don't understand. I've seen gangland executions before and they tend to send a message."

"Gutting someone—" Munro started, but Garrett was on a roll and spoke over him.

"They don't sneak around, Munro. They pick up, execute and dispose of the body. Or, as I said, they leave the body as a message. Leaving a body on the top floor of a private building isn't going to be seen by anyone except the police."

"A message to us then?"

"There were no other bodies and no evidence that our killer went through the building. A man like that has bodyguards. Where were they?"

"They could have been paid off," Munro suggested.

Garrett scrubbed at his face. "Yes, they could have, but then why that?"

"I don't know," Munro said after the other man scrutinized him as though expecting an answer.

Neither of them said anything and the warm air seem to grow heavier.

Finally, Garrett breathed out loudly. "I've taken the case."

Munro's eyes widened.

"I know, I know," Garrett said. "The numbers. But this is undoubtedly connected. We need the clues from this crime, and we need to connect it to the others. We need to catch this man."

"Or men."

"What?"

"A gang killing implies more than one man." Munro realized there was a hint of desperation in his voice.

Garrett shook his head firmly. "A gang killing, yes, but still one killer. Murderers have a signature, Munro."

He jabbed the file with a thick finger. "This is the work of the same man. One man."

Munro nodded thoughtfully. "I think you're right."

"I am right." Another jab of the finger. "Now crack on with those old files. We need to get this man."

"Yes." Munro was absently flicking through the photographs and caught sight of one. It was a shot of the exterior of a building.

"I want a report. Compare the cases." It came out as an order rather than a request.

Munro took a calming breath and used the pause to place a hand over the picture before sliding it away.

Garrett put out a hand. "You keep the report, I'll study the photographs.

For a horrible second, Munro thought the other man knew about the one under his palm. But he didn't even seem to notice when Munro awkwardly picked up the remaining ones with his left hand and hold them out.

Garrett snatched them and left.

Munro didn't dare glance at the photograph under his right hand. Instead, he slid it out of sight into another file and breathed with relief.

Garrett wanted a clue and BlackJack had left a huge one. As soon as possible, Munro needed to confront Balcombe again.

# Chapter Thirty-Six

Ten minutes later, Munro was in the secret room by the wharf. Balcombe had followed him a few paces behind. When he stepped into the room, despite the poor lighting, Munro could see Balcombe looked dishevelled.

Rather than ask about his appearance, Munro shot the issue that had been eating his insides.

"You killed Nie Pingping last night!"

"I did." It was a cold statement of fact with no apology or remorse.

Munro rarely lost his temper, but it boiled over now. Through clenched teeth, he said, "You idiot! I told you to keep BlackJack under control."

"You told me to kill the known serious criminals."

"The last time we met, I told you to keep BlackJack under control. And,"—he glared across the table at Balcombe—"you promised to give me four weeks. It's been just over a week. You killed again straight away!"

"I thought this was a special case, making amends for the more junior criminal I killed."

Munro shook his head. "And Inspector Garrett spotted the similarity to Feng's murder."

"The butcher," Balcombe said, but there was the hint of doubt in his voice.

*Doesn't he know what he did?*

"You sliced him open from here to here." Munro drew a line down his body and studied Balcombe's face, trying to read him. "Nie was still alive and staggered a few feet for dying from the shock. His guts were everywhere."

The corners of Balcombe's eyes twitched.

*God! He didn't know. He doesn't know what BlackJack is doing.*

Balcombe said, "It's nothing less than he deserved. Did they find the other bodies?"

"You killed more?"

"No. Pingping killed two boys after making them play a sick game. I don't regret killing him, Munro. He was a monster, even worse than I'd imagined."

"So a monster kills a monster?"

Balcombe said nothing.

"Our only saving grace is that he was a Chinese national in Hong Kong illegally. On the one hand, the Kowloon police won't investigate too thoroughly, especially since the logical assumption is that he was killed by the Triad. However,"—he took a breath— "Garrett has spotted the similarity to the butcher's murder. If he gets any closer, I won't be able to protect you."

"Then I'll kill him too."

Munro suppressed rising anger. "No, you will not. You step over that line... you start killing innocent people and I'll come after you."

Balcombe shook his head. There may have been humour in his eyes.

They stood in silence for a minute, facing off across the table. Munro was about to ask about Balcombe's face. Had that happened last night when he'd killed Pingping?

However Munro said, "Tell me about the rope."

"What rope?"

"I saw a rope hanging down the side of the building where Pingping was killed." He was referring to the photograph he'd secreted away.

Balcombe said nothing.

Leaving clues that it's the same murderer is one thing. Leaving a clue that it was you is another thing entirely.

Balcombe shook his head. "A rope doesn't mean it was me."

"I sincerely hope you're right, Balcombe."

"Don't worry about it. And I wanted to talk to you about the other thing."

"Before that," Munro asked, "what happened to you? This isn't from last night." He waved a finger, pointing at Balcombe's appearance.

The other man touched his head. "I had an argument with a boot or two."

"You were attacked?" Munro's voice couldn't hide his incredulity. Then he looked concerned. "You didn't—?"

"No, I didn't kill them. And it's not funny, Munro."

The detective shook his head. Had he smiled? He doubted it. "I didn't say it was funny, Balcombe. However you're a man who knows how to fight. You've taken on hardened criminals and come away unscathed."

"If you're taking about Sham Shui, then I was prepared, and they were not. It makes a big difference. These men jumped me in the dark."

"Is there any chance this is connected to Nie Pingping?"

"No."

Munro breathed with relief. "So, who were they?"

"Not Chinese. I didn't see them properly, but I'd say they were white for sure. Rough labourers. Uneducated I guess."

"They spoke English?"

"They told me to stop investigating. It was on MacDonnell, outside where Theresa Pell used to live."

"Stop investigating Theresa Pell's suicide? That seems strange."

"It could be her or Margaret Sotherland. I've spent more time investigating her and her death isn't explained. They may have been following me, and MacDonnell Road is just a coincidence."

Munro frowned. "What have you found out about Miss Sotherland?"

"Nothing too specific. Except it's looking more and more like suicide and there are similarities with Theresa's death."

"The bottle of Paregoric?"

"No. There was no sign of the drug at Theresa's. The similarity is that people didn't expect it. People who knew them were surprised, but they both had issues."

"Issues?"

"They may have thought they'd sinned. Margaret was possibly a prostitute and Theresa had aborted a child. They'd both had confessional sessions with the priest at my church. Theresa killed herself—"

"And you think it was one suicide too many?" Munro interrupted.

"It would certainly embarrass the Church. People confessing and then taking their own lives."

Munro thought for a minute. "It's not a police issue."

"Have there been others?"

"I've looked. Pell's case was the only other in the past two years."

"Classified as something else? Covered up?"

Munro shook his head. He had more pressing things on his mind. He had Garrett looking into BlackJack murders and a need to solve the Karen Vaughn case.

He said, "You've done your investigation, Balcombe. You've done what you said you would, now do something else—and keep BlackJack under control."

# Chapter Thirty-Seven

Balcombe had a restless night thinking about too many things. The cases of Margaret Sotherland and Theresa Pell were going around in his head, but that wasn't unusual. He'd investigated many things in his past life as a military policeman. He could sleep well with pieces of information in his head. In fact, he could wake up having solved crimes in his sleep, or at least uncovered relevant information. This time, it was different. This time he also had the Pingping killing in his head.

He remembered the effort of climbing the building. He remembered the depraved activity he'd spied through the shutters. He remembered waiting behind the door for the right moment to attack the fat man. He'd taken over from the masseur but after gripping Pingping's neck, the rest was a blur.

He'd taken a climbing rope to aid his escape. He knew he couldn't go down the stairs because of the guards. He also knew he couldn't climb down. Getting up had been one of the biggest challenges of his life. Up had been difficult. Down would be impossible.

So he'd taken the rope to rappel from the upper window. He had flashes now and then. He could see himself tie the rope. He could see himself on the rope.

But he couldn't see himself releasing it and taking it away. Because he hadn't. It was one thing to have BlackJack take over, but now his alter ego had made a mistake. And that concerned him more than anything.

He received a note from Albert in the morning and the return of Theresa Pell's boyfriend's photograph. She'd found out he was Petty Officer David Russell, quartered in the Murray Barracks, close to the Royal Docks. She also said that Davey bought a pastry from a bakery at five to eight each morning on the way to the docks.

Balcombe checked his watch. That was in half an hour.

Having no better lead, he decided to speak to the petty officer. It was a gamble. He might be recognized. Balcombe had changed his identity and there was always the risk that someone would realize who he was. That was why he normally avoided anyone who'd lived in Singapore or were military personnel.

Being a sailor made Russell less of a risk, but Balcombe decided he'd play this one straight—or at least straighter than pretending to be a reporter.

Balcombe wore a brown gaberdine coat and matching fedora. He knew he looked the part and showed Russell his old credentials as soon as the petty officer came out of the bakery.

"Special Investigations Branch?" Russell said, frowning. "Military police?"

"That's right."

Russell had a fresh face, sharp blue eyes and short blond hair. He was good-looking and he knew it, Balcombe judged.

Russell shook his head with a cocky smile. "You know you don't—"

"It's not about you," Balcombe said, expecting the challenge. Military police dealt with the army. He'd need Navy approval to formally question a sailor. Or he'd be accompanied by a master-at-arms. "I'm investigating a soldier."

"Oh? I only have a couple of minutes. Who is it you're investigating?" Russell now looked intrigued rather than wary.

Balcombe waved a dismissive hand. "I can't disclose... but the connection with you is your ex."

"My ex?"

"Theresa. Theresa Pell."

Russell shook his head. The cocky smile vanished, replaced by a down-turned mouth. "She has problems," he said, and Balcombe figured he didn't know she was dead.

Russell went on to say that he didn't have anything to do with her. Nor did he know who she saw.

"If she is or has been seeing a soldier, then I don't know who it would be." He spoke openly and genuinely, saying that they had been in a relationship briefly before he shipped out to Hong Kong. Then she turned up on the island and started pestering him.

"She was watching me. Stalking me. I told her it was over."

"Then what happened, Davey?"

"Then it went quiet for a few weeks. Then she started up again. She caused a scene outside the barracks. She had pretended she was pregnant. But she couldn't have been because we had taken precautions." He sighed and shook his head. "She even showed me a fake bump and then threatened to get rid of it. But she wouldn't have done that because she was Catholic."

"Catholics do a lot of things they shouldn't—especially before marriage."

Balcombe could see that Russell knew what he meant. The man had slept with her. He'd probably promised they would marry. Then he got transferred to Hong Kong and thought he'd never see her again. Maybe he even knew that before sleeping with her.

"So that crazy bitch has got a soldier in trouble now, has she?" he asked, probing.

Balcombe resisted the urge to tell him that Theresa was dead. He wanted to. He wanted to let the man know how genuine the girl had been, how he'd broken her heart. But his training prevented him. It would serve no purpose and an investigator never discloses information without a good cause. It may come in use at a later stage. So instead, he asked a question.

"Did you ever go to her house?"

"I don't know where she lives. Don't want to know."

"MacDonnell Road."

Russell's eyes flicked up the hill in the direction of the street and raised his eyes. "Not far."

"No."

Russell checked his watch. "I need to go, Lieutenant... Sorry, I forget your name." That was because Balcombe hadn't said it. The name on the military police warrant card was Lieutenant Joseph Jenkins; his given name, although he was already used to the new one. He felt more like a Charles Balcombe, especially since it had been his best friend's name.

"Thanks for your time," Balcombe said, not furnishing the man with a name. "If I need anything else I'll be in touch."

Russell frowned again, like he had when they'd first met. Then he shrugged. "Right. And whatever this is about, when you see the crazy bitch—"

"She's dead," Balcombe said, unable to prevent the words from blurting out. He felt like he was holding a rapier ready to run the sailor through.

"Oh?" The bright blue eyes were wide now and full of questions.

Balcombe started to walk away, then turned. He couldn't help it. Theresa Pell hadn't been a bitch. She'd been a good girl who'd made a mistake.

"The pregnancy wasn't fake," he said and left Russell stunned outside the bakery.

# Chapter Thirty-Eight

"Why the photographs, Charles?" Faulls asked. Balcombe was sitting with him in a restaurant overlooking the harbour. They'd ordered a seafood lunch and a bottle of French wine. "Why did you want me to process the photographs of that house?" He was referring to the property in Kowloon where Balcombe had killed the man called Pingping.

After meeting with Russell, Theresa Pell's boyfriend, he'd been thinking about what he'd said. He'd wanted the young man to know the pain he'd caused. He'd wanted the man to suffer knowing that Theresa hadn't been lying. She'd got rid of his child. She'd taken her life.

Balcombe had let his emotion get the better of him. He knew the smart thing would be to withhold that information, and he'd lost control.

Which made him think of BlackJack and two nights ago. He'd wondered how to kill Pingping and knew he mustn't squeeze the fat man's heart. That would have been too obvious. But slitting him open while he was still alive? No wonder Munro had been horrified. It had shocked the detective the first time he'd done it.

Balcombe remembered most of that one. He remembered lifting the butcher onto the meat hook. He remembered thinking he should treat him the way he treated animals.

There had been a lot of blood, much more than when he slit a chest to squeeze a man's heart.

He remembered less and less of BlackJack's activity, and this morning he'd imagined running Russell through with a sword. He hadn't been able to stop himself. The animal inside was taking control of him as he acted more instinctively.

"Charles?" Faulls said. "Everything all right? You're seeming distant today. If I didn't know you better, I'd even say you were looking worried."

Balcombe forced a laugh. "Just thinking. What were you saying?"

"I wondered what the photographs were for."

Balcombe smiled and winked, but it was still forced. It was like he was acting for himself as well as his friend.

Faulls leaned forward, intrigued. "What?"

"A rendezvous," Balcombe said. "One of my ladies gave me a challenge... you know."

"Ah, right!" Faulls said grinning. "And did you..."

Balcombe shook his head, still smiling. "I can't betray a confidence."

"Damn you, Balcombe! Can't a man get a little vicarious titillation around here?"

"Not from me, he can't!"

Their food arrived before Faulls asked how the investigation was going.

Balcombe told him.

Faulls' mouth dropped open. "I thought you looked different. That's a bruise on your face?"

Balcombe had cleaned up since seeing Munro and hoped the mark on his check wasn't obvious. Now he knew the discolouration looked like a bruise.

"I've no idea who attacked me or which investigation I'm supposed to stop."

"Have you reported it to the police?"

"Yes," was Balcombe's simple answer, not wanting to get into the detail of his relationship with Munro.

Faulls was shaking his head. "I can't get it straight in my head. Did you say you spoke to Father Thomas?"

"I did. He wasn't happy with me and wouldn't tell me about the two women."

"Surely, you don't think it's him? The Church might not approve of suicide, but they wouldn't do that!"

History was cluttered with abhorrent things committed in the name of religion. However, Balcombe didn't bother arguing the point.

"There must be someone else. Who else have you upset?"

"A few cuckolded husbands, I suspect," Balcombe snorted. "But they wouldn't mention my investigation. No, this is about Margaret or Theresa. Margaret is my best guess. She had visitors."

"Can she really have been a prostitute? A good Catholic girl like her?"

"Do you know she was a good girl?"

Faulls winced. "Well, all right, I'll give you that. I didn't know her, I just assumed. So someone who was seeing her then."

"It's possible." Balcombe shrugged. He'd given it a lot of thought since the attack but struggled with the motive. Why wouldn't they want him to investigate?

They ate and talked about other things before Faulls came back to the subject.

"Thanks for doing what you've done. Investigating Margaret's death. I feel happier that it's less of a mystery."

"I'm not," Balcombe said. "I still feel like there's more to this and I don't like that the Church seems wrapped up in it. Maybe a cover up of suicide or maybe concern that people who confide in a priest go on to kill themselves."

"You're too close to it," Faulls said. "Take a break."

Balcombe looked at his friend with new respect. It was a principle of good investigation. Sometimes you didn't see the wood for the trees. Sometimes a break led to a breakthrough.

If the person who hired the two thugs thought he'd be scared off, then they had another thing coming. Balcombe wasn't giving up. But he would take a breather. He'd do what he always did to clear his mind. He'd go climbing.

# Chapter Forty

Munro was working through the case files again, looking for BlackJack murders. Of course, he knew which ones they were, but he had to be seen to be doing the job.

When he found a case in the New Territories dated in December 1952, he decided to include it. A young woman had been found beside the road. She'd been on her way to a Christmas dance. She worked in the NAAFI at the army's Dodwell's Ridge camp and the dance had been organised by the army.

She'd been sexually assaulted and slashed. The wounds looked unusual, which was one reason for putting the file on one side. The second reason was that no one had been convicted.

Munro remembered the case. Two British soldiers were the most likely suspects, but it was hugely sensitive, and he was sure the Governor had played a part in quashing the investigation.

He had found two more cases by the end of the day when Garrett came into the office.

"What have you got for me?" he asked.

Munro handed over the three files; the Christmas '52 case and two in '53.

While Garrett read the files, Munro carried on with his next.

"Really?" the British inspector said dismissively, slapping the files onto the table. "You think this NAAFI one? Where are the similarities?"

"Knife slashes."

"Nothing like a surgeon's and not so recent."

Expecting that comment, Munro said, "Killers adapt. They grow in confidence. This could have been his first victim. This could have been unplanned."

"You think the others were planned?"

Munro cleaned his spectacles. "I don't know."

Garrett tapped the NAAFI file. "And I doubt that one has anything to do with it."

Munro inclined his head.

Garrett was clenching his teeth, glaring. "Is that all you've found? Come on. I was told you were the best investigator Hong Kong has to offer." He didn't say it like it was a compliment. His words were full of disbelief.

Munro said, "The original Squeezed-heart case: Chen Chee-hwa. Then there's the butcher and the two in Kowloon: Nie Pingping and the one I found—"

"Feng Shubiao."

"Yes."

Garrett still had clenched teeth. "And the Sham Shui Murders."

"If you say so."

"I bloody well, do say so, Munro!"

Munro said nothing. Of course, Garrett was right, but Munro had to play dumb. If they worked out it was BlackJack and hence Charles Balcombe, then it would surely come out that he was protecting the killer.

Garrett was shaking his head with derision. "Where's the report I asked for?"

"The comparison?"

"You know that's what I'm talking about!"

Munro nodded toward the last file. "I've just one more to read and then I'll get to it."

"And these"—Garrett tapped the pile of rejected reports—"aren't connected?"

"No."

"In your opinion."

"In my opinion."

Garrett picked up half the bundle. "The NAAFI girl case isn't related but if I find—" The other man didn't finish his sentence that had been delivered like a threat.

Munro waited until the Garrett had left the room before he breathed a sigh of relief. BlackJack had killed those six gang members alone. Thankfully, Garrett couldn't seem to comprehend that one man could take on so many and he mentioned a surgeon.

He picked up the last file he'd been looking at. *Saint Christopher's Orphanage*, the name read. The date of death was January 1953. Angela Newham, a carer at the orphanage, had been smothered in her room. No chance of classing this as an accident, Munro thought.

She'd been found on her bed, covered by a sheet. Her body had been washed and she was clutching a Bible to her bosom.

This wasn't a file to show Garrett, but when he looked at the photograph, he knew that Charles Balcombe would be interested.

# Chapter Forty-One

How Munro had managed to get the envelope into Albert's hands without the other detective noticing, Balcombe didn't know.

He decided to delay climbing until he'd read the file inside the envelope. He'd taken a quick look and seen the name on the file was Angela Newham.

Another suicide, he suspected.

In his rooms, he opened the file that was marked with Kowloon CID's stamp. Newham's death had been classed as murder. She was twenty-two and worked at Saint Christopher's Orphanage in Kowloon.

Balcombe was puzzled. He looked at a photograph of her. Apart from being an attractive, young white girl, it intrigued him why Munro would send him the file.

Angela Newham had died in the early hours of the morning 27th January 1953. She'd been found on her bed, covered by a sheet. Her body had been washed.

The photographs showed a girl who looked like she was sleeping. The pathologist's report said her eyes showed the tell-tale petechiae, and he had concluded that her death had been caused by suffocation.

An accompanying note from Munro said that a Chinese man called Bruce Chong had been arrested and charged with her murder. Amid a bunch of witness statements that appeared to say nothing, there was a confession by Chong, admitting that he had suffocated her with a pillow. He said he'd gone to her room to steal anything of value. He didn't expect her there and panicked when he saw her in bed.

A police report noted that stolen items were found in his possession in his lodgings, including a hair comb belonging to Angela.

Young, white Catholic girl found dead in her room. Balcombe could see the similarity but suspected there was something else that had caught Munro's eye. Balcombe read through the file and found a blood analysis report. It showed a high concentration of opium.

Balcombe changed his plans. He wouldn't go climbing after all. He set off immediately for the ferry and Saint Christopher's Orphanage.

# Chapter Forty-Two

Munro caught sight of the note in his desk drawer: the timings from Tony, the projectionist at the Queens Theatre. Previously Munro had focused on the time of the Norman Wisdom show. It confirmed when Karen Vaughn's friend and her father had left and waited outside.

But that's not what caught his eye now. It was the scribbling higher on the page.

He rang the theatre and waited until Tony came on the line.

"Inspector?" It was an old voice, almost as shaky as the handwriting on the paper.

"Thank you for the timings, Tony."

"You're welcome. Sorry it took so long to locate it. My filing isn't as good as it should be—although no one ever asks about the old shows, really. I don't know why I keep them. I sometimes think it's checking I don't repeat episodes. But my memory is pretty good."

"Do you remember the Saturday Morning Matinee?"

"I did after I found the slip."

"You've crossed something out and written a couple of words."

"At ten twenty-two, yes."

"What does it say?"

"Daffy Duck. The spool for Heckle and Jeckle episode seventy-two was damaged. I thought there'd be a problem. You know they can get stuck or break or even melt. So, I exchanged it for Daffy Duck episode fifteen. It's been a while since we showed that, so I hoped the children wouldn't remember. Some of them did of course. Or maybe it was because it wasn't what they wanted so they started booing. You know how—"

Munro interjected. "To be clear, Tony, you're saying you didn't show a Heckle and Jeckle episode on Saturday the twelfth? Not then and not later?"

"That's correct."

"I don't mean to be rude, Tony, but are you one hundred percent certain? You'd stake your life on it?"

There was silence on the line before the projectionist responded. "Yes. One hundred percent."

Munro ended the call, sat back and sucked in a huge lungful of air.

If you are a witness, Munro thought, do you question your memory? Of course you do. It happened all the time. Witnesses were notoriously unreliable, especially once information about the case spread. The longer the interval, the greater the likelihood of a mistake—or modification to match what the detective expects. Not deliberate, but the failing of the human memory combined with the psychology of conforming. Most people don't want to be the odd one out. Ask five people to describe what they saw. If the first four agree on one thing, the fifth person will say the same despite believing otherwise. Self-doubt, perhaps, Munro suspected.

If you were in the cinema watching the Saturday Morning Matinee, would you mix up Daffy Duck and

Heckle and Jeckle cartoons? The girls went every week, it would be easy to forget what you watched from week to week. Wouldn't it?

But then again, the witnesses. Why would some insist they saw Karen earlier in the morning? The newspapers reported when she went missing and yet they didn't change their stories. Why do that unless they were convinced? Why would the Frenchman in the Peak Hotel say he saw a girl matching Karen's description at half past ten?

He was either mistaken or Karen was never at the cinema in the first place.

Which would mean Mr. Prisgrove and Nicola were lying.

"Did Karen go to the Saturday Morning Matinee, Nicola?" Munro asked the girl. He'd gone into Victoria Primary School and been given a room to interview her.

"Yes."

"She didn't though, did she?" Munro said calmly.

Nicola blinked and looked left then right. Her eyes didn't return to his.

"Nicola?"

The girl then reeled off the same information that she'd given time and time again in the formal statements. Memorized.

"Why did Karen stay when you and your dad left?"

"She didn't mind Norman Wisdom and enjoyed singing the National Anthem."

"That's not true, is it?"

"It is." Nicola swallowed. "I think I have to go now."

"Tell me the truth and you won't get into trouble."

The girl looked uncomfortable, but her lips squeezed tightly together.

"Nicola, have you been to the Saturday Morning Matinee since?"

The air came out in an explosion, followed by fast words. "No, of course not! It wouldn't be right!"

"So, you remember that day like it was yesterday?"

"Yes. We all went to Queens Theatre. We all went to watch the show. Dad and I left early, and Karen never came out."

"Never came out?"

Under pressure, Nicola had used a different expression, not a practiced one.

"I mean we didn't see her come out. There must have been a thousand people, mostly kids. We didn't see her."

"Tell me about the Heckle and Jeckle cartoon."

Nicola's eyes flared wide. "I don't remember."

"But you just told me you remember it like yesterday. It was the last Heckle and Jeckle you've seen."

"I…"

"Heckle and Jeckle wasn't shown that day. It was replaced by an old Mickey Mouse."

"Oh yes," she said unconvincingly.

He shook his head. "Nicola, I want the truth."

Her eyes went glassy.

"It wasn't Heckle and Jeckle or Mickey Mouse. It was Daffy Duck."

The girl shuddered and tears brimmed in her eyes.

"Nicola?" he pressed.

"We didn't go."

"Didn't go? At all?"

She took a couple if shuddering breaths. "Don't tell… you must promise not to tell my parents."

"All right."

Her breathing was still ragged, but she forced out the words: "To the cinema that day. We didn't go in. We hardly ever went in."

"What did you do?"

"Messed about."

"Your dad was with you?"

"No."

"Where was he?"

"I don't know. He used to drop us off at Queens Theatre for the matinee and give us extra pocket money, so long as we said he'd been with us. He said it was too boring for him and we weren't to tell anyone. He said he trusted us."

"So, what did you do on Saturday the twelfth, after he left you at the cinema?"

"We walked around a bit. We bought some sweets."

"Did you go up to Zetland Hall?"

Nicola hesitated.

Munro repeated the question.

"Yes," she breathed. "There's a dirty old man…"

She was talking about Eric Cattles, Munro realized. "What happened?"

"I dared Karen to go up the steps and speak to him. She did"—Nicola smiled slightly, presumably at the memory—"and even managed to get a handful of sweets out of him before scarpering."

"Did she give him her plastic ring?"

Nicola shrugged and frowned. "I think so, maybe. I don't know."

"She was wearing a ring that morning?"

"Yes—she always had a ring on."

"Did you see it later?"

She shook her head.

Munro nodded. So the witness who'd seen Karen in the morning had been right and the ring in Cattles's special box was probably Karen's.

"What did you do next?" Munro asked.

Nicola's lips tensed and he guessed she was having difficulty admitting something.

"You didn't go back to Zetland Hall?"

"Oh no!" she said with a roll of her eyes as though it had been a stupid question.

He took a punt. "Tell me about the Peak tram."

She looked at him with scared eyes.

"Tell me, Nicola."

"We weren't allowed on the tram—not without a grownup."

"But you went on it."

"No. I—" She took a breath and asked for water. There was a fountain in the hall and Munro accompanied her to it and waited as she lapped up mouthful after mouthful. Delaying.

"That's enough," Munro said and guided her back into the private room.

"What did you do after Zetland Hall?"

"We thought about going on the tram but decided to go to the sidings instead."

He knew it. The sidings and workshops were halfway between Kennedy and MacDonnell Road stops. "There's an old tram there that can be fun to play on. But there were workmen on that Saturday, and we just watched for a while. Didn't want to get into trouble. Then we walked to the next station stop."

The Frenchman had said he'd seen two girls on the wrong side of the Peak tram at MacDonnell Road.

"You got on the tram at MacDonnell Road," Munro said.

"Yes. Karen dared me, but we both got on." She paused. We sneaked on because we didn't have tickets and we knew we shouldn't."

"You got on the wrong side."

"Yes, after people got off."

193

"All right. You aren't in trouble. What happened next?"

"We went up front. The driver was nice. He let us pretend to drive it."

A witness had said they'd seen one girl upfront.

"Was it the A-tram or B-tram?"

"B, I think."

"What happened next, Nicola?"

"We got off at May Road."

"Both of you?"

"Yes, I was worried about the time. And of course we shouldn't be on the tram."

"So where did you go after that?"

She bit her lower lip. "Well, that's just the point. We didn't. I mean, Karen didn't. At the last second, she jumped back on again. She was laughing, but it wasn't funny. We had to get back to the cinema in time for my dad.

"What did you tell him?"

"That we'd been in the cinema, and Karen and I had split up, that I'd lost her coming out. He was mad. He was worried that Karen's mum would be angry, because she has quite a temper, I can tell you! She thinks nothing of hitting you with a broom if she thinks you've done wrong. Karen was always complaining—"

The school bell rang, interrupting her. Children barrelled into the hall outside the room while Nicola sat hunched, wringing her hands. Munro waited for the commotion to die down before speaking again.

"Nicola, think back. Did your dad know the truth about what had happened?"

"No! I wouldn't dare tell him about the tram. I'd be punished for days!"

"So you went back to the cinema."

Nicola nodded. "And met my dad as planned."

"You told him Karen was still inside? That you'd come out without her?"

"Yes. I said I didn't want to watch Norman Wisdom."

"And Karen didn't come out."

She shook her head.

"What did your dad say?"

"We waited a bit and talked about what shows we'd seen—I usually checked the schedule so he'd think I'd watched it. After everyone had left, I said we must have missed her. I said she'd probably gone out the side door. There's one on Theatre Lane."

Munro nodded. "What did you do then?"

"Then we walked home. Karen usually came back with us, but she wasn't there. I don't know why, but I said maybe she'd gone to the sidings, so we looked around from Zetland up to MacDonnell Road. I didn't say everything. I didn't say we'd been there or been on the tram. I just hoped she'd still be around. Of course, when she wasn't, Dad told me what to say to the police."

"He told you to say that he was with you."

"And that we both came out before the end." She breathed and sighed. "I think he knew we hadn't watched it."

Munro nodded.

Geoffrey Prisgrove had needed an alibi.

# Chapter Forty-Three

As Balcombe arrived at Saint Christopher's Orphanage in Kowloon, a young man hobbled out into the late afternoon sunshine. He looked up and did a double take.

"Hello!" the young man said uncertainly.

"Jonah," Balcombe said. "You know me from the cathedral. We spoke on Sunday."

Jonah smiled, "Yes, yes! Sorry, I was distracted. How are you getting on with the book of saints?"

"I read the story you recommended: Perpetua and Felicity. It was fascinating."

Jonah nodded sagely. "I think so. Father Thomas says that we shouldn't emulate the saints because we are human, but they were mere mortals too."

Balcombe pursed his lips. "Well, perhaps he means that we should expect to fail and when we do, it's all right."

"True. True. I just think... well, it's good to have role models. We read about Christ, and we try to live to his standards. He forgives us our sins."

Another person came through the orphanage doors and called out. Jonah waved back at them.

"You work here?" Balcombe asked.

"Oh no, I just visit from time to time."

"And give them books?" Balcombe half-joked.

"I give the odd talk to the children. You see I like to support the orphanage because I was here. Like so many orphaned by the war. I come and talk. It's also good practise. One day I'll be a priest, so the more I practise, the better I'll be."

"It's a Catholic orphanage?"

"It is, although it's not an entrance requirement. It's because the Church funds it rather than anything more formal." He smiled. "I wasn't a Catholic when I first came at thirteen. They don't mind who they take."

Balcombe was about to bid Jonah farewell, when he thought he may as well ask: "Did you know Angela Newham?"

The young man's face whitened. He sat on a wall and Balcombe joined him. The air blew warm and carried a bitter smell from a nearby works' chimney.

"Jonah?"

The young man shook his head and when he spoke his voice trembled. "Sorry.... I... It was terrible."

"Did you know her well?"

Jonah swallowed a lump in his throat. "She... she was lovely. Everyone loved her."

"What happened—if you don't mind me asking?"

"I don't know. It was after I'd left," Jonah said, staring off into the distance. "I just heard about it and they... the staff... talked afterwards."

He paused and Balcombe waited. Then Jonah looked at him with suspicion.

"Why are you asking? Are you a reporter?"

Balcombe laughed lightly. "I'm just asking out of curiosity."

"Curiosity?"

"A friend asked me to investigate Margaret Sotherland's death."

"Pardon me?"

"Margaret—"

"Yes, I knew Margaret," Jonah interrupted. "I know she died a few weeks ago, but why would anyone investigate her death? And what does that make you? A policeman?"

Balcombe shrugged. "I used to be. I'm just unofficial these days, helping a friend."

Jonah's eyes were still full of doubt. "Why ask about Angela?"

"Because it's curious. Within a year there are three dead girls of similar ages. All were single and white."

Jonah breathed out heavily and shook his head as he stood. "Angela was lovely."

"What does that mean?"

"It means she was perfect." Jonah's voice had an edge of anger, possibly frustration. Then he shook his head. "I can't help you."

Balcombe watched Jonah hobble away, his limp more pronounced, like the weight of the world was pressing down on him and he struggled to cope.

\* \* \*

Sister Birgitta welcomed Balcombe into her office. He flashed her his old warrant card, and she seemed to properly focus on it for the moment he showed it. His chest tightened, as he hoped she didn't pick up on the name and his different appearance.

She wore a simple gray dress and a white collar. He saw a black gown on the back of the door. She had eyebrows that expressed permanent concern, a wide mouth, and with hard lines on her face but kindness in her eyes. He guessed she was late forties, possibly early fifties, and about five feet eight inches tall.

When he'd called to arrange the meeting, she hadn't asked why. Now she said, "Investigator? I thought you were interested in the orphanage. You're not here as a donor?"

Balcombe shook his head. "I'm interested in Angela Newham."

Sister Birgitta scowled, then shook her head. "I really don't think it's—"

"I know she's dead," Balcombe interrupted. "Other girls are too."

"A man was convicted of her murder, Mr. Balcombe. He's in prison."

"Two girls have died since," he said, implying that the same man could not have killed them while in prison.

She frowned but said nothing.

"I'm looking at connections."

"Well, if it helps," she said with reluctance.

Balcombe decided to soften his approach and said, "I saw Jonah outside. He used to reside here?"

"That's right. He was very close to Angela."

"He said she was lovely."

Birgitta nodded sagely. "As lovely as they come. An angel taken far too soon."

"Who found her body?" Balcombe asked. Ordinarily, he would have been more sensitive, but he judged Sister Birgitta to be a no-nonsense woman. She was built of stern stuff.

"One of the staff, but they called me straight away." She paused, thinking before she asked: "You said you're working with the police?"

"I did."

"Hmm," she said, letting the frown return. "Wouldn't the police have told you everything?"

"Not everything, Sister."

Her eyes studied him for a moment. "I think we'll keep your investigation between the two of us, for now," she said, and her tone was clear, accepting no debate.

"I've seen the photograph," he said, acting as though there was no issue; he didn't need to speak to anyone else. "Angela was lying on her bed like she was asleep. There was a sheet pulled over her."

"That's right. She looked very peaceful. The only reason we knew she was dead was because she didn't answer the knock on her door—and then didn't respond when the staff member spoke to her. She was late for breakfast."

"The report said, she'd been washed."

Sister Birgitta nodded. "That's what I understand."

"And she'd been smothered."

"Again, that's what the police said, and thankfully they caught the man."

"And yet you have doubts."

"Do I?" She sighed. "I suppose I do. I find it very hard to comprehend. Everybody loved her."

Balcombe waited a beat and she smiled at him briefly before his question made it vanish.

"Could she have committed suicide?"

Sister Birgitta breathed loudly.

"Sister?"

"I can't believe it."

"But you believe she was murdered?"

The eyebrows above her concerned eyes angled even more. "I have to accept that Bruce Chong took her life."

"Did Bruce Chong know her?"

"Yes. We all knew Bruce."

"Did he love Angela?"

Sister Birgitta took a breath. "I expect so. Where is this questioning going, Mr. Balcombe?"

"I'd like to know whether Angela ever took opium or one of its derivatives to the best of your knowledge?"

"No! Surely not."

Balcombe was thinking of the other two girls. "Not for medicinal purposes? Insomnia or diarrhoea? The medication called Paregoric?"

"No! Not drugs, not alcohol."

Balcombe's face must have shown disappointment. "Why?"

"Because she had opium in her blood."

"I can't believe it."

"It's the same with the other two deaths," Balcombe explained. "Both girls took opium derivatives. One death was classed as a suicide"—Sister Birgitta shook her head—"and the other a drug overdose. Neither, I'm afraid, showed signs of suffocation."

"Ah," Sister Birgitta said.

"But here's the other remarkable coincidence: they were similar ages, single, white females and Catholic."

She shook her head. "It's a mystery, I'm afraid. I tell myself that she was taken because it was God's will." She continued speaking, and Balcombe realized she was delusional. Angela had been smothered and she'd taken a large amount of opium.

If the police were wrong, then to Balcombe's mind, it left one possibility. But would a nun behave in such a way?

He told Sister Birgitta that he was leaving, but he questioned all the staff he bumped into. Everyone was open and friendly, and he soon found the girl who'd discovered the body. Her name was Cynthia, a petite and skinny girl. She looked younger than twenty, but he guessed the malnourishment made her look younger than she really was.

Rather than question her in public, Balcombe waited until Cynthia finished work at four.

"It must have been a terrible shock," he said to her over a cup of tea. He'd offered cake or a sandwich, but she had refused.

"Yes. A person never gets over something like that."

"Because she was such an angel?"

Cynthia hesitated before answering. "Yes, but whoever…"

Balcombe read her reaction. "She wasn't an angel?"

With wide eyes, Cynthia shook her head. "I mustn't speak ill of the dead."

Balcombe decided that since food wasn't an enticement, he'd slide some notes onto the table. Her eyes bulged again, and she slipped the cash into her purse.

"She could be… could be bad," she said.

"Taking drugs?"

"No! Nothing like that."

"What then?"

She took a breath. "Boys… men… she was… interested."

"A nun?" Balcombe said.

Cynthia shook her head. "Oh, we call them all Sister, but Angela wasn't a nun."

"So, she… misbehaved?"

"I don't think she would actually… you know, do it. But she had a lot of admirers, and she returned the attention."

"Flirting?"

"I suppose that's what it was."

"Anyone in particular?" He slid some more money across the table and watched it disappear.

"All of them, young and old. She was very attractive."

Balcombe pondered for a moment, taking a sip of tea as a delaying tactic. "I understand Jonah was keen on her."

Cynthia nodded. "All the boys were, but I suppose especially Jonah. That was until Father Thomas put a stop to it."

"Father Thomas?"

"Yes, he comes regularly... although come to think of it, not so often these days. Jonah still comes a few times a week." She chuckled.

"What?" Balcombe asked.

"Some of the girls... I shouldn't say, really."

"What shouldn't you say, Cynthia?"

Her lips twitched before she spoke. "Some of the girls joked that even the priest was keen on Angela."

"Father Thomas?"

She shook her head. "Just a joke. I'm sure it wasn't true."

Balcombe's thoughts were racing away and she interrupted them.

"What's your theory, Mr. Balcombe?"

"My theory?"

"Why are you investigating Angela's death?"

"Because I'm suspicious," he said. "There have been three deaths, all young white women, all religious—to varying degrees. Although Angela is the only one who was murdered."

"Smothered."

"And washed. That's different too."

Cynthia looked like she would speak but didn't. He waited to be sure before continuing.

"Apart from smothering and being washed—"

"Bruce didn't kill her," Cynthia blurted.

"I'm sorry?"

"He couldn't have. Bruce was a bit simple and loved Angela. She was kind to him. He wouldn't kill her."

"He was found with her possessions."

Cynthia shook her head with conviction. "He took things, yes, but we didn't mind. He was harmless."

Balcombe sat back and studied her face before speaking.

"All right, let's assume he didn't kill her. The other girls were found in a similar situation. They'd all taken high doses of opium right before they died, and they were all lying naked on their beds with the sheet pulled up."

She slurped her tea, her eyes fixed on his.

"Cynthia, think carefully. Did you see a brown bottle in Angela's room when you found her?"

"No. Nothing like that. It didn't look suspicious of anything except I thought it odd that the pillow was under the bed."

Balcombe nodded. "Ah, that's the same too."

"What about the Bible?" she asked.

He stared at her. "The Bible?"

"Did they have Bibles too?"

"One of them did."

"Held on her chest?"

"Yes!"

He said, "Think carefully, Cynthia. What happened to the Bible?"

"I don't know. I pulled back the sheet when Angela didn't answer me, and the Bible slipped. That's when I saw the note."

"There was a note in the Bible?"

No Bible or note was mentioned in the police report. "What happened to the note?" Balcombe asked.

"I didn't really read it. I was in such a panic when I realized she was dead."

"I don't know what happened." Balcombe slipped her more money. She breathed and blinked. "I think… yes, I was still holding it… I panicked," she said again.

"You didn't hand it in?"

A tear ran down her cheek. "It ended up in my pocket and I forgot it and then it was too late and so I threw it away."

"It's all right, Cynthia. I understand. It was a traumatic experience; you weren't thinking straight."

She nodded gratefully and finished her tea with shaking hands.

"One more thing. Think carefully." He paused and saw her preparing herself. "What can you remember of the note? What *did* you read?"

"I read something about forgiveness of sins," she said. "And something odd about being born again."

# Chapter Forty-Four

Prisgrove started off confidently. He was angry at being brought in again, and he questioned why there wasn't a white officer present at the interview.

Munro ignored him and simply said, "Either you tell me the truth, or I tell your wife."

Prisgrove looked like a fox staring at the barrel of a gun. His pale skin took on a green sheen.

Munro waited impassively.

Prisgrove swallowed and blinked. His eyes flickered as he processed his options. Then he looked at Munro but appeared as though his mouth wouldn't work.

Munro said, "There are two possibilities in my mind."

Prisgrove blinked and wiped sweat from his brow.

"Either you were involved in Karen's disappearance or—"

"No!" Prisgrove blurted. "Absolutely not. I wouldn't—"

"Wouldn't what?"

"Whatever," Prisgrove said, panicked.

"What do you think happened to Karen?"

"I don't know! It's been hard enough feeling guilty—feeling that I let the Vaughns down. I haven't been able to speak to Danny… they blame me, you know."

"Because they trusted you with their daughter."

Prisgrove nodded meekly.

"So where were you on Saturday morning, after you dropped the girls at the cinema?"

"Seeing someone," he mumbled.

"You have a mistress."

Prisgrove swallowed hard, thought about it and then confessed. He said they'd met in her friend's house every Saturday morning. Munro asked for the address and the name of the mistress.

"I've stopped seeing her—after, well, it all got too stressful, and that detective was convinced I was guilty and—well, it all got messy. So it's over and Mrs. Prisgrove doesn't need to know about it?"

Munro ignored the question and told Prisgrove to start at the beginning and tell him everything.

The man started jabbering as though a great weight had been lifted from his shoulders. He confirmed that he never went into the matinee show. He dropped the girls off and met them after. The 12th had been like any other Saturday except that Karen wasn't there afterward. He'd been suspicious that Nicola had been lying. She was out of breath when he met her, and he thought the girls had nipped out of the show before the end.

"They never liked the slap-slick programme," he said.

Then he said he'd tried to get Nicola to tell him what she'd really been doing, and they went up Garden Road and down Cotton Tree Drive. They looked around the lower Peak tram station and gone into Zetland Hall.

"Nicola mentioned a suspicious old man," Prisgrove said after a pause.

"Did you confront him?"

He shook his head. "The doors were locked. He wasn't there."

"Then what?" Munro asked.

"Nicola told me they sometimes went to the tram sidings, so we went there and had a look around. There was no sign of her anywhere."

"Did Nicola mention going on a tram?"

"No." Prisgrove shook his head firmly. "She isn't allowed. She wouldn't go on the tram without an adult."

Munro said nothing.

Prisgrove said again, "The mistress... I've stopped seeing her. You won't tell my wife. I've been helpful. I've told you everything I know."

"We'll see," Munro said after a long pause, letting Prisgrove sweat. "You lied to the police, and Karen Vaughn is undoubtedly dead. I would think that your wife finding out should be the least of your concerns right now."

Munro saw someone walk past the interview room and then come back. Garrett glowered through the small window.

"Progress?" Garrett asked after Munro had dismissed Geoffrey Prisgrove.

"A little," Munro said.

"But none on the more important case, eh, Munro?"

Munro didn't answer.

Garrett said, "I expect you to work late tonight to make up for spending too much of your time on that stupid old case."

Munro thought about mentioning that Garrett had encouraged him initially, but of course, it hadn't been genuine. He wanted Munro to fail, and he wanted Munro's job.

"Go through the cases again," Garrett continued. "All of them. Find that clue to identifying the Squeezed-heart murderer."

"Right," Munro said. He'd flick through the files and find nothing again. Partly because there was nothing and partly because his mind was on the Karen Vaughn case.

She'd gone on the Peak tram. The Frenchman had been right about the timings. Which meant she had been on the B-tram, riding up front with Philip Slater.

The driver had denied seeing the girls. It was too late now, but first thing in the morning, Munro would find out why Slater had been lying.

# Chapter Forty-Five

Albert dropped Balcombe at Whiteway & Laidlaw solicitors on the corner of Aberdeen and Staunton Street. It wasn't a prestigious location, but the white building stood out, clean and smart on the corner. Inside, the reception had a professional and calm atmosphere. A marble table and giant gilded-frame mirror suggested success.

It was a working day, and he'd been right to presume Mary Pilkington would be here.

"Mr. Balcombe!" she said, her smile giving away her girlish delight at seeing him.

He explained that he had a quick question about Mary and her face fell. However when her eyes blinked rapidly he could see it was more than disappointment.

"Oh," she said.

"It's about the Bible." He paused a beat and dropped his voice so that no one could overhear. "You said the Bible was on her chest. She was naked, arms crossed, holding the Bible. Sheet pulled over her, like she was sleeping?"

She nodded, took a breath, steeled herself.

He swallowed hard. It was the same as Sister Angela. Could the pathologist have missed something?

"I'm sorry to have to ask you this, Mary, but did Theresa have any spots in her eyes?"

"What sort of spots?"

"They're called petechiae. Spots suggest suffocation."

She frowned. "No. Her eyes were closed."

"There was a note."

"Yes."

"Do you know where it was, Mary? Where did the police find it?"

"Of course, I saw it," she said. "It was inside the Bible."

Inside the Bible.

Balcombe wasted no time and felt a frisson of guilt for dashing off with nothing more than a word of thanks.

Albert pulled him back across Victoria to Wan Chai.

As he'd already suspected, with the exception of the Paregoric bottle and the washing of Angela's body, the deaths were far too similar. The posing of the bodies, at least.

He had to know whether the police had missed a similar suicide note at Margaret Sotherland's. He knocked on the door of number 15, Homeville. A man answered after a delay. His eyes looked like he'd just woken up, although he was wearing a crumpled gaberdine coat.

"Yes," he said groggily. "What?"

"Is your wife home?"

The man said nothing.

"Where is Gladys?"

"She's working. Who are you?"

Balcombe ignored the question. "I understand she's a housemaid. Could you tell me where she'll be? I have an urgent question."

His eyes narrowed, and the door started to close. "You with the police?"

Balcombe shook his head. "Look, there's nothing to worry about. I just need to know about her friend who died a few weeks ago—the one from number ten."

He shrugged. "I don't know which house Gladys is at or when."

Balcombe found himself staring at a closed door. For a second he felt like pounding on it and giving Gladys' husband a hard time, but decided his frustration could be better channelled. He'd ask the caretaker instead, but when he went downstairs, he met Katie Halpern's effete neighbour coming through the front door.

"What are you doing here, Marcus?" Balcombe said, suspicious.

"Hello, Charles. I thought…" Marcus bowed his head, embarrassed. "After you visited, I thought I'd go to Margaret's grave. Which was lovely, by the way. So impressive. Then, today, I just wondered what had happened to her. How did she…" He shrugged. "You know?"

"I'm trying to find out what happened," Balcombe said. "Did you ask your friend, Timothy about her? Did he remember any male visitors?"

"Yes, and no."

"What does that mean?"

"Timothy said he was sure she had a man-friend. He'd actually seen someone sneaking in the back way—I said you could get in from the rear into her house."

"Yes, you did."

"But he couldn't tell me anything. He never saw anyone clearly enough, just knew a man visited."

Balcombe nodded and hoped he worded his next question sensitively enough: "Is it possible she was seeing more than one man?"

Marcus cocked his head to one side as though he didn't understand.

"I'm just exploring how she had money. How could she afford to live in your building on Seymour. I don't want to be indiscreet but—"

"No!" he said as firmly as his soft voice would allow. "I don't believe she was one of those, Charles and anyway, Timothy remembered."

"What did Timothy remember?"

"You asked me about whether Margaret worked. Timothy didn't know where, but Katie must surely know."

"Why?"

"Because when Katie first moved in, she told Timothy that's how they knew one another. They worked together."

# Chapter Forty-Six

"I was sick that day," Philip Slater said when Munro confronted him at the Peak Tram Company office. It was early and the trams wouldn't start for another twenty minutes.

"Another lie!" Munro growled. "Forget work today. You're accompanying me to the police station, Mr. Slater."

Slater stood ridged. "No, I was sick in the morning. I'd had a skinful the night before. The eleventh of September is my birthday. I had a hangover. Honestly!"

Munro started to pull handcuffs from his pocket.

"Philip Slater, I'm arresting—"

"Look," Slater said, shaking his head and taking a pace back. "I didn't lie. You asked about early afternoon when the girl disappeared. I didn't start until just before midday."

Munro hesitated. The Frenchman had said he'd seen them on the tram at ten-thirty, which tallied with Nicola Prisgrove's story.

Slater was either telling the truth, or he was an excellent liar.

"Can you prove you didn't start until around midday?"

"Yes!"

"Did you clock in this morning?"

"Yes."

"What time did you clock-in on the twelfth?"

"Ah." Slater's face fell. "That's the thing. We cover for one another so that I still get paid. We all do it."

"Who can vouch for you, then?" Munro asked.

"Trevor Weston, my conductor. He takes over. You'll remember he took Betty down the hill when you interviewed me last time. Him and Pat in the office. Trevor!" Slater suddenly waved to the other man, who was approaching.

Trevor Weston stopped mid-step about twenty yards away. Then he angled away and started walking again.

Slater called, "Trevor, you can vouch for me. You remember covering on the day that girl disappeared? Trevor!"

If it came to a race, Munro wouldn't have won it. His gammy knee meant he couldn't chase a suspect, but as soon as he called to Weston, the other man stopped again.

"How can I help, officer?" Weston said, as Slater and Munro closed in.

"Were you driving the B-tram on Saturday, the twelfth of September?"

Weston looked from Munro to his colleague and pondered.

"Remember, Trevor, I had a hangover after my birthday."

Weston met Munro's eyes and calmly said, "That's right, I remember now. In the morning."

Five minutes later, Munro had sequestered a room in the tram company office and was sitting directly opposite Trevor Weston. He'd let Slater take the B-tram down the hill but threatened to speak to him after the return trip.

"Why didn't you come forward?" Munro asked, his notebook open and pencil ready.

Weston stretched his legs, relaxed. "About what?"

"The girl."

"Because I didn't see her at the time she disappeared."

Munro took a note of the response. "You mean you didn't see anyone matching her description?"

"The newspaper said Karen Vaughn disappeared in the afternoon after the cinema."

"You were driving the tram in the morning."

"Yes."

"Did you see any children?"

"Of course. There are always children on the tram."

"Did you let any ride up-front with you?"

Weston rubbed his bottom, then top lip with his teeth. "I let kids ride up-front. I often do that when I can. They like it especially when we go around the corner at the top and we're so high. Feels like flying a plane," he said with a smile. "That's why I love it when I can do the driving."

"Because of the feeling or the kids?"

He laughed lightly. "Both really, I suppose, but mostly because I just love the Peak tram."

"You've been doing it for four years?"

"Almost that long, yes."

"And before that?"

"Odd jobs. I have a little smallholding that my father left me. That keeps me busy when I'm not working."

"Tell me about the girls," Munro said.

"I don't really remember them much. It was months ago, wasn't it? As I said, I'm always letting kids ride upfront. They weren't anything special that I would remember."

"You haven't answered the question," Munro said, leaning forward.

Weston remained relaxed. "What question?"

"Did you see anyone matching Karen Vaughn's description? Did you let her ride up front?"

Weston looked like he was searching his memory.

Munro pressed: "A mixed-race girl wearing a brown shirt was seen with you at the front of the B-tram around ten-thirty. That *was* you driving?"

"Yes."

"Do you remember now?"

"I think so. Sounds like it could be right."

Munro waited a beat, then said, "Why didn't you report that you'd seen the missing girl?"

"I only *think* it could be right."

"Five months later, I understand. But not straight afterwards. Her photograph was all over the newspapers. It was the big story for weeks while we searched for her."

Weston shook his head. "Sorry, I thought I did explain. It's because I didn't pay any attention, really. I was always doing it and don't pay attention to what the kids look like."

"One white girl and one Eurasian. Both cheeky and Nicola had a distinctive red skirt on. And they boarded at MacDonnell Road tram stop—on the wrong side."

"If you say so. I didn't notice." He smiled at Munro. Munro waited expectantly. Sometimes silence makes people offer information.

Weston shrugged. "What more can I say? Maybe I saw them, maybe I didn't. You say a witness saw her? Perhaps you should question him some more. Maybe he's trying to misdirect you to me? Had you thought about that, Detective?"

He looked at Munro impassively for a long time, neither man saying anything.

Finally, Munro said, "You like your job here?"

"I do."

"Good. What time do you finish today?"

Weston said his shift ended at seven.

Munro said, "I want you at Victoria police station for another interview at seven-thirty. Don't turn up and you'll lose your job. I'll make sure of it."

Weston smiled wryly and shook his head at the same time. "I've nothing to hide, Detective. I'll be there at seven-thirty."

Munro said the same thing to Slater. He also threatened that he'd arrest them both if there was any hint of collusion.

At his desk with the old murder files from Kowloon, he thought about his suspects. There was Geoffrey Prisgrove and Eric Cattles.

*Am I going to turn into the next Bill Teags?* he asked himself. Would this case drive him mad?

Teags had been obsessed by Cattles at the end. The trophy box in his house was suspicious. Prisgrove said that Cattles hadn't been at the masonic hall when he'd visited later with his daughter. Had he gone home or was he just taking a break? Then there was the Frenchman. Yes, he might be pointing the finger at a tram driver, but why do that? Why come forward as a witness, especially since the timing didn't match? Munro thought his involvement was unlikely. Slater and Weston, on the other hand, felt different. Slater had openly lied but claimed it was to cover for his delayed start and hangover. Which left Weston. Surely, he remembered. Surely, he should have come forward.

There was something about the man that curdled the juices in Munro's gut. He was cocksure and evasive.

But even if Weston was involved. What happened next? What happened after the B-Tram reached the peak before midday on September 12th?

# Chapter Forty-Seven

Katie Halpern had lied to Balcombe. She'd told him she didn't know where Margaret had worked.

Balcombe climbed the marble steps at the rear of the building at 1 Queens Road Central. It was the Hong Kong and Shanghai Bank and as he walked through the main banking hall, the Venetian mosaic on the vaulted ceiling impressed him. It always did.

He passed the US Consulate General on the second floor, under the watchful gaze of two US soldiers. The stairs narrowed, and he passed banking administrative offices over the next three floors. On floor six, Balcombe stopped. A plaque on the double doors told him that this was the office of the accountancy firm, Lowe, Bingham and Matthews.

He entered and saw a reception area followed by a long, smoky room with rows of desks. People worked with heads bent over ledgers and pencils scribbling frantically.

Balcombe moved past. On the right was a room with a hundred ledgers stacked like a library. A lady trundled a trolly laden with ledgers and files. She passed him without a glance and hurried into the smoky room.

Then he saw Katie Halpern sitting at a writing desk in the room on his left. There were only two desks in there and the other wasn't occupied. A man had his back to the door as he spoke to Katie. He was leaning close, maybe too close for Balcombe's liking.

Then her eyes met Balcombe's and her face lit up.

"Why, Mr. Balcombe!"

The man moved away from his overly close position and turned sharply.

It was Lammy, the man who had cared for Margaret in Stanley Prison after her mother had died.

"Balcombe? What are you…?" Lammy looked from Balcombe back to Katie, his face a mask of confusion. "I… I…" He started back peddling towards the glass door at the end. "Let's talk in my office."

Suddenly, Balcombe understood part of the puzzle. This was why the neighbour had thought Katie and Margaret worked together. Maybe Margaret had worked here, but the connection was Lammy.

The other man had his hand on the office door. Balcombe strode towards him, glaring.

"You replaced Margaret with Katie!" He saw Katie wince.

"Katie, go and find something to do," Lammy barked at her. "Leave us now!" He was frozen in his doorway, looking at Balcombe, his face having turned as cold as white marble.

Katie stood awkwardly, then scuttled from the room. By the time Balcombe reached Lammy's office door, the other man had recovered and was at his desk. He sat behind it as though the barrier between them provided security. His hands were shaking.

"Mr. Balcombe, please sit. I can explain. I wouldn't want your paper—"

"I'm not a reporter."

"What are you then?"

"An investigator, looking into Margaret's death."

Lammy blinked rapidly and wiped sweat from his upper lip. "I didn't replace Margaret with Katie. Margaret never worked for me."

"I didn't mean at work."

"You can't think?"

"I've a pretty good idea what happened, Lammy, but I'd like to hear it from you. You're a terrible liar so don't even consider it."

Lammy took a long breath, wiped his lip again and started talking. He explained that he and Margaret had begun an affair a few years ago.

Balcombe interrupted. "Rubbish! You seduced a young woman who was in your charge."

Lammy said, "It wasn't like that."

Balcombe shook his head. Lammy might believe it, but Balcombe doubted it was the truth. "Keep going," he instructed.

Lammy admitted that he'd set Margaret up in the house on Seymour as his mistress. But then a few months ago, Katie had started working for the accountancy firm.

Balcombe nodded. "And she became your new girlfriend."

"Yes, but…"

"You kicked Margaret out."

"No, I said she could stay. The house was big enough for two. She lasted a couple of weeks, then just left."

"And you cut her off. You'd been supporting her as well as providing the house."

"Yes," Lammy said, then paused and sucked in air. "She refused. I even went to see her in that dreadful

Homeville place, and I tried to get her to take money, but she refused, I tell you."

Balcombe said, "Did she threaten to tell your wife?"

"What? No! You aren't listening to me. Margaret was too stubborn. She didn't want anything more to do with me. She said she was going to get a job."

Balcombe shook his head. "You're scum, Lammy. I'm going to investigate this further and if I were you, I'd confess to your wife because any time soon, someone is going to tell her what you really are."

Balcombe found Katie Halpern smoking a cigarette in the square outside the building.

"You lied to me!" he said, striding over.

"I feel terrible," she said.

She may have been looking for him to comfort her, tell her she wasn't so bad, but he didn't.

"Did you force Margaret Sotherland out of the house?"

"No." she shook her head vigorously. "I liked her, I really did. And it didn't bother me. In fact, it worked well because… well, you know."

"Tell me."

She swallowed hard. "I was safer with Margaret around. Mr. Lammy could be…" she winced and waggled her hands as though grabbing the air. "It meant he couldn't…"

"You're his mistress, Katie. You can't expect the pros without the cons." Balcombe shook his head. "Did Margaret leave of her own free will?"

"Yes. She said she could manage without him. She was determined to get a job." Suddenly there were tears on her cheeks and Balcombe wondered how easily she could turn on the waterworks.

She took a shuddering breath. "I can't believe poor Maggie's dead."

Balcombe spoke to her a little more and decided he'd learn nothing else. His assessment was that both she and Lammy were now telling the truth.

She wiped away the tears and fluttered her eyelashes.

"Will I see you again, Charles?"

"No," he said bluntly. "And my advice for you is that you find another job. Find one that doesn't have ties to your boss—and find yourself somewhere else to live too. I'd do it soon because you never know when you'll become the next Margaret Sotherland."

# Chapter Forty-Eight

Garrett marched into the little office Munro had been confined to. He slapped a file onto the desk. It was one of the Kowloon cases.

"Open it!" Garrett barked.

Munro pulled back the cover to reveal the associated reports.

"All the way," Garrett said.

Munro started turning the sheets.

"Keep going."

Munro got to the back. There was a single photograph after the last sheet.

"Turn it over," Garrett said, jabbing a finger at the photo just in case Munro didn't understand.

It was a photograph of the rear of a building; the building where Nie Pingping had been found. It was the one Munro had slipped out of the large pile that Garrett had brought back from the Kowloon office.

"This is in the wrong file, Munro!"

Munro played the innocent. "Don't blame me, Garrett. You handed me the Pingping file and photographs. I didn't misplace any!"

Garrett glared. "You're blaming me?"

"I'm not the one pointing the finger," Munro said calmly.

Garrett huffed and paced the room. Then he returned to the desk and picked up the photograph. He'd spotted the black line that ran vertically from a top-floor window to three-quarters of the way to the ground.

"What's that?" he said, thrusting it towards Munro.

"I don't…" Then Munro stopped himself. Playing the innocent wasn't going to work. "Looks like a rope."

"It's how he escaped, that's what it is! Bloody hell, man, the killer used a rope." Then Garrett stopped, a thought suddenly hitting him like an express train. "Hold on a minute. Why would the killer need to escape?"

*Because it was BlackJack*, Munro said to himself.

Garrett was shaking his head. "I got this all wrong. I thought it was a gang-related murder. In which case, the killer should have just walked away, but he didn't. He had to avoid the guards. Which means he was on his own."

"Maybe," Munro said, trying to sound convincing.

Garrett said, "That Charles Balcombe."

Munro looked up, his heart suddenly in his throat. He knew he should say something but couldn't.

"You interviewed him a few times."

"Yes," Munro managed to say through his constricted throat.

"Are you all right, man?"

Munro waved his hand around his neck. "Dry throat. I need a sip of water."

"I'd expect you to know better," Garrett said as Munro went to the water fountain and took a gulp. When he returned Garrett continued: "Keep hydrated.

Too easy to forget when you're knee deep in cases, am I right?"

Munro nodded and cleared his throat. "You're right."

"OK. So, this Balcombe chap."

"Yes."

"Always in the wrong place at the wrong time."

"I dismissed—"

Garrett thumped the table. "Let's go and have a word with him. I want to talk to him myself."

# Chapter Forty-Nine

"Mr. Balcombe," the man with DI Munro said, holding out his hand, "I'm Inspector Garrett."

Balcombe had just stepped out of his building. Albert was at the end of the alley, ready to take him to the ferry and then the hills north of Kowloon. A climbing session, decided at the last minute to help clear his mind. The confrontation with Simon Lammy had sent his mind into a spin. He knew he was angry at Margaret Sotherland's treatment. However upon reflection, he suspected he was also angry with himself. He'd gone to see Katie Halpern because he thought she'd lied about Margaret working at the law firm. But the lie had been much deeper, more painful. Because Balcombe realized he'd been keen on the girl. For once he'd subconsciously believed he could have a normal relationship.

Balcombe looked from one policeman to the other. "What's this about?"

"May we have a word, sir?"

"About?"

"Could we go inside? It'll be more comfortable than standing in the street."

Balcombe considered before turning and opening the door. He stepped inside and signalled to the concierge that he would be using the reception room. He went inside and waited for the two policemen to enter before closing the door.

"I'm about to go climbing," Balcombe said remaining standing. Neither did he invite the detectives to take a seat. "I trust this won't take long."

"Not long, sir," Garrett said. "I'm hoping you can help us. You see we're investigating some incidents and I know DI Munro here has spoken to you before, but your help may be invaluable."

The man had a slightly grubby appearance, with unhealthy-looking skin behind an unkempt beard. Balcombe took an immediate dislike to him but showed nothing on his face as he waited patiently.

"You like climbing?" Garrett asked.

Balcombe nodded.

"You know your equipment?"

Balcombe looked at Munro, wondering where this was going. The other detective's face gave nothing away.

Garrett pulled a photograph from a breast pocket and held it out.

Balcombe took it. It was of the rear of the building where he'd killed Nie Pingping.

"See that black line on the right—from the window?" Garrett asked.

"Yes."

"It's a rope."

"I can see that," Balcombe said, holding out the photo for the inspector to take back.

"Is it a climbing rope?"

"Possibly. If you're suggesting…"

Garrett smiled, his mouth wide like a serpent's. "I'm not suggesting anything, Mr. Balcombe. I'm asking for your expert opinion."

"It could be a climbing rope although it didn't reach the ground. And why would there be a climbing rope hanging from a window?"

Garrett didn't answer.

Munro said, "Do you use climbing ropes, sir?"

"No."

"Oh?"

"I'm a free-climber." Balcombe saw doubt in Garrett's eyes. "Which means I don't use ropes, Inspector." It was a half-truth. He often took a rope, but not for climbing. The rope would be used for descents, just like it had been from Pingping's place.

Garrett wrote in his book, taking his time. Then he said, "May we sit?"

"I thought this was a quick interview." Balcombe glanced at Munro, whose eyes seemed to tell him to go along with it. Balcombe sat at one end of the table and the policemen pulled out chairs at the other.

Garrett cleared his throat. "You appear to crop up a lot."

Balcombe waited for a question.

"Tell me about the incident in Sham Shui... the ransom demand."

"I went to pay a ransom, but it appears to have been a fake. I met no one and returned the money."

"You were interviewed by DI Munro, here."

"I was."

"Did he ask you about the murders on the same night?"

"He did not."

Garrett looked at Munro, then back to Balcombe. "A coincidence?"

"If you say so." Balcombe kept his voice flat. "I know nothing about it except for newspaper reports—and there are plenty of deaths every day. Plenty of serious crimes."

Garrett's face pinched, and he pretended to write notes.

"You were seen at a murdered girl's house."

"Is that a question?"

"Why were you there, Mr. Balcombe?" Garrett's voice showed irritation for the first time.

"You're talking about a young Japanese woman. She was a teacher, and I was investigating a missing boy—one of her students, it seemed."

"So you're a detective?"

"Not really. I was doing someone a favour."

Garrett smiled. "Oh, don't be so circumspect. I've been told you're undercover."

"What do you mean?"

"You're connected to the British government. A spy, or something."

Balcombe shook his head. "I can't think who you've been talking to. It's nonsense." He looked at his watch. "If you'll excuse me, gentlemen, I need to catch the ferry."

Garrett stood at the same time and blocked his way momentarily in a show of power. Then he gave the serpent smile again.

"Think about the rope." He dropped the photograph on the table and stepped back. "You're the expert, Mr. Balcombe. Let us know where we might buy such a rope—a climber's rope."

# Chapter Fifty

Balcombe was outside Homeville when Gladys returned. He hadn't gone climbing. He'd spent the rest of the day going over what he'd learned about the deaths. All three young women had large quantities of opium in their systems. Only Margaret Sotherland had a bottle of Paregoric, but no one believed she would take the drug. No one believed any of the girls would take opium, and yet they had.

Had it been misadventure? They could have taken the drug elsewhere. Perhaps the Paregoric was a top up to a more powerful dose. No, he realized. The concentration in the bottle was too high. It had been doctored. Which led him to question whether Margaret had known.

Was this all some kind of bizarre pact? Did the women know one another? Did they know a supplier?

Balcombe wondered about Bruce Chong; the man arrested for Angela Newham's murder. Did he know something about the opium? He was in prison at the time of the other deaths, but he may have just been a delivery boy.

Which made him think about the men who had attacked him outside Theresa Pell's old house. Could they be linked to Chong? Were they part of a gang supplying opium to young women who wanted to keep their habit a secret?

In the perfect world, Balcombe would have asked to interview the man, although if he was as simple as he'd been told, Balcombe probably wouldn't learn anything. And there was the additional issue of Inspector Garrett. The policeman was on to him, it seemed, so Balcombe needed to be careful. Too much exposure and the policeman might just find the evidence he was looking for.

So, Balcombe was back to doing the legwork. Carrying on with his investigation to gain more information before he acted.

Which led him to Homeville and Gladys.

The young woman looked tired but smiled naturally, pleased to see him.

"Will you come up to Margaret's room for a minute, please?" Balcombe asked.

"Just for a minute," Gladys agreed.

The caretaker poked her head out and studied them both briefly before closing her door again.

"Nosy, horrid cow," Gladys said. "I hope you don't mind me saying so."

"Not at all."

They went up the stairs and as he unlocked Margaret's door, the old lady from number 8 poked her head out.

"Could I borrow you as well, Mrs. Gallshaw?"

The woman looked uncertain but soon found resolve when Balcombe pulled a five-dollar note from his pocket and held it out. When she entered number 10 Mrs. Gallshaw's eyes glistened with excitement.

"Last time we spoke, you said, Margaret had visitors," Balcombe said to the elderly lady.

"I did," she said in her crackly voice and looking at the younger woman. "Although I only recognized Gladys."

Balcombe showed her the photograph of David Russell, just on the off-chance Theresa Pell's ex-boyfriend had visited.

Mrs. Gallshaw cackled. "Oh, I'd remember a handsome young man—a bit like yourself. We don't get the likes of you around much."

Balcombe then described Simon Lammy.

Mrs. Gallshaw rubbed her chin. "Well dressed, you say?"

"Yes."

"Not handsome but looked like he had more than a few pennies to rub together. Not like the rest of us. Roundish and a drinker's face......? Yes, I'd say so."

Balcombe waited. Mrs. Gallshaw seemed to be thinking. "Yes… I think... perhaps that was who I heard arguing once. These walls…"

Gladys said, "I bet that was the man she said she wouldn't take money from."

The old lady nodded eagerly. "Yes, I remember hearing something about money."

"Did you ever hear anyone else—through the walls—talking about money?"

"No, not that I can recollect."

Balcombe walked over to the window, unlocked the bars, and opened the window. He looked back at the two ladies.

"Did anyone ever come in through this window?"

"Like a burglar, you mean?" Mrs. Gallshaw asked.

"Anyone. A friend sneaking in perhaps."

"I did hear a noise once or twice." She rubbed her chin. "I might have."

"When was the last time you might have heard that, Mrs. Gallshaw?"

"Perhaps. yes, wait a minute, maybe the night I heard her praying."

"The night she died?"

"Yes."

"And when you called the caretaker, and she found the body—?"

"Yes."

"—the door was definitely locked?"

"Yes, unless the caretaker pretended to unlock it of course." She chuckled and then coughed repeatedly.

When the paroxysm ended, Balcombe handed the old lady the money. "Thank you. You can leave us."

Mrs. Gallshaw looked at Gladys as though suspecting she and Balcombe might be up to something, possibly even a romantic liaison. She grinned foolishly and scuttled out.

"I wouldn't pay any attention to what she says," Gladys said when the door closed. "I think she might be a little mad. Or maybe the lure of your cash made her make it up."

It was possible. It was also possible that she'd been mistaken. Witnesses were notoriously unreliable and the greater the time between the event and their recollections, the more error prone they became.

Balcombe said, "The second man—the one in the suit was Margaret's lover."

Gladys' eyes bulged with surprise.

"He's a despicable married man and the reason Margaret was in this place was because he replaced her with a new mistress."

"Goodness," Gladys said.

235

"But I don't see him as climbing through this window. He didn't strike me as fit or subtle enough for that."

"But you think someone did?"

Balcombe said, "Sit down, Gladys."

The young woman took the only chair in the room. "What is it?"

"I think someone either facilitated her suicide—"

"Suicide?"

"—or she was murdered."

Gladys gasped. The blood drained from her face. She opened her mouth to speak and closed it again. Her eyes were full of questions.

"I want you to think very carefully, Gladys. Did Margaret have a Bible?"

"Yes." Her eyes darted around the room. "I can't see it."

"I didn't find a Bible when I searched her things last time."

Gladys grimaced, anger flushing her cheeks. "That bloodsucking caretaker."

"What?" Balcombe prompted.

"It was valuable. Margaret said it was a family heirloom. Really old. Gold edging on the pages, that sort of thing. It's not here, so I bet the caretaker has it."

\* \* \*

The caretaker came to her door. Toby the monkey was sitting on an armchair behind her.

"Where's Margaret's Bible?" Balcombe asked, his voice full of menace.

"Excuse—" She started to complain as he walked into her hall and then all the way back into the living room. Toby let out a shriek and scampered away.

"Where's Margaret's Bible?" Balcombe asked again. "I know you took it."

She shook her head, but her hands were shaking as she denied it. "Don't know about no Bible," she said unconvincingly.

Balcombe grabbed her by the throat. "Think again."

She gurgled into his hand, trying to speak, back peddling at the same time. He let her move but didn't release his hand as they went all the way to the rear wall.

"Either you tell me, or the police find a body here too."

The astringent smell of urine rose above the floral scent in the room. She'd wet herself and he didn't care. Her bulging eyes were looking at her sideboard.

"In there?" he asked.

She nodded; her eyes desperate for him to believe her.

He walked her to the sideboard and still held her throat as she pulled open a drawer. Inside was a black, leather-bound Bible. He could see gold lettering and gold on the paper.

He let go of her throat and she sank to her knees, holding her neck and spluttering.

"You bloody—" she started with all the aggression she could muster.

He picked up the Bible. Its heft was twice the normal weight. Maybe worth a lot to a specialist collector. But it would need to be someone who didn't know about Margaret Sotherland or, more likely, enough time had passed. The caretaker was waiting, holding onto it before she cashed in.

"The jewellery," Balcombe said.

She straightened up and looked him in the eye, defiance rising in her.

"Margaret had jewellery and it's not there now. You took it."

"I bloody—"

He slapped her head with the Bible, and it made a satisfying whack.

"I sold them," she said after blinking with the shock.

His hand darted out and found her throat again.

Her eyes lost the fight.

"I am sick of your lies. I know you didn't sell it because I saw you in her pearls." The first time he'd seen the caretaker she'd worn a pearl necklace. When she'd reappeared to show him room 10, they'd gone. It was a guess, but her eyes told him the truth. He was right.

He said, "Her friend knows everything she had. I want all her jewellery in a bag now or I make a decision."

He paused a beat and watched her thinking, wondering what he meant.

He said, "Option one is I kill you now. Option two is I go to the police and report the theft. My guess is they'll find more than Margaret Sotherland's jewellery here. I'll count to twenty. If I've not got a bag full of her stuff, I make my choice."

He let go of her throat and she immediately scampered to a cupboard and pulled out a shopping bag. He followed as she then moved into a bedroom. The floral smell was stronger here. She had a vase of flowers, either side of the bed.

The pearl necklace came out of a vanity unit along with a handful of gold. Three rings and two necklaces, he thought. She paused after closing the drawer and he guessed she was considering telling him that was all.

"And the rest!" he snapped.

She shuffled around the side of the bed, and he heard another drawer open. This one sounded like it was part of the bed, or maybe just under it. The drawer clunked shut, and she stood, came around again and handed him the bag.

He looked inside. "This had better be everything."

She considered lying, then confessed: "I sold a couple of things. Just small. A diamond brooch and silver hairpin." She swallowed, a pleading expression on her face. "Please... everything else is there."

After putting the Bible into the bag, he turned and walked out.

"By the way," he said at the apartment door. "If this isn't everything else, then I'm coming back. And in case you were wondering, it was option one."

# Chapter Fifty-One

Balcombe went to the cathedral but found he had to return to the Wan Chai district. Father Thomas was visiting Saint James's Church and was talking to someone animatedly in the office. Balcombe couldn't see the other person until they came out. It was Sister Birgitta from the orphanage, and she seemed angry.

She looked him square in the face and he thought she was about to say something. But after a hesitant step, she marched away.

There was no similar anger in the priest's face. Father Thomas smiled at Balcombe as he knocked on the door.

"Good afternoon, Charles. To what do I owe the pleasure? I trust this meeting will be more civil than the last time me spoke."

Balcombe closed the gap between them.

"I want some answers."

The priest shook his head. "Oh dear. Surely, you're not going to accuse me of a cover-up again?"

"No, but someone might be," Balcombe said. "Margaret Sotherland... You visited her at Homeville."

Father Thomas said nothing.

"I know you did. You were seen."

The priest took three steps to the door and closed it. There was no one else about, but it provided discretion in case someone walked past, Balcombe surmised.

Father Thomas spoke quietly, despite the closed door. "I told you I did home visits occasionally."

"To hear confession."

"That and other things. I see it as part of my social responsibility. Some people aren't able to attend Mass or—"

Balcombe cut him off with a question. "Did Margaret tell you she had a drug problem?"

If the priest was offended by the direct question, he didn't show it. "No, she didn't."

"You visited Theresa Pell as well." Balcombe said it confidently, although it was an assumption. Her housemate hadn't seen anyone, but Theresa had plenty of time during the day to have unseen visitors.

Father Thomas said nothing for a moment, then: "I did, and no, before you ask, she didn't have a drug problem either."

Balcombe said, "I know what they confessed about."

The priest's face showed nothing.

Balcombe said, "Miss Pell was pregnant and then got rid of the baby. Miss Sotherland had a *benefactor*."

Father Thomas didn't say anything but now his eyes showed he knew the implication.

"Simon Lammy," Balcombe said, unable to hide the disgust from his voice.

Father Thomas breathed deeply. "I'm not willing to divulge confidences, Charles. I told you that."

"Margaret felt like a prostitute," Balcombe said, watching the priest's eyes for confirmation, "but it wasn't her fault. She was young and Lammy took advantage."

241

The priest said nothing, but his eyes took on a dull, unfocussed sheen.

Balcombe pressed on. "Were there other men?"

Despite saying nothing, the priest's head moved slightly. A shake. He didn't think there had been other men.

Balcombe nodded. "Was her guilt bad enough to drive Margaret to take her own life?"

"I don't believe it was suicide. And I haven't covered it up."

Balcombe let silence grow between them hoping to make the priest feel uncomfortable, hoping he'd talk.

Finally, Father Thomas raised both hands in a gesture of supplication. "Look, Charles, I understand your concern, but I can't divulge anything."

Balcombe waited a beat, then tried a new point of attack. "I couldn't help but notice that was Sister Birgitta just now."

Father Thomas changed his hand expression, opening them like a question. "It was."

"You were arguing."

The priest smiled kindly. "With respect, that's none of your business."

"Perhaps it is," Balcombe said.

"How so?"

"Angela Newham."

Father Thomas's eyes narrowed, then he sighed, told Balcombe to sit, and took a chair behind a desk.

"Sister Angela was a lovely girl," Thomas said.

"By all accounts."

"But again, nothing to do with you."

Balcombe nodded. "And yet, Father, you're willing to talk about her even if you aren't willing to discuss your argument with Sister Birgitta."

"Funding," Thomas said. "Sister Birgitta is always complaining about funds for the orphanage. That and…"

"And?"

"Oh, I don't know. Some deep held grievance about women in the Church. I think she'd like some influence over the diocese but it's clearly not up to me!" He shook his head and for the first time, Balcombe thought he saw weariness in the priest's expression.

Hoping that was an indication that the man was softening, Balcombe said, "Tell me about Angela."

"I'm not sure what there is to say." He did the hand shrug again. "She wasn't pious. I'd say she was quietly religious. One of those who can influence gently without quoting scripture."

Balcombe nodded. "Everyone has a good word to say about her."

"Yes. It was a tragedy."

"Bruce Chong."

"Yes."

"Do you think he killed Angela?"

Father Thomas forced a smile. "I'm in no position… I'm not a detective. If the courts find a man guilty, who am I to judge otherwise?"

"There was one person who told me something interesting about Angela."

Father Thomas looked intrigued.

"She wasn't all pure."

The priest gave no response.

"She liked men."

"There's no sin in that, Charles." Thomas laughed lightly but it seemed false. "Where would the human race be if men and women couldn't unite?"

"Interesting choice of phrase," Balcombe said. "Let's call it sex, Father."

The priest looked down and back, clearly uncomfortable.

"Men and women have sex, Father," Balcombe said enjoying the other man's response. "Sexual desire makes the pulse pound. And lust—"

"And lust is a sin," Father Thomas interjected.

Balcombe struck home. "Angela felt such desire. She wanted men, and they wanted her." He paused. "Only natural for an attractive girl. And Angela was very attractive."

Thomas swallowed hard.

"She confessed to you, didn't she?"

Thomas didn't reply. Balcombe could see the man's neck flushing, but it wasn't anger that rose in the priest. Thomas swallowed again.

Balcombe held up a hand. "Here's the thing that troubles me, Father. I investigate Margaret Sotherland's death and it looks like suicide. She was a staunch Catholic and I find she confessed her sin of sex outside of marriage to you."

Thomas said nothing. His tongue moved in his mouth like it was sandpaper.

"And we have Theresa Pell, a few months ago, dying—this time confirmed as suicide—and also having confessed. She'd had sex outside of marriage that resulted in a terminated pregnancy. I can't begin to imagine what she must have been going through. And she confessed to you as well."

Father Thomas nodded meekly.

"And then we have Angela. Her death was ruled as murder and yet it was very similar in many respects. And guess what?"

Father Thomas didn't respond.

Balcombe watched as a myriad of thoughts seemed to cross the priest's mind. The air in the room gained weight, and the longer the silence stretched, the heavier it became.

Finally, the priest said, "I don't understand."

"What don't you understand?"

"How or why they died."

"Do you think Angela was murdered?"

"No, I suppose I don't."

"Do you think she took her own life?"

"It's possible."

"And Margaret?"

Father Thomas took a shuddering breath and for a second, Balcombe thought the man was having a heart attack. But the priest composed himself and finally nodded, then shook his head.

"It's also possible."

"All three. All connected to the Church. All"— Balcombe paused but could see Father Thomas was already there—"confessed to you before they died."

"I had nothing to do with—"

Balcombe stopped him with a raised hand. "I'm not saying you did. Someone provided opium. Someone helped them."

"If you are suggesting it was me, you are totally mistaken. Of course, I know people take drugs, but I don't know where they get them, and I have nothing to do with it."

# Chapter Fifty-Two

Weston sat impassively, with his hand on his chin. Munro had made him wait. It was hot, and he'd provided no water.

"So, you lied," Munro said.

"Did I?" Weston raised an eyebrow, but didn't look curious.

"You knew the two girls had got on your tram. They'd sat upfront with you."

"Did I? I don't think so. I said I couldn't remember."

"Why did you lie?"

"I was confused about the time. I told you I couldn't remember the girls because I thought it was later."

"You drove until Philip Slater took over at eleven forty-three."

"That sounds about right."

Weston remained as cool as an icicle, but Munro was sure that was about to change. Before seeing Weston, he'd interviewed Slater. In fact, Slater had brought an employee from the ticket office with him. His name was Finneran, and he said he knew all about Slater being late on 12th September. He'd been drinking with him on the evening before and expected the hangover. Finneran had been the one to tell Weston. He also said that he knew the time Slater had arrived—he'd taken a note just to cover himself in case the company found out.

Munro now struck with the other information that Finneran had provided.

He said, "I have a witness who saw you go into the Engine House."

Weston removed his supporting hand and shook his head.

"You went in with someone else."

Weston shook his head again.

Munro took a punt: "You took the girl into the building. Why did you do that?"

"I didn't," Weston said, but his eyes had reacted.

"Why did you take Karen Vaughn into the Engine House?"

"This is ridiculous," Weston said, looking away and down.

Munro waited five minutes and neither spoke. Weston kept his eyes averted until he finally raised them. His mouth tweaked with a smile, and he shook his head slowly.

"You have nothing. You know nothing. You're like that detective who beat up the man at Zetland Masonic Hall. He beat up Eric Cattles because—"

"You know his name, then!"

Weston chuckled humourlessly. "I read the papers."

"So, you can remember Eric Cattles, but you can't remember seeing the girl who went missing, and she'd spent time in your cab?"

Weston smiled then nodded.

"All right, why don't you search the Engine House— I presume you think I murdered her there."

"Did you?"

"Don't be ridiculous!"

"Where did you murder her, then?"

Weston folded his arms and refused to say another word. Munro had the man's home address. They would do a forensic search of the Engine Room before turning to Weston's home.

He had Weston sent to a cell. The man could sweat in there for a few days. Munro was sure Weston was hiding something and, with a bit of luck, the evidence would present itself.

# Chapter Fifty-Three

The young woman's hands trembled as she handed her visitor a cup of green tea.

"Don't be afraid. I am your guide."

After a minute's silence, the woman said, "Why did you come in the back way?"

"So that your neighbours wouldn't see. It is best that you don't have to talk about it."

"I don't think I *can* talk about it."

"You're nervous," the guide said. "I understand, but we have these feelings for a reason. We feel discomfort because there are things we need to do and say."

"But it's so difficult to say these things," the woman said. She had large brown eyes and shapely eyebrows. She was Chinese, but high cheekbones and fine jaw suggested another heritage. The guide thought the girl was pretty. She was also vulnerable.

"You can talk to me," the guide said after sipping the tea. "I'm here to help you. To guide you to redemption."

The young woman straightened her back and nodded. "It is so difficult in church."

"Church can be an intimidating place. But God is all around. He hears you in church, but with my channelling, he will hear you at home."

"Confession is difficult."

"Of course it is." The guide put a hand on the woman's head, who suddenly had tears on her cheeks. The guide continued: "By confessing our transgressions, we can move on. We let the Holy Spirit into our heart and cleanse it. That is the beauty of God. That is the beauty of Christ's sacrifice for us all, so that we can be saved—renewed and reborn."

"How long will it take?" the woman asked, her large eyes imploring.

"To be saved? I cannot say."

The young woman sighed. "I am not ready."

"The journey has begun. By accepting me as your guide, the battle can commence. And it is a battle. Because without a fight, victory would be meaningless. It must be difficult for you to find the release from the anguish. But confession through me takes time. I cannot say how long it will take. It may be three sessions. It may take twenty-three."

The young woman nodded, and the guide saw that her shoulders were lower, less tense.

The guide continued: "For this first session, we will just talk. If you can't talk about your guilt, then it doesn't matter. We can talk about anything. We can talk about your childhood. We can talk about your family. Whatever makes you comfortable."

The young woman looked up with moist eyes and relief.

The guide continued, "But it will be difficult. Do not fool yourself, my child. Now close your eyes and talk to me. Tell me whatever you are comfortable saying and I will help you on your way."

# Chapter Fifty-Four

The CID office was empty except for Munro. He'd moved back to his usual desk. He had the full pile of Kowloon murder reports, a cold cup of tea and a typewriter. He was writing up the bullshit report for Garrett. Knowing the perpetrator of a crime made it difficult to phrase a summary that misdirected the reader. It was clear to Munro's detective mind that BlackJack had been the killer in all the cases. The photograph of the building where Pingping had been murdered led Garrett to speak to Balcombe. He'd subsequently had one man investigating where a climbing rope might have been bought. Fortunately, of the three merchants, no one remembered selling the rope.

That may not have been true since the shopkeepers won't have wanted to be involved in a criminal investigation. However it worked in Balcombe's and therefore Munro's favour.

Munro found his mind wandering. It pained him to protect Balcombe from the murders he hadn't sanctioned, but it was necessary.

He took a sip of his lukewarm tea and then spat it out. He got up and paced the office and focused on his problem. Within ten minutes, he had an idea.

Pingping's masseur was called Kee Wan. Despite his innocence, he was being held in Victoria Gaol, a short walk across the quadrant.

Munro disturbed the night guards and surprised them with his request to speak to the prisoner.

Kee Wan had given a statement to the Kowloon detectives. He'd been knocked out and tied up. He claimed to have seen nothing. He also claimed that he knew nothing about what had happened downstairs. His statement said that he was employed to massage Mr. Nie once a week. He had to arrive by six in the evening and couldn't leave until two in the morning.

The room on the first floor had a solitary chair. It had all been scrubbed clean but according to the detective's report, the smell of blood had been in the air. Something dreadful had happened in there, but someone had removed the evidence.

The masseur had denied all knowledge. He said he saw and heard nothing.

"Two young men were killed down there," Munro said.

Kee Wan blinked his surprise. He was exhausted and hungry. His once white gown was now gray and grubby.

Munro said, "That's right, I know."

Whether the masseur wondered how Munro could know, he didn't say.

The first floor had two rooms and a toilet. There were two cots implying people stayed there. The cots had been tidied but not scrubbed like the room with the chair on the second floor. All the windows had shutters and were locked. The only way up and down was by the stairs. Pingping had gone up and been killed. The bodyguards hadn't intervened.

"They were made to fight and then Nie Pingping killed them. Isn't that right?"

"I know nothing," Kee Wan said hoarsely.

Munro nodded. "Of course, you don't because he was paying for your discretion."

"I would have been killed."

"By his bodyguards."

Kee Wan nodded his head.

The police hadn't found guards, alive or dead. But they knew a man as important as Pingping would take security seriously. The guards would have cleaned the place first before they'd known about Pingping's death. And as soon as they did, they vanished. That was Munro's hypothesis. If they hadn't then a senior member of the gang would have dealt with them. They'd failed and the punishment for failure was death. Maybe they were already dead. But whoever had killed Pingping hadn't killed the guards because he'd have left the bodies where they'd fallen.

A rival gang would kill them all. However, one of Pingping's own gang could influence the guards. Maybe they were working for the killer. Could Munro convince Garrett that it was an inside job?

The climbing rope suggested it wasn't.

"You couldn't go down the stairs," Munro said.

Kee Wan nodded.

"You killed Mr. Nie and planned to escape out of the window."

The prisoner's eyes flew wide. "No! No! I was knocked out. I couldn't—"

Munro kept a placid face. "I think you could. I think you tied a rope and planned to get away, but something went wrong."

"No!" the man said desperately.

"Was it because the rope was too short?" Before Kee Wan could respond, Munro continued: "You changed your plan. You hid and then pretended to knock yourself out."

"I didn't!"

"I can't see any other way."

The masseur erupted in a paroxysm of coughs. For a second Munro thought the poor man was having a heart attack, but it was panic and a weak chest.

Munro handed him a cup of water which Kee Wan gulped too fast, splashing it down his front.

"You're innocent?" Munro said once the man had recovered.

"Yes." Despite the water, Kee Wan still sounded hoarse.

"Then, this is what you must do," Munro said and then told the prisoner what he should say.

He could have released the man, but Munro wanted someone else to get the formal statement. Kee Wan was still suspicious that he was being stitched up for the murder, but so long as he signed a new statement Munro didn't care.

When he returned to the police station, the night clerk told him he'd received a message. The man apologized for not communicating it earlier. Two hours had passed since Balcombe had requested a meeting.

Just in case, Munro went down to the wharf and checked the secret meeting place. Balcombe hadn't been there.

When he passed Balcombe's house on Queens Road, he saw the man's lights were off. Clearly not that urgent, Munro told himself. It can wait until tomorrow.

Returning to the office, he finished his report for Garrett. His conclusion on the Pingping murder was that it had been an internal gang member execution. The rope was irrelevant.

Gangsters didn't typically kill people with medical precision. Nor did they leave witnesses alive. Which would suggest that the masseur either did it or was involved. Munro prayed his rationale would be accepted.

He went to his room, intending to catch a few hours' sleep, but couldn't. He was back in the office waiting for Chief Carmichael before the rest of the squad arrived for work. Would Garrett arrive first? Munro heard someone coming up the stairs but before the department's door opened, the desk phone rang. Munro picked up and got a shock.

Balcombe was waiting for him in reception.

# Chapter Fifty-Five

Balcombe had hoped to meet with Munro in their secret place, but after failing to make contact last night, Balcombe visited the Victoria police station in the morning.

"What are you doing here?" Munro asked sharply. He looked like he'd been up all night: bags under his eyes and a crumpled suit, but he somehow appeared more cheerful than Balcombe had seen in weeks.

"The cases I've been investigating..." Balcombe began. "Margaret Sotherland, Theresa Pell and Angela Newham all died in similar ways, and I think there could be more."

Munro ushered him into an interview room and shut the door. "More? But you have a murder, a suicide and—"

"Possibly... probably three suicides. Three assisted suicides. Someone provided them with the opium and they were all found in similar poses: a sheet over them and a Bible—"

"I didn't read anything about a Bible except for the Sotherland girl."

Balcombe nodded. "All three. And Pell's suicide note was similar to a note found in Sotherland's Bible. There was also a note in Newham's Bible."

Munro shook his head. "It wasn't—"

"It wasn't looked for. Newham's death was too easily classed as murder."

Munro looked like he was still struggling as he shook his head. "But the Newham girl was smothered."

Balcombe nodded. "Or at least seemed to be. It's possible that the pathologist made a mistake."

Munro shook his head again. "No, I trust the autopsy. Angela Newham *was* smothered—probably with her pillow."

Balcombe stared at the wall. There was another possibility; one he'd been rejecting, and yet it was there in the back of his mind. What if these weren't suicides, but murders?"

The similarity of the bodies. Pillows under the beds. Everything except the smothering.

"He changed his method."

"What?" Munro asked.

"The murderer learned from his first victim. He didn't give her enough opium. She came round and—"

The door opened. Inspector Garrett glowered at them both.

"Good," he growled. "I'm glad you've brought Mr. Balcombe in for questioning. I'll take over from here. And Munro…"

"Yes?"

"You can leave us."

Munro stood.

Balcombe said, "Speak to Father Thomas. Get a list of all the young women he's been visiting." When Munro frowned, Balcombe added: "He does home visits—home confessions."

"The inspector will do no such thing!" Garrett grabbed Munro's arm. "Is that report on my desk?"

Munro slipped his arm smoothly out of the other detective's grasp. "Yes. And you'll want to go over to the prison. I understand the masseur wants to make another statement." He let a small smile play on his lips and then he left the room.

Garrett switched his attention back to Balcombe.

"Sunday the twentieth of December," he said, taking the seat that Munro had vacated.

"What about it?"

"There was a murder in an alley off Jervois Street."

Balcombe said nothing. He remembered the fat man who lived above the laundry but couldn't recall his name. He remembered the smell of detergent and incense in the man's rooms upstairs. The fat man had conducted business there, selling young girls.

The detective leaned forward. "You were recognized."

Balcombe smiled and shook his head.

"You were there, Mr. Balcombe. You were recognized by a witness."

The detective waited for him to speak, but he didn't. He held the man's gaze, challenging him.

Garrett breathed, leaned back and glanced away. "Where were you on the night of January the second?"

"At what time?"

"Between two and three in the morning."

Balcombe narrowed his eyes. This was about the butcher he'd killed. "So, on the morning of Sunday, the third?"

"Yes." Garrett had a pen poised over a notebook.

"Asleep. At home."

"Can anyone vouch for you? A partner? The concierge?"

258

"The concierge service finishes at midnight. After that, the doors are locked, for security reasons."

Garrett frowned. "But you use a key to get in and out?"

"No, you'd be able to get out, but not back in." Which was officially true, but it was easy to set the lock so that he could slip back in. Providing that he planned it in advance.

"If you ask him, I'm sure he'll remember. I went climbing, leaving at seven on Sunday morning."

"That's a remarkable memory, Mr. Balcombe. I couldn't tell you what I did on Sunday, the third."

"Do you attend church?"

"I do not."

"Well then. I remember precisely because I needed to plan my exercise so that I'd be back in time for Sunday Mass."

"Let's go back to December the twentieth."

Balcombe waited.

"Where were you then?"

"It was also a Sunday."

"Yes."

"At what time?"

"The evening."

Balcombe smiled. "Well, on that occasion, I went to evening Mass."

"And after that?"

"To bed." He paused. "Alone again."

"For a good-looking man, you appear to spend many nights without a partner."

Balcombe chuckled. The detective had nothing. If he'd found out anything about the climbing rope or any witnesses regarding Pingping's murder, he wouldn't be fishing like this.

Again, the silence grew between them before Balcombe said, "I came in this morning in all good faith. There really is a problem with the deaths of some Catholic girls."

The corner of Garrett's mouth curled up in a snarl. "We don't go looking for work, Mr. Balcombe. It finds us."

"I think it's been missed."

"Because you're the great investigator," he said cynically.

"I don't claim that."

"But you do tell lies," Garrett said, his expression like a dog who was about to attack. "I have connections in London. You see, I'm ex-Scotland Yard and you know what that means."

"I know Scotland Yard, Inspector."

"And I know you're no spy or detective. So, tell me the truth."

Balcombe stood. "I'll tell you the truth, Inspector. The truth is, you're wasting my time. Instead of pestering me with false witnesses and claims, how about you investigate those girls?" He took a step to the door, opened it. "Because if I'm right, then there will be more deaths."

He walked out of the interview room. Garrett watched him go with his face still set in a snarl.

# Chapter Fifty-Six

When Munro came out of the interview room, he caught sight of Chief Carmichael going up the stairs to the CID office.

He followed but then spotted Balcombe's rickshaw boy, Albert loitering outside. By coming to the police station, Balcombe had clearly been desperate. However Munro had a major lead on the Karen Vaughn case and that was his priority. He urgently needed Carmichael's approval and Garrett off his back. Balcombe's problem could wait.

Munro detoured and passed a quick message to the boy. He'd meet with Balcombe in the usual place later. That done, he hurried up the stairs and found Carmichael settling into his office, hanging up his raincoat and hat.

At first, Munro thought the Chief was in a good mood, but he scowled when Munro leaned into the room and asked for a meeting.

"What is it, Munro?"

"You wanted some good news from me?" Munro provided an encouraging, friendly smile.

Carmichael sat behind his desk and lit up a cigar.

"That would make a welcome change, Munro."

Munro provided an update on the jewellery theft and stabbing. He'd told his men to keep the progress quiet until he was ready. And now was the time. He'd worried that Garrett would have learned about it and taken the case as his own, but he hadn't. The other detective was obsessed by solving the Squeezed-heart case and had missed an obvious opportunity.

The fence had provided a lead that resulted in a witness pointing at a new suspect. Under pressure, this new man had confessed to the stabbing and Munro was sure more information would lead to the stolen goods.

Carmichael cleared his throat and said, "Very good. Very good indeed."

"And there's good news on that gruesome Kowloon murder—the one where we're holding the masseur."

"Garrett's case."

"We all need to work together." Munro opened his hands in a shrug. "The murderer is from the Walled City. Both the murderer and the victim are Chinese nationals. This isn't a Hong Kong problem."

Carmichael's eyes brightened. If they were both from China, the murder wouldn't appear in the Hong Kong statistics.

"You're certain?"

"The masseur will confirm it," Munro said confidently.

"Excellent."

"I've more good news, sir. The Karen Vaughn case…"

Carmichael set down his cigar. "Yes?"

"I'm getting closer." Ordinarily, this type of update would annoy the Chief, but Munro could see enthusiasm in the man's eyes. The other good news had clearly softened him.

Munro continued: "I'm holding someone who was probably the last man to see her alive. And has been lying about it."

Carmichael picked up his cigar and took a satisfying drag.

Munro said, "He works for the Peak Tram Company, and I'd like your permission to search the Engine House at the top of the line. I'd also like permission to search his home.

"Of course, man!"

Approval by the boss meant that no search warrant was required.

Munro said, "The reason I ask, sir, is that Inspector Garrett…"

"What about him?"

"He thinks the case is a distraction." As Munro said it, he could read that the Chief had thought so too. The man's left eyebrow raised quizzically before he spoke.

"How's Garrett getting on with the Squeezed-heart murders?"

"He's had me working… well, I was writing up summaries of old Kowloon murders all night."

Carmichael shook his head.

"I think he's becoming obsessed," Munro pressed on, certain this would worry the Chief. "We don't want another problem like we had with Bill Teags."

"Fine," Carmichael said after blowing a plume of blue smoke into the air. "You get me other results, Munro. I'll tell Garrett you're no longer working with him."

Munro said nothing for a moment.

"Dismissed, Inspector," the Chief said, surprised he was still there.

Munro took a breath. "One other thing, if I may?"

Carmichael drew a circle in the air with his cigar. "Go ahead. If it's quick."

"Suspicious deaths of white girls," Munro said, knowing that emphasising *white* would get the Chief's attention.

"Who? I've not heard—"

"All Catholic girls. One, a year ago, was classified as murder. One, last year, was suicide and a recent one just filed as misadventure." Munro was talking fast, and he could see doubt forming in the Chief's eyes. "Sir, the thing is that they are all similar. There's something odd and… whatever it is… there could be more, you see. They're suspicious and—"

By the time the Chief interrupted, Munro knew he'd been gabbling.

"Enough!" the Chief said, shaking his head. He pointed the cigar at Munro. It was a gesture the men knew well. It meant listen to what I'm about to say and follow my instructions. "You know as well as I do, Munro, we have limited resources. We don't go looking for crimes. We solve them. The Karen Vaughn case is your opportunity to change my impression of you. Go and get the guilty party convicted. Don't mess up by getting distracted by a crime that isn't there."

# Chapter Fifty-Seven

Munro took three men and searched the Peak tram Engine House. It didn't take long. The building was only about twenty-four feet by thirty-five. It had massive steel cables running down to the tracks. Inside were two pairs of horizontal engines with boilers that the staff member described as multi-tubular. There was one huge flywheel and pistons bigger than a man.

The air was thick with the smell of coal and oil. The heat and noise were so unbearable that Munro insisted they stop the tram while they carried out the search.

He upset a florid-faced duty manager and then the company director, who needed persuading that Munro had the authority. But following twenty minutes of debate and phone calls, the motors ground to a halt.

Once quiet, the duty manager was helpful and to the point. He was under instructions to get the search over with as quickly as possible and get the trams moving again.

As his men looked for potential blood stains and collected samples, Munro learned that there was a door at the back. He also learned that the manager didn't like Trevor Weston.

He said, "I know you're holding him for questioning."

"Why don't you like him?"

"He's a slacker."

"Slacker?"

The manager shrugged. "Any opportunity to take a break, he does. And he sometimes comes in the Engine House. He thinks I don't know, but he takes sneaky breaks in here."

"Do others?"

"Would you? As you found out, it's damned hot and smelly in here."

"Sir!" One of the policemen called. He was standing by a tall cupboard.

Munro stepped over and saw greasy overalls hanging from a hook and a pair of old boots. There were packets on a shelf and a clear glass jar containing fluid. There were also rags and an oil can.

"What's in the boxes?" Munro asked the manager.

"Bleaching powder. With a solvent it's used as a degreasant."

"And in the jar?"

The manager shrugged. "No idea. One of the men's drinks. Probably water."

Munro instructed and his man unscrewed the lid. The policeman sniffed, then screwed up his face and coughed. "Not water!"

"All right, we'll take the jar and powder for analysis." They searched the pockets of the overalls but found nothing inside.

"Have you ever had to clean up any blood in here?" Munro asked the manager.

"There have been a couple of accidents in my time, but never any blood to speak of. So, no, I haven't."

Munro walked to the rear door. There was a key in the lock, which turned. Outside was a coal bunker and track.

Munro stepped back inside. "If there's a problem in here—"

"Yes?" The manager cocked his head.

"If there's a tram problem or an accident... anything urgent. What do you do?"

"If there's someone in here, you mean? Well, then they'd call the office or the lower terminal. Depends on the problem."

"Call? I don't see a telephone."

The manager took Munro back to the entrance and opened the lid of a green wooden box. Inside was a telephone.

"Kept in here for protection," he said.

"Do the men use it? I mean generally."

"No, it's against regs. Just in an emergency."

"And then just the office or lower terminal?"

"Correct. Can I start her up again now?"

Munro looked at his men. They had a sack each with items for analysis and waited expectantly by the entrance. They were done here.

Munro nodded. "Fire her up and thank you."

He stepped out into the sunshine as the immediate whir and grinding of the engine was followed by the clank of moving cables. Munro told one of his men to take the sacks back for analysis and then had a thought. He looked back at the telephone box and addressed the duty manager.

"Please ask in the office and the lower terminal if anyone remembers a phone call from the Engine House on September the twelfth last year. For any reason."

★ ★ ★

Trevor Weston's house was off Peak Road, two miles south of the engine house. It was an old log-built property on a narrow track, alone in a clearing at the edge of the forest.

It had chickens and pigs and Munro wondered if it had been owned a hundred years ago by someone working the forest and living simply off their land.

Weston had said he lived alone, and there was no sign of anyone else there when the police entered the house.

It smelled old and earthy, and Munro wondered whether it hadn't been cleaned properly in a long time. Before taking anything for analysis, Munro walked through the house on his own.

There were five rooms on the single floor: a kitchen with a reasonably stocked panty and a tin-bath tub; a living space with two chairs and lots of old photographs; a bedroom which was just big enough for a double bed and little more space; a smaller room that may have been a bedroom once but now had the floor covered with miniature soldiers and models; and finally, another room that was empty. And clean. The only spotless room in the tiny house. All that was inside was a battered suitcase.

Munro instructed his men to begin the search.

Would they find anything? After his enthusiasm at getting a green light from the Chief, Munro doubted himself. Weston was just an odd chap who lived on his own in this miserable place. His only joy appeared to be his job and playing toy soldiers.

Munro stood in the room with the soldiers and tried to imagine Weston here, moving the little pieces about. There were fake hills and trees, painstakingly made. Munro didn't know his British or French military history, but from the look of the generals, they could have been Wellington and Napoleon.

Waterloo? Munro wondered.

Ironic, he thought. This could be his own Waterloo after convincing Carmichael that he was close to solving the Karen Vaughn case.

However a minute later he was back in the spotless room. The suitcase was open and inside appeared to be children's clothes. In the pantry they found bottles of ethanol. Munro felt more positive again. Weston wasn't just a sad old man, after all. He undoubtedly had something to hide.

# Chapter Fifty-Eight

When Balcombe arrived at the disused office, Munro was already there. The detective's bright eyes suggested he'd had a good day despite the lack of sleep the night before.

Balcombe said, "Have you learned something about the case?"

"The Catholic girls?"

"Yes."

Munro shook his head. "I've got enough on my plate without worrying about your investigation. Not least, about Inspector Garrett's suspicions of you."

"He has nothing."

"He has threads and threads can be pulled. And that's when things start to unravel."

Balcombe took a seat at the table and said, "You're referring to the rope at Pingping's place?"

"No, I've sorted that," Munro said. He went on to explain that this morning, an officer had taken a statement from the masseur. The man had confessed to knowing who the killer was.

"Triad?" Balcombe said when Munro told him.

"From the Walled City and outside our jurisdiction. Despite the death occurring in Hong Kong, the politics of it means the crime will be ignored. Not our problem. More specifically, it's not our statistic."

Balcombe was both impressed and relieved. He asked about the issue with the rope. Could Garrett let that go?

Munro explained that the masseur's statement included using the rope to winch up items he needed. He said it looked too short in the photograph because it was partially withdrawn.

"Does Garrett buy it?"

"Doesn't matter whether he does. It's explained. Pingping's murder is not Garrett's concern. BlackJack didn't do it." Munro's eyes widened. "I need to know, Balcombe."

"What? You know BlackJack did it."

Munro sighed. "I need to know that you have your alter ego under control."

Balcombe said nothing.

"Have you killed anyone else? Anyone since?"

"No."

"Would you know if BlackJack had?"

It was a good question. Balcombe did black out. He was missing parts of what BlackJack did, but not totally—as far as he knew.

"I'd know," he said convincingly. "And I've cut down on the booze."

"That's good to hear because I think I need your help." Then he told Balcombe about the Karen Vaughn case. He said what they'd found.

Munro said, "He was probably the last person to see her and he lied. We know he was spotted going into the Engine House during the day."

"You found evidence that she was there?"

Munro pursed his lips as his head shook. "We found nothing incriminating. But it was months ago."

"And yet, you seem cheerful," Balcombe said.

Then Munro told him what the forensic analysis had found. "Chloroform in a jar. It was homemade from calcium hypochlorite and ethanol. We found the chemical powder in the Engine House with the jar of chloroform. There were rags there that could have been used with the chloroform, but any evidence evaporated long ago."

"OK," Balcombe said with doubt.

"Do you know how to make chloroform, Balcombe? You mix it with ethanol. And guess what? We found bottles of the stuff at Weston's home."

"And you're sure he's guilty?"

"Certain of it."

"What about other evidence that Weston had anything to do with her after she was seen in the tram. Karen Vaughn's fingerprints perhaps?" When Munro shook his head, Balcombe continued: "It sounds like you're not there yet. You're here asking for my help, and you also tell me you've done nothing about the Catholic girls."

Munro sighed. "What do you want me to do?"

"Question a priest," Balcombe said. "You do what I need and I'll help you, Munro."

Before they parted, Munro said, "Keep your eye out for Inspector Garrett. He's frustrated about Pingping and about your murders. Don't do anything stupid."

"Like killing this Weston chap, you mean? You haven't got enough evidence, Munro. I've told you before, I don't kill just anyone. I need to know he's guilty."

# Chapter Fifty-Nine

Munro had delayed interviewing Weston again. He wanted the man to stew in a cell for a few days. But he also wanted time to build a better case.

"What really happened?" Munro asked after making the man wait in the hot interview room for two hours. Weston had been in jail for two days and nights, and he already stank to high heaven.

Weston said nothing. His tired eyes stared blindly at the wall behind Munro.

Munro said, "I know what happened, Trevor. Now is the time to hear it from you."

Weston continued to stare into space.

After a long wait, Munro decided to speak. "On the morning of Saturday, September the twelfth, you were driving the Peak tram. Two girls got on at MacDonnell Road. They slipped on from the alighting side and you let them ride upfront."

Munro paused and saw no acknowledgement in Weston's eyes.

He continued: "It was about ten-thirty. Nicola Prisgrove got off at May Road but the other girl, Karen Vaughn stayed on. She rode with you to Peak Station."

Munro waited and eventually Weston said, "We agreed all this, although I couldn't remember the girl."

"You remembered her," Munro said. "You told her about where there had been a bomb in the Engine House. And you took her to see it."

The florid-faced duty manager from the Peak Tram Company had called in the morning with two pieces of information. No one reported seeing Weston with a girl, but more than one member of staff said they knew the man liked to show kids the Engine House, especially where a Japanese bomb had been found.

Weston made eye-contact.

"You were seen with her," Munro lied.

"Your witness is mistaken," Weston said. "Anyway, I went down on the next tram. Slater arrived, and we both went down on Betty."

"You had ten minutes."

Weston shook his head.

Munro said nothing as he studied Weston's eyes. The man stared into the distance again.

"We know about the chloroform," Munro said eventually. "You used it on Karen."

Weston's eyes focused again and when he spoke, it was as though he'd practiced the speech. To Munro's ears, the intonation was all wrong.

"You found the jar. I get tense sometimes and when I do, I take a break. I go into the shed and sniff the liquid. It's just a mixture of the bleach and alcohol. It's harmless. It relaxes me."

"It's chloroform," Munro said. "You used it to knock out Karen."

Weston's eyes swung to Munro and focused. "You've been reading too many crime novels, Inspector. Chloroform doesn't just knock people out. It doesn't work like it does in fiction. Do you know how long it would take to knock out someone with chloroform?"

Munro didn't.

"Five minutes. Maybe more. I don't know, I've never tried it. It's an anaesthetic. I just sniff it to relax myself now and again. How long did I have between trams?"

"Ten minutes."

"Ten minutes to wait until everyone had got off, then take the girl to the shed, then locate the chloroform. Then I'd have to hold it over her nose for at least five minutes. Then I'd have to come out and meet Slater, get in the tram and leave. And not be flustered! Did Slater say that I was flustered when he arrived at work?"

Slater hadn't mentioned it, but Munro ignored the question.

"Why did you make the phone call?" That was the second piece of news he'd gotten from the duty manager. Someone had called from the Engine House on that day. The witness couldn't remember the timing or who'd taken the call.

"What phone call?" Weston said, his eyes narrowed.

"You called the lower terminal."

Weston shook his head, but Munro wasn't convinced. "Why did you call?"

"I didn't," Weston said. Then added: "Maybe I did, maybe I didn't. I don't remember."

Munro's heart rate quickened. Did Weston make that a call. If so, what was it about? Was it a signal that he had the girl?

"Why did you use the phone?"

Weston breathed in and out. "Look, Inspector, I don't think I did. Why would I? Your witness is lying. People are trying to stitch me up, just because they don't like me."

"Who doesn't like you, Trevor?"

"Slater... others. Anyone who claims to know something." He was agitated now.

Munro said, "From what I saw, you were very friendly with Slater."

"If Phil's stitching me up, then he's a snake in the grass. Have you thought that it was him? He wasn't at work until later. Maybe I got the time wrong. After all, I was covering for him. Maybe the girl—"

"Karen."

"Yeah, maybe Karen... maybe Slater met her after the tram. I don't remember her very well. I don't remember her getting off or where she went. I didn't take her into the shed."

Forensics had found nothing incriminating. There had been no blood or a fragment of clothing that they could link to Karen. In fact, nothing from Weston's house said she'd been there either.

But Munro's gut instinct and the voice in the back of his brain wouldn't shut up. Weston was guilty.

Then it struck him. "You said chloroform takes five minutes to knock someone out. How would you know that?"

For a second, he thought he had Weston. The man's eyes flew wide with panic, but then he got it under control. "I read it somewhere. I have to be careful." He smiled. "I don't want to sniff it and knock myself out, now do I?"

Munro stayed silent, letting Weston sweat over his answer. Then he spoke sharply: "What did you do with her, Weston?"

"Nothing. I tell you I did nothing with her." For a second he was flustered, then Weston took a long breath and smiled. "Hold on. What am I supposed to have done with her? Knock someone out with chloroform and it doesn't last long. I didn't finish work until seven. A couple of days ago you accused me of killing her in the shed. Now you're saying I knocked her out with the stuff. It doesn't make sense. And I'm not a detective. What am I supposed to have done with her for over seven hours?"

Munro said nothing. It was a hole in his logic, that was for sure.

Weston was on a roll. He grinned now. "And there's another problem. What did I do with her afterwards, eh? Did I just walk out of there after my shift. Did I have her rolled up in a carpet, slung over my shoulder? Now I think you've been sniffing something, Inspector."

He leaned back and put his hands being his head.

"You walked home that night?"

"I always walk home. And you found nothing there, did you?" It was a statement rather than a question.

"Tell me about the children's clothes."

"Dressing-up clothes," Weston said shaking his head. "They're old from my sister's kids. From when they used to stay. I don't know why I keep them. Sentimentality, I suppose."

Munro stood. "All right, Weston, you can go."

"What, just like that?" Weston said, his face full of surprise before he stopped it with a scowl. "I'm going to complain to the Police Commissioner. You held me without good reason. If I've lost my job... And you didn't interview me with a white officer present. You're supposed to do that, aren't you?"

Weston was still ranting, but Munro was at the door. He told the guard outside to escort Weston off the premises. Then Munro went to the toilets and kicked the wall in frustration. He'd hoped Weston would break.

After splashing his face with water, he looked at himself in the mirror. Weston was guilty. Munro knew it and he also knew he would need Balcombe's help. Which meant he had to do what Balcombe wanted. He had to confront Father Thomas.

# Chapter Sixty

Munro returned the priest's smile, but he knew it looked fake. He didn't know where it came from, but Munro disliked the clergy—all clergy, irrespective of their denomination. His wife thought it was distrust. He certainly saw them as disingenuous with overly soft and friendly personas.

Father Thomas was no different.

"How may I be of service, Detective?"

"Detective *Inspector* Munro."

"Ah, my apologies, Inspector. How may I help?"

"You know the name: Margaret Sotherland?"

Munro noticed a facial tic before the priest's reply. "I do."

"Theresa Pell."

This time, Father Thomas let the pleasant façade slip from his face as his eyes and mouth hardened. "Yes."

"I would like to—"

"Inspector," the priest interrupted with a shake of his head, "this is because of Mr. Balcombe, isn't it?"

Munro said nothing.

Still shaking his head, Father Thomas continued: "Look, Mr. Balcombe is worried about a couple of young women who died—"

"And you're not?"

"Of course, but—"

Munro raised a hand and took half a step closer, within the priest's personal space. "Will you let me ask my question, Father?"

"Of course. Go ahead."

"I would like to know whether the young ladies sought your counsel before they committed suicide."

"Miss Sotherland didn't commit suicide, Inspector."

"Please answer my question."

"Many people... most of my parishioners, come to me for confessional. In fact, I encourage it, no matter how big or small the sin. It's important to recognize that we are all sinners, Inspector."

"Indeed," Munro said pointedly. "But my main question is why you visited the young ladies in their homes?" He said it with confidence, and the confirmation in the priest's eyes pleased him.

However, Father Thomas shook his head. "This is preposterous. You can't be taking Mr. Balcombe's accusations seriously."

"You aren't above the law, Father. I'm more than happy to take you to the station for questioning if it comes to that."

Father Thomas turned his face away and stared at the pews for a moment.

"I'm not covering anything up," he said, switching his focus back to Munro, "if that's what you're thinking, Inspector. I know Mr. Balcombe believes—"

Munro raised a finger again. "Let's start again. You visited them in their homes."

The priest took a breath. "Yes."

"Is that normal?"

"When I deem it necessary."

"And why was it necessary on those occasions, Father?"

"Because they were very troubled."

"Their sins?"

Father Thomas moved his head in a slow nod.

Munro said, "Do any other of the priests do it?"

"No."

"Then what I would like from you is a list of all the young, single, white women you are currently giving home confessional to."

The priest said nothing for a moment then: "The whole point is that it's confidential. These are potentially vulnerable women."

"All the more reason that we should protect them. No?"

"Mr. Balcombe thinks we're—either me or the Church in general—are covering up suicides."

"Are you?"

"No!"

When they'd talked last night, Balcombe and Munro had considered the possibility of murder. Assisted suicide seemed the most logical answer. There was the problem of Angela Newham's death, which looked like murder. Was Balcombe right when he thought she'd been given opium but not died as expected? Could it have been a killer's first victim.

Munro took a breath. "The other possibility is murder."

The priest's eyes bulged.

Munro said, "Angela Newham."

"I know Sister Angela was... but the others?"

Munro nodded and made his voice more reasonable, deferential. "We really need your help, Father. By giving us a list of your ladies, we may prevent another murder."

Munro could see the priest considering it so he quickly added: "And it's not breaking a confidence. You won't be telling us what they confessed. And when we speak to them, we won't say anything about confessional. As far as they'll know, we'll be interviewing all single women from the Catholic churches."

"That would work," Father Thomas said. "I can accept that. I'll have the list sent to you by the end of the day."

"Names and addresses."

"Names and addresses," Father Thomas agreed.

# Chapter Sixty-One

On Saturday, Munro had a drink with his pathologist friend Fai Yeung after work at the Wellington Inn. He shared his frustration with the Karen Vaughn case and the inability to find evidence against Weston.

"What would your predecessor have done, Babyface?" Yeung said.

"Beaten him up and then crashed his car."

Yeung chuckled into his pint. "Ah, you're talking about that Cattles man. He was probably guilty, too. But no, that's not what you said he'd normally do."

"He'd normally find another felony, possibly something minor."

"But something that would stick."

"Yes. However, I have nothing on Weston except for a few lies. The best I can come up with is accusing him of changing history. As far as I could tell, from his model armies, Napoleon was beating Wellington."

"Shush," Yeung said. "You can't say that here! Not in the drinking house named after that very famous British general."

Munro smiled. "I have nothing."

"What about other cases? How are you getting along with that hairy inspector you work with?"

"He's still trying to solve the Squeezed-heart case."

Yeung raised his eyebrows. "You can't have that."

"And you know better than to try and get me to discuss why," Munro said, sipping his own drink.

"Of course. And what about those other cases? The Catholic girls?"

Munro told his friend everything he knew.

"You think murder? All three of them?"

"Yes."

"But the Sister Angela case—the one from the orphanage. It was definitely smothering rather than an opium overdose."

"It may have gone wrong, and he had to use a pillow," Munro said. "Nearly everything else is the same."

"And the man who was arrested?"

"Bruce Chong. The more I look at it the more I suspect he was innocent—or her murder at least. He undoubtedly stole things, but the sister's body was also washed."

"That's right," Yeung said. "I remember. That was odd. Definitely washed afterwards."

"First, it seems out of character for the man, who is quite the simpleton and second, there's something ritualistic about it."

The pathologist shrugged. "More likely, the killer was removing any evidence."

"Fingerprints."

"Anything, real or assumed." Yeung nodded.

Munro said, "And now I have a list of six other young women who are in a similar situation. I interviewed them all today."

"And?"

"Nothing. I'd hoped there would be something obvious. Some clue. But there was nothing."

★ ★ ★

An hour later, Munro was saying the same thing to Balcombe in the disused office.

He added, "And before you suggest it, I can't go posting a sentry on each of their doors, just in case. We don't know for certain that the other two were murdered and even if they were, we don't know when the next would be."

Balcombe said, "What I find odd is the time between the first and the second. Angela died in January a year ago. Theresa Pell was nine months later and then Margaret Sotherland last month. The next could be soon or it could be months away."

"And that's why I can't allocate any resources to protecting these women. All I can do is warn them, tell them to be vigilant."

"I don't like it," Balcombe said.

Munro shook his head sadly. "If you have a better proposal, I'm all ears. Otherwise all we can do is sit tight and wait. Maybe there won't be another case."

"Oh, there will be another," Balcombe said. "You can count on it."

# Chapter Sixty-Two

The guide held the girl's hands. "You are almost ready."

"Am I? I don't feel ready," the girl said as the guide felt her hands shake.

"How many times have we met?"

"Five."

"And you have done so well. Remember the first time we spoke like this? I told you it would be challenging. I told you to face your fears. You have to confess your sins for them to be forgiven."

"I have." The girl gave the guide a questioning look, almost pleading for the end of the sessions.

"You have to believe it in your heart. I have to know you believe it and are ready for the final step."

"Yes," the girl said quietly, with acceptance.

"So, let's begin with the words of John. Let's go over what you have learned."

The girl recited the passage, ending with the words: "For I will forgive their wickedness and will remember their sins no more. No one can see the kingdom of God unless they are born again."

"Good. And why must you be born again?"

"To put the past guilt behind me. To be forgiven."

"And why must you be forgiven?"

"Because I transgressed. I stole from my mistress. I took what was not mine to take."

"And the consequence?"

"She became ill. She needed those drugs to help her ailments. I was selfish. I was thoughtless. I was wrong."

The guide smiled and stood. "Wonderful. You have done so well. Together, we have overcome your trials. You are ready for the next step. I will let you know when I will come for our final appointment." The guide smiled kindly again. "And you will be reborn."

# Chapter Sixty-Three

Munro was surprised to find Fai Yeung at his door in the morning. The pathologist shared what he'd found out, handing over three reports.

Twenty minutes later, Munro was calling on Balcombe at his home.

"It's urgent," Munro said. "Forget the office, we need to talk here."

Balcombe hesitated before showing the inspector to the meeting room on the ground floor. When he shut the door, Munro took three reports from his satchel and spread them on the table.

"You got it wrong," he said.

Balcombe picked up a report. The autopsy of a young woman dated 6th July 1953. She died of respiratory failure because of a massive opium overdose. She was twenty-six years old and Catholic.

"My God," Balcombe said. He picked up another and read the same thing. This girl had been nineteen and found dead on 7th May. The third report was dated 19th November.

Three more victims. All Catholic, single and young.

The difference was that these weren't white.

Munro said, "We were looking for white girls. Two of these are Chinese and one Filipino by birth. All three classed as death by misadventure. All opium overdoses. And these aren't assisted suicides."

"I agree. Someone is murdering them."

Balcombe took a pen and piece of paper and wrote the details in chronological order of the deaths.

Margaret Sotherland - 12th January 1954
Agnes Cheng - 19th November 1953
Theresa Pell - 1st October 1953
Maria Lee - 6th July 1953
Rose Escalo - 7th May 1953
Angela Newham - 27th January 1953

When he'd finished, he said, "It makes much more sense. The timing between the murders. There wasn't a long break."

"The longest was between the first and second." Munro nodded. "Which is likely for multiple murders."

"Yes. Although the gap between Maria and Theresa surprises me. Almost three months."

"Then made up for by a shorter internal to Agnes Cheng."

"Unless there was another between Maria and Theresa."

"I doubt it," Munro said. "My pathologist friend would have found it, I'm sure."

"Then another reason?"

"Holiday? Away for business? I looked at the day of the week and there's no obvious pattern: two Tuesdays, two Thursdays, a Monday and a Sunday."

Balcombe stared at the details he'd written. "There will be logic to it."

"Is there a pattern to BlackJack's killings?"

Balcombe shook his head. "I'm not this kind of killer. Each of these is the same in many respects. There *is* a pattern and when we work it out, it will tell us who the next victim will be. There's only one problem."

Munro looked curious.

"You need to go back to Father Thomas. We need a list of everyone. We need to know about the non-white girls he's visiting at home."

# Chapter Sixty-Four

The following day at Mass, Father Thomas read passages from Corinthians and the Proverbs. He said that being single was a blessing because you could devote yourself to God rather than a partner. That seemed reasonable, but Balcombe never liked the emphasis of some passages that implied that God made woman to be a blessing to her future husband.

However Father Thomas didn't dwell on that aspect, instead he provided a warning to single women to be vigilant. He said that evil may come from unexpected quarters and to take care when alone, whether on the street or at home.

Munro had spoken to him and the other Catholic priests of Hong Kong yesterday. He'd obtained a full list of women who Father Thomas had paid home visits to and asked the priests to be specific in their warning.

So when Father Thomas said, "Lock your doors and windows. Let no uninvited visitor into your home," Balcombe was expecting it.

However he saw others in the congregation exchange glances of puzzlement. The priesthood wasn't normally so frank. They wouldn't go as far as being specific, despite Munro's pleas. He'd wanted the priests to report the deaths and explained that the single women had all been members of the Catholic church.

Informed that it wasn't just white, single women, Father Thomas provided more names. The list of potential next victims wasn't six it was now thirteen.

Munro had said he couldn't provide security for six, let alone thirteen. They debated using the newspapers to warn people, but that raised a problem in Balcombe's mind.

The killer was following a pattern of some kind. If he thought they were on to him, he might change that pattern. Worst case: he'd accelerate the killing. Maybe he'd find a new pattern, a new justification.

It was a month since Margaret Sotherland's death. The shortest time between murders was around seven weeks.

Munro said, "If he isn't accelerating, I think we have at least two, maybe three weeks before he strikes again."

"I hope you're right."

They discussed using the police to warn the girls individually, rather than provide security, but neither of them was convinced. Munro pointed out that his Chief would have to accept that there had been more murders, which would affect last year's crime statistics.

"Even though it's real?" Balcombe asked.

Munro sighed. "You and I know it, but it's just common sense. We don't have evidence against the suicide theory. And he'll throw Angela Newham in my face. Her killer is behind bars. Without proof, Carmichael isn't going to admit we got it wrong."

So they agreed to ask the priests to include a warning. Balcombe would follow-up over the next few days by speaking to the women individually.

After the service, Jonah limped hurriedly, making a beeline for Balcombe.

"Mr. Balcombe!"

"Yes, Jonah." Balcombe stopped in the cathedral gardens. He stood under a cherry tree in full bloom.

"Can we... can I have a word?"

"Of course."

"I heard about the deaths. Those poor girls... and Sister Angela."

Balcombe said nothing.

"I loved her." Jonah shifted his stance awkwardly and watched as people passed. "I thought..."

"What did you think, Jonah?"

"I believed Chong had killed her. You know, gone a bit mad. I think he probably loved her too. She was so kind and... and..." The boy's voice caught in his throat.

"And now you think differently."

Jonah blinked, perhaps because tears threatened, although none appeared. "Who could have done it? You're an investigator... you said. So, who do you think did it?"

Balcombe said nothing.

Jonah continued: "I understand. You're still investigating and can't talk about it but I keep thinking. Since I heard Father Thomas's sermon this morning. The warning. I keep thinking about Angela."

"What are you thinking, Jonah?"

"Why was she washed? We should have known Chong didn't do it. Even if he'd smothered her with the pillow, why would he wash her?" His eyes pleaded, as though Balcombe had the answer.

"I don't know."

Jonah gulped in air and seemed to compose himself before speaking again. "Someone who cared about her, that's who."

"Everyone cared, Jonah. You said everyone loved her."

"Yes, but it struck me that the person cared about afterwards. He cared about preparing her."

It was an interesting comment. The other girls hadn't been washed and Balcombe's theory was that Angela Newham was the first. The killer had needed to smother, but it was more than that. The killer had truly cared about her—more than he cared about the others.

Roy Faulls sauntered over with a grin. "Pressuring my friend to confess his sins, Jonah?"

The boy swivelled abruptly.

Faulls continued: "He won't do it you know. You're wasting your time. My friend here is a lost cause."

Jonah's expression had changed. He'd gone from distressed to determined. His jaw set and his eyes hardened. "No one is a lost cause."

Faulls held up his hands. "Whoa, I was just joking."

"Right," Jonah said, dubious.

Faulls said, "But I can report that Charles is reading your book."

Jonah turned his attention back to Balcombe. "You are?" He seemed more relaxed now, as though their previous tense conversation was forgotten.

"Avidly," Balcombe lied. The truth was, he hadn't picked up the book of saints since Monday evening.

"Which is your favourite?"

"So far, Perpetua and Felicity," Balcombe said, which was the only one he'd read. "Who's today's saint?"

"Peter Damian," Jonah said, clearly not impressed. "Saint Polycarp next Tuesday is interesting. Others I included were last Saturday's. Francisco and Jacinta Marco were the youngest of all the saints. They saw an apparition of Mary who encouraged them to convert sinners." Jonah grinned. "If you are against Confession,

Mr. Balcombe, you could always follow their instructions, which was to sacrifice lambs."

"I think I'll stick to the more accepted method," Balcombe said. "When I'm good and ready."

Faulls was smirking, and Balcombe shot him a critical glance.

Jonah didn't notice. He said, "Saint Polycarp is the next in the book. He's the saint for the twenty-third of February."

"Thank you, Jonah, I'll read about Polycarp."

The boy bobbed his head and smiled before limping away.

"You're too kind to him," Faulls said as they left the garden and Balcombe headed for Albert's rickshaw. "Join me with some friends at Jazzles?"

"Not today, Roy. I've got some home visits to do."

# Chapter Sixty-Five

Of the thirteen young women on the list, four lived on the island and the rest in Kowloon.

After leaving the cathedral, Balcombe visited the first girl. He and Munro had discussed how he should play it. There were two options: Scare them or be more circumspect. The former approach would be to tell them about the other deaths and provide all details. He could say that young Catholic girls who had been to confessional were being murdered and their deaths made to look natural, as though they had taken an overdose.

They decided that if a girl believed she was a target, she would panic, and people who panic don't think clearly. They needed the girls to think.

The second issue with providing a direct warning was that the girl would likely change her behaviour. Locking doors and windows was one thing, but changing a route to work or looking at people with suspicion could influence the killer. Maybe it could warn them, which was something Munro and Balcombe desperately wanted to avoid.

So Balcombe went to each of the island-girl's homes and introduced himself as working with the police. He told them that there had been six suspicious deaths that looked like opium overdoses. He did not mention murder. Nor did he mention that the girls were on his shortlist. He reminded them of Father Thomas's sermon and asked whether they had experienced anything out of the ordinary lately. He asked about new people in their lives—anyone who had been especially friendly or asked lots of personal questions.

By the end of the day, he'd spoken to all four and been given a handful of names that were common between no more than two girls at a time. And all of them related to the Church.

In the evening, Balcombe sat in his armchair and pondered the list of victims from Angela to Margaret. He limited himself to a single glass of whisky. Alcohol affected his control over BlackJack and he knew Munro was right. He had to be careful while Inspector Garrett was investigating his murders.

He finished the glass with a toast to his dead friend Eric. "What's the pattern, here?" he asked the photograph on the mantelpiece without response.

Before turning in for the night, he flicked through Jonah's book of saints and read about Polycarp. The man had been tied to a stake and set alight. But he hadn't died because the flames hadn't consumed him. However he was then stabbed to death. Which Balcombe thought unfortunate. It seemed that God could prevent death by burning, but not the blade.

During the night, his mind spun with thoughts of his problem with Garrett and the pattern of the girl's deaths.

By the morning, he knew how to distract Garrett, although no similar insight had come regarding the case.

He travelled on the first ferry to Kowloon and told Albert of his idea. When they arrived, he sent her off to implement his plan while he hired a trishaw to take him around the city.

He had nine more girls to visit and hoped to manage it in a day, but he hadn't accounted for work. Yesterday had been Sunday and today, only one girl on his list was at home during the morning.

By the end of the day, he'd managed to speak to six. Again, he found some common names, but none of them cross-referenced with the names he'd received yesterday.

On Tuesday evening, he spoke to the final three girls and compared all his notes when he returned home.

Nothing.

The clues he'd hoped to find just weren't there. He was sure of was that none of the girls took drugs. They all appeared to be clean-living, good Catholic girls. The only thing that linked them all was Father Thomas and his home-confessionals.

Albert came back on Wednesday and said that she'd spoken to people. Which meant she'd found the right contacts and hopefully influenced them with information. Only time would tell whether Balcombe's plan would work.

Each night, he sat with a glass of whisky and his notes and found no answers.

He settled back into the old routine of betting on the horses, parties and liaisons with his various ladies. What he didn't do was drink to excess.

He also found that the challenge of Munro's plan was also providing a good distraction. On Thursday he took the ferry across to the island of Macao and met a collector. The man had exactly what Balcombe needed. Would it work? Only time would tell.

Faulls noticed Balcombe's change in behaviour. He also noticed Balcombe's appearance was slipping. That evening, as Balcombe limited the booze to two glasses, Faulls asked whether everything was all right.

"You're not just limiting your consumption in front of me, are you, Charles?" He pointed to Balcombe's unshaven face. "I'm concerned about what might be going on."

Balcombe shook his head. "No secret drinking, my friend. Then he gave Faulls an update on the Catholic girls' case. "It's not just about solving it," Balcombe said.

Faulls misunderstood. "You can be proud of solving why Margaret Sotherland died. I asked you to investigate, and you proved it wasn't misadventure."

Balcombe shook his head. "When the next girl dies, I'll know I failed."

"How long have you got?"

"Worst case, within the week. But that's just a guess. I've no idea what pattern he's working to. It could be tomorrow night."

"Why night? I thought Theresa Pell was during the day."

"Because all the girls left on the list have jobs. Theresa didn't and her housemate wasn't home during the day. There was no way to get into the house secretly." Balcombe had figured that the killer had come in and left via Margaret's window. That's why the bars hadn't been locked. And the key had been in the door, on the inside. Similar situations applied to the other murdered girls.

The only other exception was Angela Newham. She had no accessible window. Her killer had walked along the hall and into her room. Bruce Chong had managed it, but he wasn't the killer.

The killer would most likely enter through a window. That's why they'd had Father Thomas tell the congregation to lock their windows.

Would it stop the killer? Balcombe doubted it. The man was driven by rules. He would strike the next person on the list when the time was right for him. Locked window or not.

The questions for Balcombe were: Which of the girls would it be, and when would he attack?

★ ★ ★

On Friday evening, Balcombe and Faulls visited Homeville, where Margaret had lived. The caretaker opened her door, saw him and quickly shut it again. Her alarmed expression made Faulls laugh.

The old lady in number 8 also peeped out, although she watched as Balcombe unlocked Margaret's door.

After checking that the room hadn't been disturbed, he left a leather bag on the chair, then went up to number 15. Gladys answered.

"Oh, hello." She looked from Balcombe to Faulls. "Is everything all right?"

He handed her the key to number 10. "Since I paid for the room and there's no one to inherit... well, there were some nice shoes and clothes in there. I'm sure Margaret would have liked you to have them."

"Thank you," she said.

A shout came from somewhere behind her. The husband, complaining, Balcombe thought.

Balcombe said, "There's also a bag"—it contained the jewellery and Margaret's Bible that he'd recovered from the caretaker plus some extra cash—"Take it. My advice is to get out of this place. You're too good for it."

The husband shouted something again.

Balcombe shook his head. "For him too."

She flung her arms around Balcombe briefly, smiled gratefully, and then shut the door.

Faulls said, "You could have handed her the bag."

"Yes, I could have."

"But you didn't in case the husband got it?"

"Maybe she won't tell him," Balcombe said as they went down the stairs.

"You're a good man."

"I try to be, Roy. I try."

Mrs. Gallshaw from number 8 was waiting on the ground floor with another woman. "Ah, good. I caught you before you left," she said. "I told you about the visitor and the chanting, didn't I?"

"Yes, thank you, Mrs. Gallshaw."

The woman smiled and took a drag on her cigarette between her yellow fingers. It was a mere stub.

"The priest."

Balcombe was moving away. "Yes. Thank you."

"There were two of them."

Balcombe stopped. Was Father Thomas here with someone else? "Together?"

"No," she said firmly. "Definitely a different one. I remember, see, because the gown—you know, the thing priests wear was different. Didn't fit as well. At least that's what I thought. I only saw the second one briefly, but I'm sure it wasn't the same man." And it wasn't one of those others."

"Others?"

"That's right." Now the other woman spoke.

"And you are?"

"Barbara Edwards from number one."

Balcombe said, "What others Mrs. Edwards?"

"Two men were looking for you. They were rough men. Came looking for you after your first visit they did. Did they catch up with you?"

And then Balcombe realized who she meant. He hadn't seen much of them but described the two who had attacked him outside Theresa Pell's old place.

"That sounds like"—the old lady gave a phlegm-filled cough—"sounds like them. And they knew where Margaret had lived."

"Simon Lammy," Balcombe said to Faulls as they left Homeville. "I'd thought the two thugs were to do with the other girl, but he didn't want me to investigate Margaret because it would lead to his affair."

"Shall we go and beat *him* up?" Faulls said with enthusiasm, although Balcombe doubted his friend could go through with it. The man probably couldn't even punch.

Balcombe patted him on the shoulder with a thanks. "No," he said. "Revenge can be much sweeter than that."

# Chapter Sixty-Six

Balcombe climbed the crags at the Peak until his heart pounded and his fingers ached. It was Saturday and the first time he'd been on the rocks since Faulls had challenged him to investigate Margaret's death.

Exhausted but happy, Balcombe returned home and pondered the case, looking for the pattern that still eluded him.

Most evenings, he'd taken to reading about one of Jonah's chosen saints. At the end of the book, he'd found a list of the saints by date. He thought he'd better check whose day it was tomorrow, in case Jonah cornered him again. Tomorrow, Sunday 27th, was Saint Oswald's day. He wasn't included. Balcombe opened the book and read a random page. It was the distressing story of Saint Maria Goretti. As a young girl, she'd been sexually attacked. She told the young man that what he was trying to do was a mortal sin and that she wouldn't be party to it. He stabbed her multiple times, but she didn't die straight away and on her deathbed, she forgave him.

The words moved Balcombe but there was something else, a niggling idea. Saint Maria. He flicked to the back of the book and checked. Then he went to the list of girls murdered, and he finally had it.

He knew the pattern. It had to be.

Another check of the list and he felt sure he knew when the killer would strike again.

Tonight.

Balcombe rang the cathedral office. Jonah answered.

"Is Father Thomas there?"

"He's at Saint Jude's. I can put the call through," the boy said. "It's about the list, isn't it?"

"Just put me through, please."

Jonah was still on the line. "Are the police doing anything about it, Mr. Balcombe?"

"Jonah!" Balcombe failed to suppress his irritation. "Put me through now. It's life or death."

There was a pause, a series of clicks, and then he heard the phone ringing again.

A clerk answered and two minutes later, Thomas was on the line.

"How can I help you, Mr. Balcombe?"

"What do you know about the murders?"

"Nothing. We've been over this, Charles. I know what you've told me."

"Single women. Catholics. Confessed a sin to you."

"Yes."

"They died on their saint's day."

"What do you mean?"

"Margaret was killed on twelfth of January. Saint Marguerite Bourgeoys' day. Marguerite, like Margaret."

"I really—"

"And Sister Angela was killed on Saint Angela Merici's day. All of them, Father. They all died on their saint's day."

The priest said nothing.

"Did you know?"

304

"No! How could I?"

Balcombe thought back to what the old woman at Homeville had said a few days ago. Another priest.

"Is it you?"

"You're asking whether I killed those poor girls?"

"Well, did you?"

"No! I heard their confessions, and that is all. I tried to help them."

"Who was the other priest?"

"What *other* priest? Doing home visits? I am the only one who does the home-confessionals."

"There was someone else. If it wasn't you, then another priest. A witness... Either it's you or another priest," he said again. "Think about it, Father."

He put the phone down. He was wasting time. He needed to speak to Munro and get protection for the next potential victim. However, as he hurried to the police station, he thought back to the phone call and another click on the line. Had Jonah been listening in?

# Chapter Sixty-Seven

Munro looked at the list of names that Balcombe had written, matching the victims with the saints' days.

Angela Newham - St Angela Merici - 27th January
Rose Escalo – St Rose Venerini - 7th May
Maria Lee - St Maria Goretti - 6th July
Theresa Pell - St Therese - 1st October
Agnes Cheng - St Agnes of Assisi - 19th November
Margaret Sotherland - St Marguerite - 12th January

"The names don't match perfectly," Munro said, "but I can't deny—"

"They're close enough. It's the pattern," Balcombe said firmly. "This is it, Munro!"

"And the next? Do they all have saint's names?"

"Most Christian names are, and I think the next murder will be tonight. It's Saint Gabriel's day."

Munro looked at the list of thirteen names they'd received from the priest. "Gabrielle Li?"

"Gabrielle Li of fifty-three Kai Yan Road."

"Kowloon." Munro waved Balcombe out of the interview room and hurried to the reception desk and had the clerk place a call.

Garrett came down the stairs fast. He was smiling and then pulled up sharply with a scowl when he saw Balcombe.

"What are you doing here?" he snapped.

Balcombe held up a hand. Munro was trying to be heard on the phone.

"Fifty-three Kai Yan Road," he repeated. "Get someone outside now and don't let anyone enter. Understood?"

He put the phone down and said to Balcombe, "Let's go."

"What?" Garrett said, closing in and barring the exit.

Munro quickly explained.

"Gabrielle-Gabriel sounds like a stretch to me," Garrett said.

Balcombe started moving. "We haven't got time—"

"We?" Garrett said. He brought up a hand. "You, Mr. Balcombe, are going nowhere. This is a police matter now. Thank you for bringing it to our attention, but your involvement ends here." Then he smirked. "Use the time to wash and clean up."

Balcombe hadn't shaved for the past few days, deliberately letting his usual well-groomed appearance slip. He looked at Munro for support, but the other inspector said nothing.

Garrett turned and started for the door. "Munro with me." Then he called over his shoulder. "Don't get involved, Mr. Balcombe. I don't want you in Kowloon. I don't want you meddling in police affairs. And if I find you do, then I'll throw the book at you."

Balcombe watched in disbelief as the door swung shut behind the two inspectors.

# Chapter Sixty-Eight

"You really think you've solved this Catholic girl case, Munro?" Garrett said aboard the Polar Star. The sun had just gone down, and the darkness was rushing in from the east.

"Balcombe's been looking for a pattern. I think he found it."

Garrett let a small smile crease his hairy lips as he scratched under his chin. "Gabriel is a man's name."

"Gabrielle's the feminine form."

Garrett leaned against the railing and looked towards the rising darkness. "It's a stretch."

"I don't—"

"And where are you with the Karen Vaughn cold case?" The way he said *cold* made it sound frozen, impossible to solve.

Munro said, "Getting closer."

Garrett let out a spluttered laugh. "I heard you got news about the phone call. Your theory was that Weston had the girl in the engine house then signalled the lower tram station."

Munro stared across the water.

"And then yesterday," Garrett said, "you got a message from the tram company duty manager who had found that one of the engineers had made the call. You have nothing. You're not getting any closer and that's why you let your key suspect go."

Everyone in the office knew Munro had released Weston. What they didn't know was that he had a plan. The tram driver was guilty, and Balcombe would prove it.

Garrett continued: "Now getting involved in this other case—well, do you really think that's going to help your career, Munro?"

Even if Balcombe was wrong about Gabrielle Li, he was right about the dates. If the killer didn't strike tonight, then it would be the next on the list. There was a Julie on the list from Father Thomas. Her saint's day was 8th April.

Garrett was clearly asking a rhetorical question because he continued after a pause. "I'm not getting involved. You see, I think I've cracked the Squeezed-heart murders."

"You have?" Munro felt his heart push up into his throat. "What—?"

"Wait and see," Garrett said mysteriously. "By all means, you can go to Gabrielle's house, but I'm the one who's going to get a result tonight. The Squeezed-heart case, Munro. The killer works at Kowloon Hospital."

# Chapter Sixty-Nine

Constable Kwee had run half a mile to the address in Kai Yan Road. Sweat prickled his eyes, and he cursed that he'd not spent more of his eighteen years keeping fit.

His sergeant said that there was a threat to a young woman. As he neared the property, he slowed to a jog and then walked, taking gulps of air to calm his heart.

The street showed no sign of trouble. Faces watched him, curious and concerned, but no one said anything. There were no shouts, no calls for help.

He went up the steps of number 53 and opened the shared front door. The rooms he was looking for were at the back of the house.

He could hear voices, children playing in the room on the right. On the left there was a scuffing sound and then rapid chatter. Not trouble.

He passed two more doors and reach number 6. He listened and heard nothing but the sounds behind him. Then he heard sounds on the floor above, but the rooms beyond door 6 were quiet.

Kwee rapped three times on the door and waited.

He heard footsteps and breathed with relief. His mind had been spinning with possibilities, not least that he was too late.

A young woman opened the door. About his own age, she wore a white cotton shift. Her eyes looked inquisitive and without fear.

"Excuse the interruption," Kwee said. "Has there been any trouble here?"

"Trouble? What kind of trouble?"

Kwee smiled awkwardly. "I don't know."

"Perhaps you are at the wrong address?" she said reasonably.

Kwee bobbed his head. "Yes, that's probably it. So sorry for the intrusion."

She closed the door, and he returned to the front door. Standing on the top step outside, he looked up and down the street, then back at the property. Yes, this was the one the sergeant had given him.

He waited for a few minutes, wondering whether to go back and check or perhaps go to the next bar one street with a similar name. Kai Yee Road was shorter, with nicer properties than Kai Yan Road. Could the sergeant have made a mistake? What to do? Stay or go? Eventually, he decided to stay and stand guard on the bottom step. The trouble clearly hadn't happened yet. He'd arrived ahead of time and was doing what he'd been instructed. If he left and the trouble was here, then he'd have no excuse for the sergeant. And he'd said something about not letting anyone enter. Kwee had thought that meant anyone after the trouble. Now he realized it was to prevent the trouble.

Faces on the street continued to scrutinize him. He ignored their critical looks and stood like a soldier at ease, hands clasped behind his back, staring straight ahead.

To his left was a side road with shops and street vendors. He watched people coming and going. He saw people buying food, and it made his stomach grumble. How long would he have to wait? Would someone relieve him? What if they forgot he was here? He could be up all night, standing guard for no reason at all.

A man appeared to be walking down the street with purpose. He didn't go into a shop or deviate to a vendor. He wasn't even walking on the pavement.

Then Kwee realized what had drawn his attention. The man had a limp. He also looked out of place, dressed in a black cloak and hood. The rapid walk also looked awkward and unbalanced.

*He must be old*, Kwee thought. But as he came within forty paces, the policeman saw the limping man was young.

At twenty paces, Kwee realized the cloak was more than a simple robe. It was a cassock, the sort of thing a religious man might wear.

Their eyes met as the man closed in.

The man crossed the road and stepped right up to the policeman.

"What has happened?" the young man asked, his voice straining.

"Nothing."

The young man nodded, then sidestepped.

Kwee blocked his way. "I'm sorry, sir, but I can't let you pass. Orders."

"I need to speak to the person who lives in room six."

Kwee shook his head.

"Have you checked on her?"

"Yes, sir. She's fine."

"When did you last check?"

Kwee bristled with annoyance. Who did this kid think he was? He might be in a cassock, but he was no priest.

"Please," the young man said. "Please, would you just check again?"

"You wait here."

The man nodded his acceptance and Kwee half-expected the strange young man to follow, but instead he appeared to be scrutinizing a piece of paper. Kwee mounted the steps, checked again that the young man wasn't following, and hurried to the door of number 6.

Kwee listened and then knocked.

The same young woman eventually answered. Her face registered annoyance through the small crack she'd opened.

"Yes?"

"I'm sorry, but are you still all right, miss?"

She sighed. "Of course I am. Please stop pestering me. You must have the wrong address."

He apologized, and she watched him walk away before closing the door.

Outside, the young man with the limp had disappeared. Kwee resumed his position, but his head was full of doubt. He looked up and down the road. Nothing looked suspicious. A trishaw turned off Sai Kung Road and raced towards him.

Reckless, Kwee thought and signalled for the boy to slow down. He did. There was a European in the back, no doubt late for an appointment. Their eyes met, and Kwee wondered what the man was thinking. Was he going to stop? Did he think the policeman wanted to have a word?

Kwee signalled for them to continue. He was too busy guarding the property to reprimand the trishaw rider for speeding dangerously.

The European said something to his rider and the boy picked up speed again.

Kwee watched them go. The street went quiet. Night was falling fast, and lanterns were being lit outside the shops.

Doubts crept in again. Maybe the sergeant hadn't got it wrong. Maybe Kwee had misheard.

Better check 53 Kai Yee Road, he told himself. It wouldn't take long. A quick check and if nothing was amiss there, he would return to his position here.

Better safe than sorry, he thought.

# Chapter Seventy

"Thank you for coming," the young woman said to the guide.

"I said I would. I said I would help you. I said I would guide you to redemption."

"I am ready."

The guide opened the Bible and read a passage from Paul to the Romans. Then John 3:3 just like the guide had done on each occasion they had met.

"Now you must express yourself," the guide said. "Do you have the pen and paper ready?"

"I do." The young woman knelt by at the bedside table and held her pen ready. "Do I write my sin?"

"There is no need," the guide said kindly. "You have confessed your sins. Now you must prepare to be reborn. Write what comes into your head."

The guide watched as the woman wrote what they always wrote. They regurgitated the readings they'd had. Which was fine but a little disappointing. Creativity, at least a little variety, would have been appreciated.

A rap on the door made them both turn and look.

The guide's face registered a question, and the woman said, "I don't know."

There was another knock, more insistent this time.

The guide inclined her head. "You need to get rid of them."

The woman gave a tiny nod and hurried to her front door. A man's voice carried down the hall. He sounded nervous, asking questions. The guide heard the woman say everything was all right. She sounded irritated and suggested he had the wrong address. Then the door closed, locked, and then the young woman came back.

"I'm sorry," she said.

"Finish your letter."

The woman wrote two more lines, then handed the sheet to the guide who placed it inside the Bible.

A brown bottle appeared in the guide's left hand. In the right there was a teaspoon. The label read *Paregoric*, and the guide made sure the woman could see it.

"Three teaspoons," the guide said. "It is just enough to make you sleep."

"Yes," the woman said. She took the spoon, and the guide poured from the bottle. The woman drank the sweet liquid, then held out the spoon for more.

"How long will it take?"

"Just a few minutes. You will soon feel drowsy. Now take off your clothes and lie down."

The woman was wearing a simple dress that pulled off easily revealing no under garments. She swung her legs onto the bed. It had a plain white sheet with no pillow, prepared in advance. There was another white sheet ready.

The guide placed the Bible on the woman's chest and pulled the sheet, covered the young woman's nakedness and stopped at her throat.

From the Psalms, the guide quoted, "Blessed is he whose unrighteousness is forgiven, and whose sin is covered. Blessed is the man unto whom the Lord imputeth no sin, and in whose spirit there is no guile. I acknowledged my sin unto thee; and mine unrighteousness have I not hid. I said, I will confess my sins unto the Lord; and so thou forgavest the wickedness of my sin." After a pause, the guide pulled the sheet all the way up, covering the woman's face.

"Now close your eyes and think of Jesus. In your thoughts, ask him for forgiveness. Ask him for rebirth. You are so lucky, Gabrielle. This is your special day." Then the guide began reciting Psalm 103.

"Praise the Lord, O my soul; and all that is within me, praise his holy name. Praise the Lord, O my soul, and forget not all his benefits: Who forgiveth all thy sin..."

The guide tucked the brown bottle that contained opium beneath the cloak. It had been a mistake to leave it. It had been a mistake to leave any clues. This time the Bible should also go.

The young woman continued to breathe slowly.

The guide continued with the Psalm and watched the sheet rise and fall. Rise and fall. Already starting to slow down.

# Chapter Seventy-One

Munro's taxi pulled onto Kai Yan Road. He saw activity at the far end outside a temple. There were people shopping in the road to his right. A couple of old men sat on the steps of one house, smoking and shooting the breeze. There were no policemen outside number 53.

*Perhaps they're inside*, he thought. *I damned well hope they are, and the Kowloon division hasn't failed me!*

He jumped out of the taxi and mounted the steps. Gabrielle Li lived in apartment 6. It was straight ahead; the door shut. There were no police in the hall. He heard random voices and sounds from the other rooms and pressed his ear to the girl's door.

He heard a low voice. Someone was reading a religious text.

He knocked loudly and counted to five, listening.

The voice stopped, but no feet approached.

A door opened behind him. There were voices in the hall but no more sounds from within.

"It's the police. Open up!" he shouted and barged the door with his shoulder. Wood splintered around the lock and Munro was inside.

It took a second for him to understand what he was looking at: a priest in a robe, the hood up and hiding his face. His hands were out, beseeching as he whispered a prayer.

"Look how wide also the east is from the west; so far hath he set our sins from us," the priest incanted, speaking faster. His voice was strange, high and fast. Manic.

On the bed was a white sheet with a body underneath.

Gabrielle Li.

Munro charged forward. His only thought was to pull back the sheet and save the girl. The priest got in the way, still chanting.

As Munro grabbed the sheet, he felt the priest grabbing him. Instinct kicked in. Without thinking, he spun and punched wildly. His fist made solid contact, and the priest crashed away.

Munro pulled back the sheet. The girl's eyes were shut but her chest still moved.

*She's alive!*

Munro slapped her face and her eyes opened, white and rolling back. Munro pulled her up, arms around her middle, squeezing hard. She flopped back, loose in his grasp.

He hit her chest, breathed into her mouth, tasted the sweet poison but kept going.

Behind him he heard movement. The priest was up, but Munro wasn't going to stop. Would the man grab or barge him? Neither it seemed. He felt a hand touch his waist.

Then, too late, he realized.

The priest had taken his sidearm.

He heard a click but didn't turn. He didn't stop.

The priest wouldn't shoot. But the priest did shoot. The gunshot rang loud, then searing pain immobilized his right arm. Blood spilled onto the white sheet and Gabrielle's body.

He spun, desperate.

The priest was there over him. The gun shook in his hands. He was speaking, but Munro couldn't hear what the priest was saying.

In slow motion, he saw the trigger finger tighten and the gun kick up as it fired.

Something shadow-like moved in the corner of his eye.

The Grim Reaper, he thought. The Grim Reaper has come for me.

His brain registered a second bang, but not the pain. The world quickly shrank to black.

# Chapter Seventy-Two

Seventy minutes earlier, when Garrett and Munro had left the police station, Balcombe dashed out and instructed Albert to get him to Kowloon. He couldn't take the ferry, so he had Albert race to the docks and persuaded a boatman to get them across the strait.

Balcombe directed the sampan to the wharf on Hung Hom Bay, travelling twice the distance across the water than the ferry. He'd be out of sight of the police inspectors and almost a mile closer to their destination, so he judged the delay would be fine.

After reaching the other side, Albert hurried to pay a trishaw rider so that she could ride it. Balcombe had given her enough cash to buy the transport, so the haggling to borrow it took seconds.

As soon as Balcombe was aboard, Albert cycled north along Chatham Street, which became Ma Tau Wai Road. They'd left the industrial docks behind. On the left there were parks and then shophouses, packed in along parallel streets. Somewhere ahead he knew was the airport, but Albert steered away and left until Balcombe no longer knew where he was. The daylight had almost gone. To the east, he could see the indigo of night chasing across the heavens.

Albert continued confidently, despite the growing darkness. It came in long stretches as lanterns created pools of light.

They crossed Argyle Street and Balcombe figured where they were. He thought about the plan he'd discussed with Albert. Kowloon Hospital would be a couple of miles to the west. It had been three days since Albert had spoken to people, following Balcombe's plan. Maybe it wasn't going to work. Maybe he'd have to try something else.

"Almost there," Albert said breathlessly as she pressed harder on the pedals. They'd crossed Prince Edward Road and entered Kowloon City.

They went right, then left, and a few seconds later were turning into Kai Yan Road.

It wasn't long, maybe a little over a hundred yards. Halfway along, they passed a young policeman jogging.

"Police," Albert said.

"Slow down."

Albert eased off, and they cruised towards the policeman.

"Slower," Balcombe instructed and checked the house numbers. Had the policeman been outside number 53?

*It could be good news*, Balcombe thought. Should he speak to the man or not?

There was no sign of a car. Munro and Garrett might not be there yet.

*The killer doesn't appear to be here yet either. Maybe he's been put off by this policeman.*

Balcombe told Albert to continue.

They went to the end of the road and turned.

"Back along?" Albert asked.

"No," Balcombe said, having counted the properties. "Take me to the rear. I'll tell you when to stop."

★ ★ ★

It was too narrow a passage for Albert's borrowed trishaw, so Balcombe hurried along it. Garbage and rotting things mingled with the smell of cooking. Each of the properties had a yard and he counted then carefully until he reached the back of 53.

Faint light spilled from barred windows. He didn't know which rooms were apartment 6. Crossing a yard with bins and boxes and a pile of junk, he heard sounds.

Chanting. Then a scuffle.

There was a window with the bars unlocked and angled open.

A gunshot jolted him into action, and he sprang for the window, leaping into the room. A person in black robes stood over Munro, gun aimed.

They swivelled and fired a wild shot as Balcombe leapt into the room.

As BlackJack, the slashing of the attacker's throat had been easy and instinctive. But as he struck, he registered that the attacker wasn't a man. The woman from the orphanage.

Sister Birgitta.

Arterial spray covered BlackJack normal clothes. Munro was shot, possibly badly injured. That could solve all his problems.

Should he let the inspector die?

# Chapter Seventy-Three

"Tell me what happened," Garrett said.

Munro was groggy with painkillers, but not as groggy as he pretended to be.

"What day is it?"

"Monday. You've only been out for a few hours."

Munro was in a hospital bed. The light from the window opposite suggested it was now late morning or early afternoon.

Garrett put one hand on the headboard so that Munro felt crowded. "Tell me what happened?"

Munro had had nightmares while he slept. In them, the Grim Reaper really had been there for him. Last night, the priest had shot him. A woman. He remembered the shock of realizing BlackJack had killed a woman.

His mind went back. He'd lost a lot of blood through the wound in his shoulder. He must have fainted. When he opened his eyes, surprised to be alive, Balcombe had been there. He had torn a large section of the white sheet, balled it up and jammed it against Munro's wound.

"Press it tight," Balcombe said, then switched his attention to the girl on the bed.

Munro saw him check Gabrielle's breathing and pulse. He pumped her chest and breathed into her mouth.

"She's gone," Munro said weakly.

"No!" Balcombe persisted, and she started to cough, then as he stuck fingers down her throat, she wretched. Balcombe called for water. A second later, barely conscious, Gabrielle vomited. Balcombe held her until she stopped, then he took the cup of water Munro had poured. Balcombe helped Gabrielle drink the liquid and then forced her to be sick again. She fought him, confused and with no strength. Balcombe made her be sick again, before putting her in the recovery position.

"I think she'll be fine," he said.

Munro turned his attention to the body of the priest on the floor. Scarlet blood had sprayed from her neck and was now rapidly darkening in a large pool on the floor.

"It was a woman," he said. "You killed her, slit her throat!"

"Good. It was you or her." Balcombe stepped over and pulled back the cowl. "Sister Birgitta!"

"You know her?"

"The head of Saint Christopher's Orphanage."

"Where the girl was murdered."

"Angela Newham."

Noises from the hall attracted their attention.

"Quick," Balcombe said, "we need to agree the story. I wasn't here."

"I broke the door open. You need to stop them. Lock it. Block it or—"

Balcombe was already hurrying away. A moment later he was back.

"Jammed it. It'll hold them for a minute. Now this is what you say."

★ ★ ★

When Munro finished his version of events, Garrett said cynically, "So, you stabbed the woman?"

"Yes."

"How?"

"I just slashed at her."

Garrett said nothing for a beat. His eyes were narrow and cold. Munro focused on the nasal hairs protruding from Garrett's flared nostrils.

"So, again, you're telling me you were attending to the victim and the woman grabbed your gun?"

"Yes."

"Where did your knife come from?"

"It was on the side."

Balcombe had placed the kitchen knife in Munro's hand before he'd left through the window. He'd also dipped it in the woman's blood.

"Tell me about the second shot."

Munro's heart raced. "Second shot?"

"Well, it can't have been the first." Garrett smiled with his mouth but not his eyes. "She didn't shoot at the window and then you. That wouldn't make sense. I'm asking why there was a bullet lodged in the wooden window frame."

Munro shook his head and kept his face blank. "Must have been a wild shot. Yes, you're right. It will have been the second." He turned away from the other inspector's critical gaze. "If you don't mind, Garrett, I'll sleep now. I'm tired."

"I'm just trying to make sense of this, Munro." The bearded inspector leaned closer so that he could be seen. Munro could smell the man's sour breath.

Garrett said, "She shot you with your weapon, then you had the peace of mind to find a knife and slash her."

Munro closed his eyes. "Yes. I was lucky—"

"You could have died."

"It was chaotic. I don't remember the detail. I remember tussling with her and the pain and thinking I would black out. Somehow, I found the knife."

"And the second shot?" Garrett pressed again.

"Wild, during the tussle."

"A miracle."

Munro opened his eyes and met Garrett's icy stare.

"Luck happens. If it didn't, I wouldn't be alive to tell the tale."

"It's definitely a wonderful story," Garrett said, his voice suggesting he didn't buy it. Again, he paused a beat and then leaned close to whisper in Munro's ear. "I'll be looking closely, Munro. If there's a discrepancy…"

Garrett pulled away, nodded and then spun on his heel as a young policeman, DC Reece, called his name. The junior man spoke urgently, although Munro couldn't hear. After a brief exchange, Garrett hurried from the ward. Reece remained.

Munro was wishing his brain wasn't so foggy with the drugs. Were there any holes in the version? Had Garrett accepted the constructed story?

He realized Reece was still there, smirking.

"What is it Reece?"

"Sorry, sir."

"No, I want to know." Munro wondered if he sounded paranoid. "What is it? Out with it, man."

"Garrett, sir. He's… he's in trouble."

And then Reece told Munro what had happened last night. While Munro was dashing to save Gabrielle Li,

Garrett had marched into Kowloon Hospital and arrested a surgeon. He charged him with the Squeezed-heart murders and others, stating that he had information that the man was an illegal gang member.

"It turns out the informant got it wrong," Reece said. "The surgeon is a respected member of the Hong Kong Club. He even knows the Commissioner. Can you believe it? Garrett really put his foot in it. The Chief is furious."

*What a shame*, Munro thought.

# Chapter Seventy-Four

Two days later, Fai Yeung met Munro in a Chinese bar rather than their usual Wellington Inn drinking place.

"How are you Babyface?" Yeung said as they sat in a dark corner with their full glasses. The assistant pathologist had ordered, so they shared a bottle of his preferred baijiu.

"The painkillers help."

"You are a cat with nine lives."

"I was lucky," Munro said. It was becoming a stock phrase when asked about the incident.

"Tell me about it," Yeung said. "Why was the woman doing it?"

"I may have nine lives, but I can't speak to the dead," Munro said, knocking back his first glass and letting his friend pour another.

"She was killing sinners."

"Young women who couldn't confess properly to a man, is what I think. And based on the passages, I wouldn't be surprised if she convinced them to experience rebirth in order to redeem themselves."

"In death?"

"Based on the strengthened opium drink, I think she tricked them. They thought they'd sleep and wake up.

Sister Birgitta was handing them to God for his judgement." He paused. "Of course, I'm only guessing. She could just have been a sadistic murderer."

"Angela Newham was smothered."

Munro nodded. "She was probably the first. I don't know what she had to confess. We'll probably never know, but the Sister hadn't perfected her technique. The drug was probably too weak. I've been thinking that her victim started coming round. Her breathing didn't stop, so the Sister used a pillow. I think she also washed Angela out of respect. She was the only victim that Sister Birgitta knew well."

"The bottle of Paregoric wasn't found every time."

"No. I suspect she didn't think about it or didn't want the deaths ruled as suicide. That may seem crazy, but the minds of murderers aren't as logical as your or mine."

Yeung knocked back his drink and sniffed.

"What?" Munro asked.

"Logic and not thinking."

"Right?" Munro said cautiously.

"I know the story of what happened. Everyone is talking about it."

Munro waited.

Yeung said, "I hear that Inspector Garrett isn't buying it. He's had forensics in the house, examining everything."

"Which is perfectly fine."

"And he's asked for the weapons to be examined. Your gun and the knife you used."

Munro took a sip of his drink. The burn in his throat suddenly seemed more intense.

Yeung said, "The gun had her prints on it. The knife has yours."

"Of course."

Yeung took a slow sip of his drink as his eyes flicked around the room.

"It's a good job Dr. Swift didn't examine the knife. I looked at it."

"Yes?" Munro failed to hide the tension in his voice.

"I know."

"What?"

Yeung sighed and dropped his voice. "Your secret is safe with me." Their eyes locked, and he thought Yeung was on the verge of tears.

"What?"

"I'd hoped you could tell me, my friend, but I suppose I understand the risk." He paused and again checked no one was listening. "The blade that killed Sister Birgitta was razor sharp. The kitchen knife was too big and too blunt. The wound didn't match."

"I'm sorry," Munro said with a dry mouth.

"And those other murders. The gruesome ones…"

"Yes. I know who it is."

Yeung said nothing for a minute, then knocked back his drink.

"You might get a medal."

"That's not my motivation."

"No," Yeung said, waving to be brought another bottle of baijiu. "Just be careful."

"I will be, my friend. I will be."

# Chapter Seventy-Five

Munro stepped up beside Chief Carmichael and faced the body of senior policemen. Apart from Garrett's, the other faces were friendly.

It was his first day back on duty since the incident. His right arm was still in a sling, but the wound was healing well. He received his commendation and public handshake from the Chief.

"You've done our reputation a lot of good, Munro," Carmichael said when they stepped into his office with the applause still ringing in Munro's ears. "This is a high-profile case with a newsworthy outcome. For once—and I stress for once—I'm impressed."

"Thank you, sir."

"However there is still the general matter of results. The Governor will give us some leeway, but detection rates have to improve. You probably heard Inspector Garrett made a mistake by arresting the wrong man."

Munro nodded.

Carmichael continued: "He's keeping the Squeezed-heart case, but he won't be overseeing your activities going forward."

"Thank you, sir."

"You promised me a result with the Karen Vaughn case. I heard you thought Trevor Weston was guilty."

"I still think he is, sir. Give me time and I'll have it solved for you."

"You have a week," Carmichael said.

★ ★ ★

Garrett beckoned Munro into his cubbyhole of an office. He'd moved back into it and vacated Munro's official desk.

"Good to see you back, Munro."

"Good to be back."

"You're a hero," he said, a smile fixed beneath his unkempt beard. "And so very impressive with a knife."

"You had it checked. You didn't believe it was me."

"Who else could it have been?"

Munro nodded. "Exactly."

"Which has got me thinking." Garrett sat on his desk and placed a hand on a bundle of files. Munro forced his eyes away from the man's hand.

"Let's see," Garrett continued. "The Squeezed-heart murder of Chen Che-hwa."

Munro raised a hand. He wasn't taking any more nonsense from the man. "You don't tell me what to do any more, Garrett."

Garrett continued: "I know, but bear with me, old chap. You'll remember, the fat man who was buying and selling girls."

"I remember."

"Killed by an expert with a knife."

"That's right."

"One of your cases."

"Of course," Munro straightened. "I'm the detective inspector."

"And the butcher, Feng. He was sliced open with great skill. Someone very good with a knife." His mouth pulled a disingenuous smile. "Again, one of your cases, Munro."

"What's your point, Garrett?" Munro said, no longer able to suppress the disdain he felt for the man.

"You visited the scene of the crime where those six gangsters were sliced up."

"But not my case, if that was your point."

"And the other Squeezed-heart murder—the one you had transferred from Kowloon."

"What are you suggesting, Garrett." Munro forced a laugh. "Are you trying to say I had anything to do with all these deaths? I thought you were looking for a big doctor. And then, after the murder of Pingping, you were again convinced of gangster ties. So, I'm a gangster too, am I?"

Garrett grunted and folded his arms. "I don't know what you are Munro. But I know for damn sure, you're no hero, no matter what the Chief says publicly."

Munro started to leave.

"How's the Karen Vaughn case?"

"Progressing, thank you."

Garrett smiled. "Shame about Old Teags."

Munro stopped. "What's happened?"

"I heard he had a stroke. Not in a good way. That's what happens when you get obsessed by a case. I heard you visited him, Munro. Looks like you got him all het up again." He paused and shrugged unconvincingly. "I'm not saying it was your fault…"

Munro walked out and shut the door behind him.

# Chapter Seventy-Six

Munro's plan was for Balcombe to befriend Trevor Weston. Balcombe first made contact with another tram company employee who then introduced him to Weston. He posed as a miniature soldier collector and enthusiast. He didn't like his appearance but with his unshaven face, he hoped he looked the part. He hoped Weston would see him as a loner and kindred spirit.

He played it softly-softly, and it wasn't until the week after Gabrielle Li had been saved that he made the first significant move. He showed Weston a rare model of Napoleon on a rearing horse.

He'd bought it from the collector in Macao. It had cost a ridiculous amount, but it worked a gem. Weston almost wet himself with excitement.

On the Saturday after Gabrielle Li's rescue, Weston invited Balcombe back to his house to see his Waterloo campaign set-up, and they played for hours. Balcombe learned that the other man had a usual partner but with the chance to use the new Napoleon, he gave Balcombe priority.

Weston like to play scenarios where the French won. They talked about military strategy, but Balcombe also managed to make small talk. He needed to build rapport, especially around being misunderstood, and unlike other men.

After their first session, Balcombe took his Napoleon home afterwards. Weston wanted him to return on Sunday, but Balcombe left it a further day before returning in the evening.

On the second occasion, Balcombe had learned about the *playroom,* as Weston called it. He said he had a secret and was clearly proud. Balcombe could see the man wanted to boast and made sure he didn't press too hard. When he left on Monday night, Balcombe said he'd return on Tuesday. He left his Napoleon.

During a break in their gameplay on the next night, Balcombe pulled the photograph of a girl from his pocket. He handled it nervously.

"What?" said Weston, studying him with curiosity.

"I feel like I can trust you," Balcombe said quietly, nerves edging his voice.

"You can trust me."

"We're... the same, aren't we?"

Weston's lips twitched with anticipation. "We are."

Balcombe left a reasonable pause. He passed the photograph to Weston.

The man's face gave nothing away.

"Sometimes... Sometimes I get these feelings," Balcombe said with a hushed voice as though they might be overheard.

Weston nodded but his expression still didn't confirm anything either way.

Balcombe swallowed hard. He wasn't a great actor. He'd been over this conversation in his head multiple times, unconvinced that he sounded genuine. Would Weston see through him?

Balcombe said, "I feel... I'd like to know her better."

Still Weston said nothing, his stone-cold eyes on Balcombe's. Finally, he returned the photograph and said, "Let's get back to the game, shall we?"

Balcombe didn't bring the subject up again, and they met again to play with the soldiers the following night.

Out of the blue, Weston said, "What would you do?"

Balcombe didn't know what he meant. "Attack with calvary on the left flank?" he said.

"I mean about the girl. You know… the photograph."

"I…"

"Touch her?" Weston raised a knowing eyebrow.

"Yes," Balcombe said quietly and then waited as Weston's eyes tried to read his.

"Touch her," Weston said again.

"It feels so wrong. To… you know."

"It's not wrong, Charles. It's natural." Weston smiled.

Balcombe rubbed his face with a slow movement, hoping it would calm his discomfort. His hand shook, but if Weston saw it, he didn't read the truth in Balcombe's nerves.

Balcombe said, "I see her on Tuesdays. I saw her yesterday. Alone. I could… Perhaps…"

Weston leaned forward, his eyes shining. "Yes?"

Balcombe breathed, then shook his head. "I couldn't."

"I could help."

"How?"

"I've done it before, Charles. I'm experienced. It would be easy."

"You've done it…?"

"Many times." Weston looked proud, a smug smile on his face. "And Chinese girls are easier."

Balcombe said nothing, fearing his discomfort would show.

Weston said, "You read about Karen Vaughn?"

"The name rings a bell… wait! Of course, the girl who disappeared a few months ago. It was in all the papers."

"That was me." A wider smile. "It was easy. She wasn't my first either. It's bad, you know, how the papers don't care when a Chinese girl disappears. They paid a bit more attention when the girl had a white father."

"What happened? She went to the cinema with a friend and just disappeared."

Weston grinned. "They were never at the cinema. They were on my tram. They got on at MacDonnell Road and then got off at May Road. But then the half-caste girl got on again. She was cheeky and excited by the risk."

"She didn't understand the risk."

"No, she didn't," Weston giggled. His eyes rolled back as though he was visualizing it.

"No one saw?" Balcombe said.

"There are so many passengers, but no one really pays attention. We got talking, and I told her about the unexploded bomb that had been in the Engine House. Once everyone was off, I took her in there."

Balcombe waited. His heart thundered in his chest as he waited for Weston's confession.

"You know, in crime stories, they use chloroform, and it works instantly. On a kid, it usually takes a couple of minutes. And you can't expose it to air for long. It's got to come straight from the bottle." He nodded. "I make my own—extra strong with the solvent they use, plus ethanol."

"You used home-made chloroform?" Balcombe tried to sound impressed.

"It works for at least a couple of hours, so I put her in the cupboard."

"And did what?" Balcombe breathed and hoped it came across as awe rather than revulsion. "Did the deed there, later... no wait. You brought her here... your playroom."

Weston chuckled.

"A risk though, wasn't it? Keeping her in there for so long... you wanted until your shift ended. What time did you say that was? Seven?"

Weston said, "Yes," although his eyes betrayed him. Something else had happened.

Balcombe knew Weston didn't drive. After 7pm it will have been dark but carrying a girl for three miles to his home, without being seen, seemed unlikely.

"I had help,"

"Who?" Balcombe tried to sound casual.

Weston shook his head. "You don't need to know about that. Now that I have you."

The Vaughn girl wasn't the best though. I managed to get two girls here, walking. They'd been out looking for their teacher. I said she lived with me, and they just came straight here."

He chuckled. "I said that she was my cousin and loved to see her children dressed up, especially as nurses, so they agreed. They didn't suspect a thing. I got the case of clothes, and they were down to their knickers before they realized there was only one nurse's uniform in the box. Did I say I'd never had two girls before? I wasn't prepared. It's more complicated." He blinked and smiled. "So I improvised. I hit the first girl. It took two blows to knock her out and... Anyway, shock is a funny thing. The other girl didn't scream.

She just came with me to the other room where I'd set things up. Normally I'd get much further though before they realized what I was doing. They're very accepting, at least Chinese girls are. So, then the second girl went in, but then I had to hit her to make her behave." He giggled childishly again. "She wet herself. They all wet themselves and then apologize for it. It's so funny that they do that."

Weston carried on talking. His eyes were unfocussed and moving rapidly, like he was visualizing it all.

Balcombe's throat burned with bile. He needed to stop Weston before he went into too much detail, but took a few breaths before he could trust his voice.

"How do you get rid of the bodies?" Of course, Weston had killed them, but the police hadn't found a trace.

"My pigs," Weston grinned. "They'll eat anything. You have to wait for the blood to go hard, otherwise it's a mess. Then I chop them up and feed them a few chunks at a time. The small bones don't matter, but afterwards I use the barrel burner to get rid of the bigger bones. It's so easy, Charles. What's this girl's name?" Weston held up the photograph. "We could do it next Tuesday. So easy."

Balcombe wasn't listening anymore. Karen Vaughn wasn't alive. Munro hadn't expected her to be. But there was a chance she'd been kept alive and hidden somewhere. That had been his vain hope. But no. Karen's existence had been obliterated. There was no evidence except for Weston's confession, and no way would he repeat that to the police.

"Do you believe in hell?" Balcombe said.

Weston was in a reverie describing what he'd done. His neck was flushed, and he didn't hear the change in Balcombe's voice.

He focused on Balcombe and smiled uncertainly. "Pardon?"

"Do you believe in hell?"

Now Weston's eyes widened with realization.

BlackJack got up and grabbed the other man by the throat, squeezing hard but allowing Weston to speak.

"So, do you, Trevor?"

"Well... I... I don't suppose," Weston managed to splutter.

BlackJack drew his knife. His hands were still shaking from the rage, but Weston didn't notice. He was trembling too, only his was fear as he looked into BlackJack's dark eyes.

"I'm going to make you suffer, Trevor. You're going to discover what hell on Earth means. And by the time I'm finished with you, you'll think the real hell is a relief."

Within the first hour, Weston pleaded and screamed at the pain because he no longer had a penis.

He lived for another ninety minutes, fading in and out of consciousness, whimpering and full of contrition.

And BlackJack heard none of it. He just kept thinking that this was for the girls Weston had tortured and abused. Although he also learned something important. He discovered how Karen Vaughn and others were transferred from the upper Peak tram station to Weston's house in the woods.

# Chapter Seventy-Seven

Munro drove up to Oceanview nursing home with a smile on his face. Two weeks ago, Garrett had arrested an eminent surgeon and friend of the Commissioner, and this morning he'd blundered again. He'd charged into the Hong Kong and Shanghai Bank building and arrested an accountancy firm partner. A set of surgical knives had been found at the man's home along with a token that linked him to a gang—the one thought to have been behind the Sham Shui murders.

Munro chuckled at the thought. Of course, Balcombe had planted the items as revenge against a man called Simon Lammy. The incrimination served them both.

Garrett would look a fool again and Lammy would be embarrassed and uncomfortable after a few nights in Victoria Gaol.

Munro walked into reception and asked for Bill Teags. He wasn't in the garden this time; he was in a conservatory. There were six residents lined up at the window in armchairs.

Teags had a tartan blanket over his legs and an unfocussed expression in his eyes. The right side of his face was slack.

*The stroke*, Munro thought.

"Old Bill, it's me, Babyface."

The man's pale eyes stared back without recognition.

A nurse stepped forward. "Ah, sir, I should have mentioned that he's just had his medication for the morning."

Munro knelt and held Teags' hand. "The Karen Vaughn case—I have an update for you."

He couldn't say much. He couldn't tell Teags the whole truth. Balcombe had been supposed to get a written confession out of Weston, but he'd lost control. He'd killed the man and disposed of his body.

He said that Weston had done it, but not alone. Before he died, Weston admitted that his sometime game-playing partner had helped. After using the chloroform and locking Karen in a cupboard, he'd met Slater, and they'd travelled down on the tram. At the bottom, he got one of the boys to deliver a newspaper. They'd thought he'd phoned from the engine house, but the signal had been simpler than that.

Two hours later, after Weston had checked on Karen and topped up the anaesthetic, his partner had arrived in his car. He'd parked behind the engine house and put Karen in the boot. He'd driven her to Weston's remote house and waited. He'd tied Karen up in the playroom and started their game when Weston had arrived. Only that night it hadn't involved toy soldiers.

Yesterday evening, after an alleged anonymous tip-off, Munro had found the partner in his bathtub. This time there was a confession, written as a suicide note.

Assistant pathologist Yeung had confirmed death as exsanguination. The man's wrists were slit. But what Munro's friend hadn't noted in his report was the surgical removal of Cattles's genitals. Blackjack couldn't stage a suicide. He couldn't resist the torture and punishment of the second man guilty of Karen Vaughn's abuse and murder.

Munro realized he'd been holding Teag's hand for a while with no response. Should he return when Teags would understand?

He stood, thought to leave, but then said, "You were right, Bill."

A flicker of understanding appeared in Teags' eyes.

"Bill, you were right. It was Eric Cattles. He did it. The bastard did it and we got him."

A tear appeared in the corner of the old man's eye. It burst over the ridge and ran down his cheek.

Munro drove back to Victoria. The Peak was on his right, and he knew Balcombe was up there climbing. BlackJack had lost control by killing Weston without getting a written confession, but they'd got Eric Cattles. However, Fai Yeung now knew his secret. How long would it be before Garrett worked it out as well?

How long before BlackJack decided he could no longer take the risk? How long before he killed one of them?

# Acknowledgements

Again, Dr Samson Chan was an immense help regarding the Hong Kong prisons and penal policy in the 1950s.

I would also like to thank Helen Moran and John Alexander for their assistance regarding religious matters. Pete Tonkin stepped up as the main editor for this book and I'd like to thank my wife and other beta readers for their feedback.

A final thanks to my sister Dr Kerry Bailey-Jones who provided advice on medical matters.

murraybaileybooks.com

## IF YOU ENJOYED THIS BOOK

Feedback helps me understand what works, what doesn't and what readers want more of. It also brings a book to life.

Online reviews are also very important in encouraging others to try my books. I don't have the financial clout of a big publisher. I can't take out newspaper ads or run poster campaigns.

But what I do have is an enthusiastic and committed bunch of readers.

Honest reviews are a powerful tool. I'd be very grateful if you could spend a couple of minutes leaving a review, however short, on sites like Amazon and Goodreads.

If you would like to contact me, I'm always happy to receive direct feedback so please feel free to use the email address below.


Thank you
Murray
murray@murraybaileybooks.com

Printed in Great Britain
by Amazon

29070647R00199